T0171306

Also by Arthur Wenk

<u>Fiction</u>
The Quarter Note Tales

<u>Non-Fiction</u>
Claude Debussy and the Poets
Introduction to Nineteenth-Century Music
Claude Debussy and Twentieth-Century Music
La musique et les grandes époques de l'art
Une esquisse de la pensée musicale
Analyses of Nineteenth- and Twentieth-Century Music: 1940-1985
Musical Resources for the Revised Common Lectionary
A Guide to the Bookstores of Toronto, with P. Warren

New Quarter Note Tales

Axel in Québec

ARTHUR WENK

iUniverse, Inc.
New York   Bloomington

New Quarter Note Tales
Axel in Québec

This is a work of fiction. All of the characters, names, incidents, organizations, and dialogue in this novel are either the products of the author's imagination or are used fictitiously.

iUniverse books may be ordered through booksellers or by contacting:

iUniverse
1663 Liberty Drive
Bloomington, IN 47403
www.iuniverse.com
1-800-Authors (1-800-288-4677)

ISBN: 978-1-4502-5477-9 (pbk)
ISBN: 978-1-4502-5479-3 (cloth)
ISBN: 978-1-4502-5478-6 (ebk)

Printed in the United States of America

iUniverse rev. date: 9/10/2010

For Patti

Preface

I BEGAN MY CAREER AS a musicologist at California State College, San Bernardino (whence Chihuahua State in "A Faltering Trust"). The unsettling experiences of earthquake, forest fire, mudslide and smog, coupled with the academic amphigory of California in the early 70s, led me to compose a Biweekly Chronicle for incredulous friends back east. Chronicles of my life's misadventures and absurdities, continued in Boston, Pittsburgh, North Carolina and Québec, provided background material for my mystery stories. It seemed as if only the murders needed to be invented—the rest was simple reportage.

The title of the first set of *Quarter Note Tales* emerged from the name of its protagonist, Axel Crochet. In British notation, a quarter note is a crochet, and in French, a *croche*. Claude Debussy, the composer to whom I devoted my scholarly career, wrote music criticism under the *nom de plume* of Monsieur Croche, anti-dilettante. The surname Axel comes from a play, *Axel*, by the composer's friend Villiers de l'Isle Adam, from which Debussy hoped to produce a theatre-piece.

While I recognize a certain kinship between myself and Axel Crochet, I must observe that he is even more naïve than I and a good deal more reckless, particularly when it comes to rushing headlong to the rescue of a female companion or colleague. For me, as for Axel, Québec marked the end of a twenty-year career as a musicologist and the start of a twenty-year career as a calculus teacher. As to whether Axel will follow my footsteps into my latest career as a psychotherapist, you'll have to ask him.

Regarding this new set of *Quarter Note* Tales: my predecessor at Université Laval (Fleur de Lis University in "A Faculty Affair") really did disappear after trying unsuccessfully to move musicology from the School of Music to the Faculty of Arts. Was he murdered? No one knows for sure. The leading man of a production of "The Music Man" that I directed during this period really did suffer a near-fatal encounter with at truck, although I took a few liberties with the circumstances. And Eric the Rat, from "Fire and Ice," really did dwell beneath the stage at the Sedbergh School, model for Galton, though to my knowledge suffered no ill effects therefrom, although the school did experience a catastrophic fire.

Those interested in the original *Quarter Note Tales* can read excerpts on my website at www.arthurwenk.com/my_mysteries.htm.

New Quarter Note Tales

A Faculty Affair   1

The Music Man Mystery   101

Fire and Ice   187

A FACULTY AFFAIR

Chapter 1

A FEW MONTHS SHY OF my fortieth birthday I found myself teaching music history at Fleur de Lis University in Rochambeau, Québec: a new country, a new culture and a new language. Especially a new language. Memories of my initial visit to the university, six months earlier, remained something of a blur, so concerned was I with trying to make a good impression on the Search Committee members who served as my hosts and guides, so in order to orient myself I asked a student to direct me to the library. "Pouvez-vous me dire," I asked, "où se trouve le bibliothèque?" She kindly and subtly corrected me by saying "La bibliothèque est là, après la tour à gauche."

I half-expected her to exclaim, "Le bibliothèque? Le bibliothèque? Send for the grammar patrol and take this poor idiot away. He can't even keep his articles straight, for God's sake! What are they letting past the border these days anyway?" And were I to confess that I was Axel Crochet, the new professor of music history, I anticipated a disdainful response. "Professor? You? Don't kid me! What can you teach anyone here and say le bibliothèque? Yes, here he is, officer. I'm glad you arrived quickly. He's already contaminated the language enough. Take him away and deport him." Even my prematurely gray hair wasn't going to save me from an ignominious fate.

Eventually I traced a path to my office in the École de Musique, located in Pavillon Desjardins, the most distinctive building on campus, a Monty Pythonesque version of a chapel, built during the 60s to hold hundreds of Jesuit priests in training, then sold to the university at fire sale prices in the late 70s after the Quiet Revolution saw the decline of church influence in the province. Students graduating with advanced degrees in musicology went on to teach in music departments across Canada; those in music education taught in secondary and primary schools; no one knew what happened to the performers. My office on the fourth floor had been constructed by tearing down the wall between two cells in the erstwhile seminary, providing ample space for several bookcases and a fair-sized desk under high windows admitting sunlight but no distracting view.

Rochambeau being a tourist as well as a university town, I encountered a variety of responses to my efforts to speak French with the Québecois:

- They spotted me as a foreigner from my first sentence, addressed me in English, and refused to budge. This happened only in the tourist district and felt rather insulting.

- Their English was better than my French. If I made even a simple request to repeat a remark, they switched immediately to flawless English and refused to budge.

- They maintained French no matter what. This produced the best learning environment for me. They'd repeat their remarks more slowly if necessary and would help me with vocabulary, but always in French. This happened when I opened two bank accounts and purchased a mattress. I couldn't pretend to understand everything the salesman was saying, but when you order Sears' best you have a pretty good idea what you're getting. Renting an apartment also took place entirely in French, requiring a fair amount of patience on the part of the *locataire*.

- They spoke English but returned to French when I persevered. This happened while getting directions on which bus to take. The number eleven bus ran to the university from an intersection near my apartment. On several occasions I heard passengers remark on the approaching vehicle, "Bon, v'là la onze." This bothered me because the noun *autobus* is masculine: surely it should be "le onze." Finally I checked this out with my colleague Valéry Turgeon, a musicologist from Geneva. He simply shrugged and said that Québeckers thought that the word "bus" was feminine.

- I just plain chickened out. In the tourist district everyone spoke English anyway, so I just made like another dumb

American. I can't say I was proud of this strategy but sometimes the burden of living in a different language simply became too heavy to endure.

Valéry Turgeon, as a non-Québécois Francophone, proved to be an excellent friend for a stranger in a strange land. A shock of silver hair, brushed straight back in the style of conductor Herbert von Karajan, gave him an air of masterful authority, frequently undercut by a boyish grin. Each morning Valéry would wander into my office with an infectious "Hey, man!" (in English), would listen sympathetically to my latest tales of woe in wrestling with the French language, and then ask my advice about some arcane English metaphor that he wanted to incorporate into a paper he was preparing to read at the November meeting of the American Musicological Society.

I would exclaim in disbelief that the only way to say "what we need" in French is "ce dont nous avons besoin." He would just smile and say, "That's the way it is." Then he would proudly show me a sentence using the phrase "run with the hare and ride with the hounds" that he'd found in his French-English dictionary, and refused accept my insistent opinion that no contemporary English speaker would ever use it. The closest substitute I could come up with was "kill two birds with one stone," which he found unappealing.

Musicologists probably have no monopoly on the sadistic practice of assigning whatever courses nobody else wants to teach to the "new guy." They typically excuse the practice by saying, "Perhaps he'll be able to make a go of it," a breathtaking exercise in wishful thinking. In the fall term my teaching responsibilities included the exquisite frustration of "La Méthodologie de la Recherche." Masters degree candidates in performance—that is to say, most of them—were required to submit an essay. Some students were better equipped for intellectual activity than others, and one imagines that the negotiations in writing the requirements rather resembled the haggling between Abraham and God over the fate of Sodom and Gomorrah.

You remember the story. God got so fed up with all the wickedness and corruption in the Twin Cities—they had pornographic movies and massage parlours and child molestation and people coveting their neighbours' asses and idol worship and punk rock and toxic waste and drug addiction and MTV and who knows what all else—that he decided to destroy them. Abraham pleaded with God saying, "What if there be fifty righteous in the city?" (They knew how to use the present subjunctive back in those days, so Gomorrah University must have had something going for it.) "For fifty righteous, I will spare the city," was God's reply. "But what if there be only forty-five righteous?" Abraham kept at it and finally got God down to ten righteous people.

I imagine that the Curriculum Committee must have functioned somewhat along these lines. The original requirement called for all instrumentalists to write an essay of some length illustrating their ability to present and solve a research problem. Then the violin professor, let us say, thought of his star pupil and asked, "What about students who can't write an essay?" So a second option was added—an instrumental recital thirty minutes long accompanied by a brief essay explaining the choice of these pieces, their interrelationships, style, historical context, et cetera. But the clarinet professor still had his doubts. "What about students who can't write even a brief essay?" So a third option was added—an instrumental recital accompanied by an oral presentation. But even this requirement was found to be too stiff—what about students who can't express themselves orally? So a final option was added: the student would play a thirty-minute recital then answer questions posed by the jury.

After reading the first disastrous essays, the committee added a further requirement—the semester before undertaking the essay, a student must submit a *projet d'essai* explaining the historical context, *problématique,* objectives, methodology, outline, calendar, and bibliography for the eventual essay. When students turned out not to be able to produce even a *projet d'essai* on their own, the committee invented a course to teach them how, for good measure made it obligatory, and gave it to me to teach.

Whether my conjectural history was accurate or not, the requirements were exactly as I have presented them. No one seemed to mind that students got the same degree whether they chose the most difficult option or the easiest. Some students understood this right away. One young woman in my class proposed to resolve the question of apparently anomalous fingerings and bowings in Fritz Kreisler's violin works by comparing the written scores with the composer's own recorded performances. Of course, this student already held a master's degree in performance from Yale and came to Fleur de Lis University only in order to get her teaching credential. Another student planned to contrast instrumental and vocal ornamentation in Baroque music. Other students had more difficulty, including one South American chap whose heavily accented French I had trouble understanding. (He also stammered.) It would have been far easier to lecture to ninety students in the undergraduate history survey than to change the manner of thinking of ten instrumentalists, many of whom weren't into thinking to begin with.

"La Méthodologie de la Recherche" brought me in contact with the most annoying student of my career, a young violist whom I came to call Screaming Annie, after one of the more flamboyant characters in John Irving's *Hotel New Hampshire*. The moniker seemed appropriate for the student who came to my office early in September to deliver a ninety-minute harangue to the effect that the work-load in my course on Methodology of Research was more than she could handle.

How much time did she devote to completing the assignments, I inquired? Six hours a week, she replied. I suggested that six hours a week seemed entirely appropriate for a three-credit course on the graduate level, whereupon she produced several pages full of calculations offering conclusive proof that she could not give that kind of time to this course and still practice her instrument, play in an ensemble, cook for her husband, and maintain her health. She couldn't drop the course because she planned to graduate in December, so the only solution was for me to reduce the workload.

The foregoing suggests the content of our conversation but hardly the tenor. The Québecois speak exceedingly rapidly and Screaming Annie was easily the most voluble person I had ever encountered. Whenever I tried to raise a question or offer an explanation she would redouble her efforts so that my participation mostly confined itself to stunned silence with an occasional inutile demurral. When Screaming Annie showed no signs of tiring after an hour and a half I decided that waiting her out would not likely succeed. I suggested instead that her argument lay not with me but with the École de Musique who required even instrumentalists to write a graduate essay and take the course preparing them to do so. I encouraged the young woman to plead her case with the Director himself, and with that ploy managed to get her out of my office.

Chapter 2

NEXT TO TRYING TO SURVIVE in a language not my own—a language I had first encountered only in my mid-twenties—my chief activity in Rochambeau was trying to overcome loneliness. The single newsstand carrying *The New York Times* provided an essential lifeline to home, but the absence of companionship, preferably female, haunted my waking moments and a fair proportion of my dreams. Valéry Turgeon proved to be a sympathetic friend and frequently invited me to his house for supper, where I entertained his young children with the kinds of acrobatic games that easily cross the language barrier.

Early in the fall I asked Valéry whether he planned to take his family to Expo-Rochambeau, the Canadian equivalent of the Texas State Fair, which *Le Soleil*, Rochambeau's French-language newspaper, had been touting for several weeks. Turns out he'd never heard of it. When I asked whether I might take his children, six and five, to the fair he was pleased to let them go.

That afternoon I received confirmation of something I had suspected about Valéry: he genuinely considered his house to be on Swiss soil (and not simply financed by a low-interest mortgage on a family property in Switzerland). As we got into the car and the kids waved goodbye to their parents, they shouted, "We're going to Québec!" Not the city of Rochambeau, mind you, but the nation—well, at least the Québecois insist that it's a nation—of Québec.

Hélène and René didn't show much interest in the displays of animal husbandry but enjoyed the rides (carousel, Ferris wheel, rocket ship) and the food (hot dogs, fries, coke and ice cream).

In the afternoon came "Walt Disney's World on Ice," with all your favourite Walt Disney characters plus Linda Frattiane, a host of other fancy skaters, and what I suppose might be called the *corps de ballet*, which appeared in one spectacular costume display after another. We watched skaters jump through fiery hoops and sail over barrels, suffered through the inevitable dog act, and covered our faces with cotton candy, which provided the occasion for yet another French lesson.

My command of academic French enabled me to talk in polysyllables about music and literature but everyday objects, well within the grasp of any Francophone six-year-old, frequently baffled me. When the Turgeon children pointed to the large glass cylinder housing the mechanism that generated spun candy, I couldn't understand what they were saying, though I was happy to buy them the puffy confection. Later Ghislaine, Valéry's wife, explained the French term, *la barbe à papa*, literally "Daddy's beard."

Sitting in the very first row, right on the ice, the children and I could practically touch Pinocchio, Goofy and Donald Duck, and while I knew that there were just ordinary people underneath all that plastic and rubber, when the French voice for which Linda Fratianne was lip-synching announced the entrance of "your favourite inhabitant of Walt Disney World," I unexpectedly burst into tears. All those childhood afternoons watching the "Mickey Mouse Club" and all those evenings viewing progress reports on the construction of Disneyland had planted deep seeds of association. If you had asked me what I treasured most about being American I might have responded in terms of my admiration for Thomas Jefferson and his ideals, but my profound, mostly unacknowledged homesickness had been triggered by an ageless mouse.

The same thing happened toward the end of the show when the *corps de ballet* skated out in western garb. Suddenly the house lights blacked out and their costumes lit up as they glided into a skater's version of the square dance routine that the Disney organization had designed for the Orange Bowl some years earlier. The Orange Bowl game, always scheduled on New Year's Night in that era, maintained a tradition of elaborate halftime spectacles, and the Walt Disney people had taken advantage of the darkness to put on an electric square dance. Now I was seeing it live, ten feet away, and all the associations of New Year's Day football games came together and overwhelmed me. (Clearly I'd been reading too much Proust.)

A week later I experienced an unexpected interruption in teaching caused by a surprise strike by the university maintenance workers. The union locked all the university buildings for a one-day work stoppage, with no guarantee that it might not be extended. The maintenance workers had been operating under the terms of a government decree reducing salaries for an indeterminate period of time. Now the university wanted to negotiate the new contract on the basis of the status quo. "Nothing doing," said the union, and to bring the point home, locked up the university. The University obtained a court injunction enjoining the union from blocking the doors. The union retaliated by letting students and professors cross the picket lines but refusing to admit the secretaries, who were members of the union. And without secretaries the university, for all practical purposes, ground to a halt. I guess I should not have been surprised that labour relations in this extremely liberal province might not be the same as south of the border—after all, I had had to endure a postal strike for nearly ten days shortly after arriving here—but I still found the experience disconcerting.

I tried to be imaginative in my search for a partner. I consulted a *psychothérapeute* with the engaging name of Marie LaBienvenue, who instructed me to spend several evenings hanging out in a small bar on Avenue Cartier observing guys picking up women. I obediently located the establishment, auspiciously named after one of my favourite Truffaut films, *Jules et Jim*, nursed a ginger ale for several hours and took notes on my observations. I finally decided that this just wasn't my style, and that a non-drinker was unlikely to find the woman of his dreams in a tavern.

Instead I joined a diner's club called La Bouffe des Courtesans, founded by a Montréal divorcée tired of always eating out by herself. The Rochambeau branch was run by a black chap from Teaneck, New Jersey, who wore his hair in curled braids. Each month the management chose a fancy restaurant and organized a dinner for the membership. My first time there I met a Venezuelan chap who taught medieval English literature at Fleur de Lis. (Given the nature of the university, there's no way I would ever have made his acquaintance on campus.) Now I don't make a point of my peculiarities, but the woman sitting next to me was evidently keeping track during the course of the evening, because when I ordered a glass of milk at meal's end she could contain herself no longer. "You don't drink wine, you don't drink coffee or tea, you don't own a house, or a car, or even a television set—what kind of American are you?" That didn't seem to merit a response so I just smiled sweetly and made a valiant effort to resist the temptation to empty my water glass into her lap.

Chapter 3

EARLY IN OCTOBER THERE CAME an official notification from Marie-Claude Contretemps, the Vice-Rector of Academic Affairs, that the three-year term of the Director of the School of Music was approaching its end and that elections would be held to name a successor. We were asked to choose among three fairly complicated procedures for carrying out this process. I threw the ballot away. I'd had more than enough of mindless bureaucracy at Chihuahua State College and had no interest in participating in its Québecois equivalent.

A choice having been made to hold an election (the other two processes were too technical to explain), we received another letter from the dean soliciting nominations. I threw that ballot away, too. These people took this nonsense even more seriously than their California counterparts. Didn't they have anything better to do with their time?

A third letter from the dean informed us that the only nominee was the incumbent but that we were still required to turn up for the election. I dutifully turned up. I didn't think anyone would be monitoring the contents of my wastebasket but presumably attendance would be taken at a command performance like this.

The election was held in a $200,000 chamber with a great round table surrounding an empty carpeted pit, individual high-backed, upholstered swivel chairs, microphones (inoperable) at every place, great rows of chevrons hanging from the high ceiling, a fleur de lis emblazoned on one wall, and huge tied-back curtains decorating floor-to-ceiling windows: in short, a thoroughly intimidating location.

Mme Contretemps explained at some length that we constituted a carefully selected deliberative body representing (in measured proportions) faculty, students, professional employees and non-professional employees, gathered *in camera* to render our considered opinion on this weighty question. One of the instrumental teachers, who always embarrassed me not only because he was such a jerk but also because he spoke French with such an awful American accent, raised his hand to ask what would happen if the incumbent failed to gain a majority of the votes cast. The Vice-Rector earnestly explained that in the event that the assembly was unable to arrive at a decision, she would duly report this result to the Rector and the selection process would begin all over again.

There being no further questions, the Vice-Rector went on to explain in wearying detail the process to be observed. The powers that be presumably having decided that electing a Director didn't merit hooking up the electronic voting system, yellow ballots would be distributed bearing the name of the incumbent followed by the words POUR and CONTRE. We were to indicate our choice by making a mark—such as an X, a circle, a line, or some other device of our imagining—alongside one of the two words.

After duly marking our ballots we lined up, marched past the Vice-Rector, and deposited the ballots in an official container. Valéry asked "So it's over— we can go now, right?" But in fact not a soul stirred until the two official scrutinizers, one professor and one student, had finished scrutinizing the ballots, tabulating the results and transmitting this information to the Vice-Rector. During the period of scrutiny I whispered to Valéry, "What's with this woman anyway?"

"That's just the point," he whispered back enigmatically. Mme Contretemps then announced that the incumbent had been officially re-elected and we all filed out of the hall. On the way I asked Valéry to explain.

"Marie-Claude Contretemps is the first woman to hold the position of Vice-Rector of Academic Affairs."

"Bully for her."

"That's just the point."

"Will you please stop that!"

"She's contending with the Old Boy network—'bullies' wouldn't be too strong a term. She also feels like a second-class citizen academically."

"Why's that? She has her doctorate."

"In education. Do you personally hold that in as high regard as a Ph.D. in philosophy or history?"

"Not really."

"So she's opted to compete in a bureaucratic rather than an academic playing field. Actually, she's at a double advantage."

"Because she knows all the rules?"

"Not just that—she really likes regulations and hates exceptions to the rules. You have to be careful with those people, Axel; they can be dangerous."

"Why's that?"

"Let's just say that they don't have much patience with mavericks like you, and can always find a weapon somewhere in the regulations to cut off your legs if they think you're getting too far out of line."

We went to resume our activities, in my case a meeting with the song seminar.

Sisters Isabelle and Paule Bascombe transferred from Montréal to follow Isabelle's voice teacher, Jeanne-Françoise Trébuchet. Small wonder. Isabelle displayed complete control of a very beautiful voice, making entrances on high A's seem effortless. Slender and dark-haired, she projected an aura of demure innocence belied by an erect posture resulting either from formal training as a dancer or considerable practice keeping "chest high, shoulders straight, back erect." Her sister accompanied her in a Mozart aria and "Monica's Waltz" from Menotti's "The Medium" with as much vigour and sensitivity as if she'd been performing a piano solo. Paule, the older of the two by a year and slightly fuller of figure, had quick eyes and a mouth always poised for a smile, as if in readiness for whatever amusement the world might next bring her.

All through October students in the song seminar scheduled presentations with an eagerness I had seldom encountered elsewhere. When I asked Isabelle to explain this enthusiasm she said, "It's because of the strike." While training for a marathon in the fall I had noticed shrubs, bushes, even fully developed trees being wrapped in burlap as if preparing for some cataclysmic event. "Winter," people told me. Clearly Rochambeau winters occurred on a grander scale than anything I'd experienced. But a strike? It turned out that Rochambeau was undergoing a periodic crisis, as inevitable and predictable as winter, a ritual performed every three years with the expiration of the collective agreements by which labour and management (in this case, the government) regulated their special forms of non-violent warfare.

I didn't pretend to understand it. All I knew was that all the secondary schools had been shut down for three weeks in a teachers' strike, now in a state of *trève*, or truce, while the principals negotiated some more. The government professionals were still *en grève* while the *cols bleus*, after letting garbage mount up for a while, had gone back to work and hospital workers, who had threatened a shutdown, were persuaded not to strike.

The maintenance workers of Fleur de Lis University, Isabelle informed me, had scheduled a strike for the following week. This would be a legal strike, unlike that of the schoolteachers, and could go on for some time. Or, since only 52% of the employees actually supported the strike, it could last just the week preceding reading period. I hoped for a short strike. Not only was it annoying to have my teaching schedule interrupted, but my office, books, scores, etc. would be off-limits for the duration: striking maintenance workers locked all the doors and threw away the keys.

If the maintenance workers didn't strike and the schoolteachers went back on strike, Isabelle continued, the professors at Fleur de Lis threatened a sympathy strike. So there seemed to be a waiting line of groups eager to shut down the university. I took the threat seriously enough to move the midterm exam up by a week, inspiring a bit of grumbling from students who had been counting on the strike to get them off the hook.

The loudest grumbling, not surprisingly, came from Screaming Annie, who reported that she had been to talk with the Director and that he wanted to see me. I presented myself at the Director's office, uncertain what to expect. Although the Venetian blinds were partially closed against the afternoon sun, I could admire the Director's view down the plaza toward the twin towers in the centre of the campus. Usually you can tell a person's specialization by studying the bookshelves but the diverse collection in this office gave no clue of what he had been up to before becoming Director. I did notice the absence of any personal effects: no photographs of wife and children, no mementos from former students, just the obligatory framed diplomas on the wall.

The Director told me that Screaming Annie (he didn't call her that) had come to him with her calculations, that he had listened at great length, and had explained to her that this was a university, not a conservatory, and that six hours a week was a reasonable expectation for three-credit course, but that she had remained unmoved. I asked him how he'd gotten rid of her. "By promising to talk with you," he said (thus completing the circle). I apologized for inflicting Screaming Annie on him and he said, not at all; he welcomed the opportunity to hear about how my courses were going. Aside from her complaint about homework, Screaming Annie had nothing but praise for my teaching.

But I hadn't heard the last of her. The next day she barged into my office to demand whether I'd talked with the Director and whether I'd decided to make any changes as a result of our conversation. By that point I had run out of ideas and simply told her to go away and, after a few scathing remarks, she did.

It occurred to me that the local YMCA might assist me in my search for a social life, so I called the executive secretary, who described the organization's offerings in the upbeat tones of a paid publicist. "We've got volleyball, racquetball, basketball, three kinds of swimming, and an eight-week course in jogging," he told me enthusiastically. "Or, if sports aren't your racket (get it, racquet? Heh heh) there is a committee that plans international events: each month they pick a country. This month's country is Africa. You could be our music advisor. You are interested in African music, aren't you? Or why don't you try the Literary and Historical Society?"

Great idea, I thought—there must be other Proust lovers in the city. Alas, the LHS turned out to be a group of aged but indomitable Anglophones who met annually to celebrate another year of having successfully defended their archives against unnamed but fearsome enemies. When I stopped at the Rochambeau Hotel de Ville, or town hall, I discovered that the community sponsored a wide variety of socio-cultural activities. By paying a substantial fee you could take courses in ceramics, bridge, chess, creative dance (ages five and six), Spanish, enamel on brass, weaving, horticulture, yoga, water colors, batik, needlework, quilting, pillow-lace, painting, woodworking, photography, stained glass, and guitar, half of which I had to look up in the dictionary.

Come Halloween I was beginning to get discouraged, but I thought that the page on "Where to go in Rochambeau," published each Friday in *Le Soleil*, might give me some ideas. I discovered a masquerade ball at the Hilton. Disco. Forget it. Another *Soirée d'Halloween*. More disco. A *Grande Mascerade* for UNICEF. Nope–just for kids. Then I came upon an announcement for *Danses folklorique internationales*. I had enjoyed folk-dancing during a summer French immersion program; maybe this would be fun.

Toward the end of the afternoon, after spending several hours hunting for a particular harmonic progression in Wagner, I rode my bike over to Valéry's house to present him with the problem. We spent an hour marvelling over the Ring cycle and he invited me to supper. Afterwards, while Valéry and Ghislaine cleaned up, I played the catching game with Hélène, instructing her to keep her feet together, arms at her sides, and lean backwards—I would catch her. René took a turn and then Hélène again; the children seemed captivated by the thrill of deliberately losing their balance, trusting that I would catch them. When Ghislaine came into the room to see what we were doing, I commented that adults couldn't play this game because they could never trust another person enough to keep their feet together—they would invariably flinch and take a step back at the last moment. "Don't be silly," Ghislaine said and, instructing Valéry to stand behind her, she confidently let herself fall back into his arms.

"You've been practicing!" I protested.

"Never did it before in my life," she said as I marvelled at a relationship that would inspire such complete trust.

Ghislaine decided she'd like to go to the folk dance, so we left Valéry, still recovering from Legionnaires disease (of all things), to mind the children, and we drove off to the community center.

Well, it turned out to be a party for a folk dancing course—no instruction, just continuous folk dancing. Why they advertised it in the newspaper remained a mystery. So mostly we watched; both the music and the dancing were pleasant. By the time a dance had ended, we could usually figure out the pattern, but by that time they were off on another. I felt a bit like Alice at the tea party: every time she lifted the cup, the Mad Hatter would cry "Move down!" Was the only alternative to learn to like disco?

Chapter 4

EARLY IN NOVEMBER I RODE beside Valéry on the final leg of our flight back from the annual meeting of the American Musicological Society. The excursion had begun inauspiciously. In the absence of buses I took a taxi from my apartment to the Rochambeau airport. Arriving half an hour before the flight I discovered to my chagrin that I'd left my ticket at home. Searched pockets, emptied suitcase, beat the bushes, and kicked self, cursed in two languages. (That's not really true: while I had a sixth grader's command of French vocabulary, any normal Francophone sixth-grader could swear rings around me.)

I went to the ticket counter and explained the problem. The agent verified that my reservation was in the computer, but said he couldn't help me. "Your ticket was an excursion fare, purchased 14 days in advance. If I sold you a ticket now, it wouldn't be 14 days in advance, would it?" He suggested I buy a new ticket full fare and then redeem my excursion fare tickets, at enormous loss, after I returned to Rochambeau. No way. So I found another taxi, went home, retrieved the tickets, kicked myself some more, and returned.

"You're back!" The agent exclaimed, expecting, one supposes, that I would have given up the trip altogether. I asked him whether I could make the next flight to Toronto and he said he'd have to charge me the difference between my ticket and a full round-trip fare. "But I'm going to use the return portion of the ticket as scheduled," I protested. Finally he punched buttons, made a ticket materialize, scribbled "tickets lost, found too late" on the bottom, and told me to hurry over to Gate One, where I could catch a flight to Montréal, switch to another flight to Toronto, and pick up my original itinerary.

At the meeting I hosted a session on the music of Debussy. In addition to the four presenters, I had invited three more Debussystes to join us at the panel table for announcements, comments and questions. One presenter spent about five minutes at the beginning of his talk trying, a bit prudishly, it seemed to me, to discredit the idea that Debussy had slept with Blanche Vasnier, the singer to whom he dedicated his early songs. The speaker based his argument in part on the relatively innocent dedicatory inscriptions on the songs. In the course of introducing the next speaker I speculated about what one might accept as confirmatory evidence, perhaps "To Blanche Vasnier in gratitude for an unforgettable weekend in Pourville"? When all the formal papers had been given I invited the panel members to comment on each other's offerings. Our *eminence grise*, a spry 90-year-old amateur musicologist, archivist, and *grande dame*, returned to the question of Blanche Vasnier and produced evidence from certain unpublished letters of Debussy (I later learned that she *owned* these letters) leaving no further doubt as to the actual liaison between the young composer and his favourite interpreter. A minor point from a scholarly point of view, but it added interest to a session which also included recorded performances of works no one had ever heard before, as well as ideas that compelled us to listen to familiar works in new ways.

Outside the session I experienced once again the brutal psychological stresses of AMS meetings, in which no credit is given for lots of things that matter in one's "real" life, but rather everyone is judged by a single inexorable standard. That I was not the only one to be affected became evident any time I stood in the lobby overhearing snatches of conversations of musicologists trying desperately to assert their value in front of other desperate musicologists, somewhat in the manner of men who constantly touch their own clothing as if to reassure themselves of their corporeal existence. "I've published an article...," "I'm giving a paper ...," "I'm in charge of ordering all the books ..." At one point, to escape all this nervous hot air, I walked to the wharf to visit the calliope and to admire the changing patterns of steam as each pipe blew its lid.

I shared these and other observations on life in the academic grove with Valéry as we flew back to Rochambeau. After running out of other topics I asked Valéry why my predecessor had left Fleur de Lis.

"Andrew Girard? He'd been trying to maintain a trans-Atlantic marriage with a professor of medieval studies at the Sorbonne. Finally it became too difficult and he returned to Paris to join her. It happened just before the end of fall term last year."

Flight attendants in their blue and white Québecair uniforms moved along the aisle, cleaning up after what they imaginatively called a meal. After a time Valéry turned to me and asked, "You bought your tickets on a fourteen-day excursion discount, right?"

I nodded.

"When you get to the airport, find a ticket counter that's not too busy and if you slip the agent ten or fifteen dollars they'll print you out a receipt for a same-day purchase."

"What's the point?"

"It's worth several hundred dollars more than the ticket you actually bought. You submit the new receipt with your expense report and the school will reimburse you for it."

"But, that's ..."

"Cheating? Sure, but everybody does it. Of course, you don't want to submit a receipt for a first-class ticket, because we're not supposed to travel first class, but nothing in the rules says that you had to purchase your ticket fourteen days in advance."

I didn't say anything but my expression must have spoken for itself, for Valéry continued, "Come on. It's just a way to bring your salary up to a reasonable level. You think this is something? Some guys go really overboard, like the Dean of Letters. He'd never survive an audit of his budget."

"Why does he do it?"

"I hear he's got a gambling problem."

"But how does he get away with it?"

"Nobody checks that carefully around here."

"I don't know. In my experience it's always the little fellows that get caught."

At that point the pilot warned us to fasten our seatbelts for landing and I didn't hear Valéry's response, if he said anything. A short while later we were back in Rochambeau.

Chapter 5

DURING MY LAST YEAR OF teaching in the States I noticed that the papers my students turned in looked better than the outlines I was handing out. I used an electric typewriter but it didn't seem to make the sharp, dark impressions that I saw on the papers of at least some of my students. So, at some considerable expense, I had my machine overhauled, which pleased the local office supply dealer but still didn't give my typing the appearance I wanted. When I went back to complain he beckoned me to draw closer, then whispered "Silk."

"Silk?" I asked.

"Silk," he repeated. "Nylon doesn't cut the mustard."

Sure enough, when I started using silk typewriter ribbons, my work took on the professional appearance commonly associated with an electric typewriter. Late in the fall I went back to restock and learned that the supply was temporarily exhausted. "The ribbons have to be imported from the East."

"How far east?"

"Connecticut." Well, the Pony Express from the East took several months, and by that time I'd discovered that another store up the street also carried silk ribbons for my machine.

In the spring I told the office supply man that I was moving to Canada and he said, "You'd better stock up on silk ribbons. They probably don't even have silk ribbons, or if they do, they'll probably be twice as expensive." I didn't care much for his attitude, and supposed that in a city several times the size of the college town in which I was employed one could surely find silk typewriter ribbons. "You'll be sorry" were the last words I heard as I drove off to my new job.

After a dozen telephone calls to every office supply store in Rochambeau I had to conclude that he had been right. Oh, there were the usual glimmers of false hope along the way. When I called the Olympia dealer a clerk told me, "Oh sure, we have two styles of silk ribbon, one at $4, one at $6." So I hopped on my bike and rode halfway across the city to the Olympia store, where a different clerk informed me that silk ribbons weren't being made anymore—they'd been replaced by nylon. I tried to explain that you can't replace silk with nylon, but to no avail.

After a few more calls I came across the local A.B. Dick representative. "Silk ribbons? Sure thing. How many do you want? … Of course we deliver. What's the address?" Next day there arrived a box of *nylon* ribbons. Finally I placed a long-distance call to an office-supply store in the States and asked them to ship me a box of silk ribbons. By mid-November I was still waiting.

The next time the musicologists met I recounted my experiences with Screaming Annie, and without even hearing the name of the student one of them said, "A violist, right? Don't worry about it. She does the same thing in all her courses. We've each had to put up with her at one time or another."

The following day, while I was working at the library, Screaming Annie came over to object to library policy. I led her, swiftly and firmly, to the office of the music librarian, Claude Beaudoin, a calm, helpful, and infinitely patient man, who listened to her complain that sometimes the books she'd been assigned to look at for my methodology course didn't appear on the shelves. She demanded that the library put all the books on reserve. The music librarian observed mildly that this involved a very large number of volumes and what with the paperwork involved, putting them all on reserve would be impractical. Screaming Annie remained unmoved and cranked up for a ten-minute tirade— articulate, logical (at least from her perspective), loud and fast. I began feeling dizzy and begged to be excused.

My office, as I've mentioned, represented the conflation of two monastic cells. I never found out whether the two sets of doors to the corridor, an arrangement found in many Swiss hotels, belonged to the original design for the building or came as an after-thought to reduce the impact of practicing instrumentalists on thoughtful musicologists. The right wall of the office contained bookcases running down to the desk in the corner.

As I brought more and more books from my apartment to my office I found myself running out of shelf space and so requisitioned another bookcase, which finally arrived in mid-November. In order to place this new bookcase alongside the others I had to slide the desk to the left, and in so doing dislodged a sheet of paper that had evidently gotten wedged between the desk and the wall.

I looked at it—a handwritten note on ivory paper: nothing of mine. I reflected—new professors often receive the offices of their predecessors. The office had probably belonged to Andrew Girard. I was about to throw the sheet away when the word "*mort*" caught my attention. My translation does not do justice to the elegant French, but conveys the gist of the message: "*Persisting along this path will lead to your imminent death.*" Underneath the words, in another hand, I read "M.C.C.? A.V.? posse?"

I took the note next door to Valéry's office and asked what Andrew Girard had been up to that might have led to a death threat.

"What do you know about the structure of the university?" Valéry asked.

"Not a lot," I said.

He pulled a binder from a bookshelf and opened it. "Fleur de lis has twelve faculties," he explained. "Administration, arts, education, engineering, food and agriculture, law, letters, medicine, nursing, science, social sciences and theology. Each faculty comprises a number of departments or schools, ranging in size from theology, with no departments at all, to a number of the larger faculties that have as many as six departments."

"I'm with you so far."

"The École de Musique belongs to the Faculty of Arts, along with the School of Architecture, the School of Visual Arts and the Department of Urban Planning. Andrew wanted to move musicology from the Faculty of Arts to the Faculty of Letters."

"What for?"

"Have you talked to any of the musicology students?"

"Sure. They seem bright and able."

"How would you describe the performers—not as performers, you understand, but as academic students?"

"Somewhat less so, I'd have to say." And thinking of Screaming Annie, the voluble violist, I would have said considerably less so.

"Andrew thought that the performance and music education divisions of the School of Music had a negative influence on the academic side. He wanted a graduate degree in music to have the same intellectual validity as a graduate degree in history or literature or philosophy."

"And he thought this would happen if he moved musicology into the same faculty as history, literature and philosophy?"

"That was the general idea."

"But what would happen to performance and music education?"

"He would never give a direct answer to that question but I suspect he hoped that music education would find a home in the Faculty of Education and that the performers would eventually transfer to the conservatory."

"And this campaign caused a fair amount of controversy?"

"That's putting it mildly. Andrew was brilliant, persuasive and persistent."

"But not conciliatory, sympathetic or tolerant?"

"I might almost think you knew the man."

"So the main dispute occurred between the Faculty of Arts, which would have lost influence, and the Faculty of Letters, which would have gained?"

"It started out that way, but before long the entire university became embroiled in the argument."

"How so?"

Valéry read from the notebook: "'*On matters affecting the internal organization of the university, the regulations governing the Faculty Senate call for each faculty of the university to have a single vote, presumably representing the majority will of its constituent members.*' Some faculties— notably letters, law, medicine, nursing, engineering, and science— applauded Girard's campaign as a way of restoring academic rigor at the university, which they saw as moving too far in the direction of open admissions as a way of generating funding from the province."

"I take it that not everyone favoured academic rigor."

"That's right. There were two camps opposing Girard's campaign: faculties most of whose students could barely make it into university in the first place and faculties who needed every student they could get in order to maintain their faculty status."

"And those would be ..."

"Arts, Education, Food and Agriculture, Social Sciences, Theology, and Administration."

"Looks like something of a stand-off."

"It was going to be a very interesting vote. I understood that toward the end Girard had cut some kind of deal with the Dean of Theology to garner his support."

"You mean it never came to a vote?"

"No. As it happened, Andrew had to return to Paris for a family crisis on the day of the vote. In his absence one of his opponents moved to table the proposal until Andrew's return. And when he failed to come back, the whole issue just evaporated."

"But did anyone really take the issue seriously enough to write a death threat?"

"It would seem so. It doesn't look like Andrew's handwriting."

"What about the initials at the bottom of the page."

"It appears that he wrote that part."

"What does it mean?"

"Well, M.C.C. would probably be Marie-Claude Contretemps."

"The Vice-Rector of Academic Affairs?"

"Right."

"Why would she try to stop Andrew's campaign?"

"As I said, the dispute had spread from Arts and Letters to the university at large. In some faculties nobody was getting any work done. I imagine she was under a fair amount of pressure from the Rector to put an end to the matter, one way or another."

"I guess I'll need to obtain a specimen of her handwriting if I'm going to connect her with this note," I said. "Do you have any ideas?"

"As it happens, I can help you with that." Valéry opened a file cabinet, withdrew a manila folder, and showed me a sheet of writing paper clipped to a typewritten document."

"I didn't know anyone wrote notes any more," I said.

"Marie-Claude is of the old school," Valéry said. "She not only approved the grant proposal I'd submitted for the Frescobaldi edition but she congratulated me on it. See for yourself," he said, passing me the folder.

I held the note I'd brought from my office beside the message from Mme. Contretemps. "These don't look anything alike," I said.

Valéry stood beside me. "You're right. Your mystery writer uses vertical lines while Marie-Claude's slant backwards."

"And look here: her b's and p's are completely closed but those on my sheet remain open."

"And look at her capital G—I've never seen it made like that. There's a capital G on your note—they're not at all the same. I don't think she's the person you're looking for."

"How about A.V.?"

"That would be Alain Valcartier, the Dean of the Faculty of Arts."

"I take it his influence would diminish if he lost the École de Musique?"

"It's not just influence, it's money. Funding at the university is calculated on the basis of student hours, and much as Valcartier despises the legion of instrumental students in music—he considers them incapable of meeting the university's academic standards, and as you've seen, mostly with good reason—they do generate a ton of hours. It was personal, too. He considered Andrew the incarnation of the pushy upstart American. So I don't think he shed any tears when Girard moved back to Paris."

"And what's this 'posse'?"

Valéry chuckled. "I understand that a number of students got interested in the campaign. Although Girard was born in the States, he perfected his command of French in Paris, partly with the help of his Parisian wife. He would infuriate Québecois students by correcting their French."

"So what was the posse?"

"I don't know all the details, but I understand the Bascombe sisters were part of the group. You have them in your song seminar, don't you? Why don't you ask them?"

I mulled the question over as I returned to my office. The success of any seminar course rests on the quality of student presentations. Our most recent class offered a magnificent argument in favour of the system. I spent the first hour lecturing on Mahler, then one student gave a fine comparison of two settings of a Mörike poem, one by Brahms, the other by Wolf. This was followed by a report on the Wolf Italienisches Liederbuch by the Bascombe sisters, which for sheer theatre could hardly have been surpassed. Isabelle would read the German text line by line and Paule would follow with a French translation. Then one or the other would offer a few precise, succinct observations on Wolf's setting, after which the Paule would go to the piano and accompany Isabelle in a polished performance. (Earlier in the fall the two girls had offered the songs at a recital broadcast on CBC Radio.) They discussed and performed four songs in this manner. I could have listened all day. But would they have issued a death threat against one of their teachers?

I could easily have imagined Screaming Annie leading a posse, except that knowing her, it might have turned into a lynch mob. Earlier in the day I had been working in the music library when she asked for help on a term paper she was writing on the physiology of violin playing. She wanted to know how you could find articles on that subject. I asked if she'd looked in RILM.

"What's that?" she demanded.

"Don't you remember our musical scavenger hunt?" I asked.

At the beginning of our course on "La Méthodologie de la Recherche" I'd organized a *chasse à l'énigme* (Valéry had supplied the term) in which students, presented with a list of twenty questions of the sort that reference librarians constantly encounter, proceeded to the reference section of the library, where I joined them as a kind of resource of last resort. A number of the students sailed into the exercise without hesitation, deducing from the question "Where would you expect to hear a tedoc?" that the term in question was probably some kind of musical instrument, and after failing to find it in the New Grove Dictionary sought a more specialized lexicon which would describe the tedoc as a Cambodian cowbell.

Others hadn't mastered the fundamental fact that a library is a repository of information systematically arranged. One girl was frustrated by the question "Who composed the following melody?" I asked her to imagine what kind of book would help her. "A dictionary of musical themes, I suppose." I suggested that she look in the card catalogue under "D" and she soon had the appropriate book in hand, but returned a few minutes later to complain that the theme she was looking for didn't appear in the book. I asked whether she'd read the instructions on how to use the dictionary. No. "You have to transpose the theme into C and then look up its pitches in alphabetical order." I reckoned that eventually they'd get the hang of library research. I hadn't counted on Screaming Annie, who claimed to have forgotten everything from the first half of the course.

So I pulled out a volume of RILM (*Répertoire International de Littérature Musicale*), found the section on physiology of music and showed her the list of entries, each accompanied by an abstract of its contents, and went back to my work.

A few minutes later she returned. "How do I find the journals?" I asked her if she hadn't had a bibliography course. "Yes, but I forgot it all." So I showed her the computer printout that listed all the journals received at the university and the call number for each one. She still didn't understand, because a few minutes later she came back and said, "I looked up the authors in the computer printout but they weren't there." I explained that the computer printout listed only the journals; hadn't she noted the full citation from the entries in RILM? No.

So we pulled RILM out once more. "At the end of each entry it gives a citation," I explained. "In the case of a book it lists city, publisher and state; in the case of journal, it lists title, volume, number, year, and page reference. You look up the title of the journal in the computer printout to see whether Fleur de Lis has it, and if so, to locate its call number."

"That sounds awfully complicated," she complained. I asked if she'd looked in earlier volumes RILM. "Earlier volumes?"

"Yes, it comes out once a year and lists every book and article of musical interest published anywhere in the world during that year."

"You mean I have to look up each year? That'll take a long time."

"Well, that's the nature of research. Think how long it would take if we didn't have RILM." There are times when it becomes difficult to maintain my policy of infinite patience with students, times when I wish someone would suggest that they might be happier in other fields—fields that didn't require logical thought.

Screaming Annie returned at full volume later in the week, storming into my office to complain again that my assignments were too hard, that it was unreasonable to ask graduate students to spend six hours a week studying, and that if she had to drop the course and delay her graduation by a term it would be my fault and her curse would be upon my children's children unto the seventh generation. I didn't bother telling her about my vasectomy.

Perhaps a penchant for argumentation forms an essential part of the Québecois character, at least its academic side. At the end of November the music faculty, without the benefit of students, professional workers or non-professional workers, re-assembled in the intimidating assembly chamber to approve an announcement of vacancy for a voice teacher.

Or actually, for three quarters of a voice teacher, that being all the Vice-Rector would authorize.

First the pedants went to work on the description. A Paris-born choral conductor pointed out that the phrase "Direction and instruction of courses in chamber music" contained an unfortunate solecism since (at least in French) you can instruct only students, not courses. She proposed an inversion in sentence order to resolve the problem. The Vice-Dean of Research countered that her inversion destroyed the parallelism with the other phrases of the description, and offered a rephrasing. But given the size of the hall, the non-functioning of the individual microphones and the soft-spokenness of the participants, it took some considerable time to work this matter out.

Then came the legalists, armed with copies of the Collective Convention, the official document by which the faculty conducted its academic life. "As a deliberative assembly, we are empowered to amend the job description. Why don't we just amend the three quarters of a position into a full position?" Nobody seemed to have an answer to that one.

Finally the politicians weighed in, declaring that we should reject the job description and send it back to the Vice-Rector with the demand that we be given a full position. Someone suggested that the resolution might be stronger if we passed a few whereases, so a flurry of whereases flew about the chamber:

- whereas we have enough students to keep three or even four voice teachers busy, God knows;

- whereas the university has resolved its current fiscal crisis so where does the Vice-Rector get off telling us that we can have only three quarters of professor;

- whereas the Vice-Rector himself will come up for re-election one day and had better watch his step, et cetera.

At this point I had to leave, but Valéry told me that after the better part of an hour, the faculty decided to reject the description and send it back to the Vice-Rector heavily laden with whereases.

Chapter 6

By THE BEGINNING OF DECEMBER my social life had hardly improved, unless you count a date with an angry Francophone feminist who took it as a personal affront that in French the nouns referring to the female sex organs are of the masculine gender. My forays into the tiny Anglophone community hadn't produced any better results. As organist at the Anglican cathedral, I'd met members from the city's several Anglican parishes. Once a month I'd hold a dinner party, inviting three couples to my apartment. I reasoned that with each return invitation I'd meet more people, in a grand exponential progression, and that among them I'd find some connection to a suitable partner. My mathematics may have been correct but the plan came to nought for want of return invitations; perhaps Anglophones disliked the uneven table arrangement produced by an unattached man.

Then I received a dinner invitation from the Bascombe sisters, who were about to return to Montréal, having completed their graduate studies at Fleur de Lis. Their parents, the young women explained when I arrived at their apartment, had rented a place for them during their time in Rochambeau. I couldn't help observing that it was nicer than mine and certainly more attractively decorated. A grand piano occupied one corner of the living room with a sliding door leading to a balcony containing a small table, two chairs and several planters that must have produced the effect of a garden during the summer months. The dining room table had been set with tall candles for illumination and a centerpiece of votive candles floating in a spherical bowl.

Paule and Isabelle served and cleared each course with the same graceful partnership that I had observed in their performances in the song seminar. I learned that while Paule had always been a pianist, Isabelle had originally been destined for the violin and had studied that instrument for several years before the development of her extraordinary voice made that the better choice for university study. Both parents were musicians, their mother an oboist with the Symphonie de Montréal, which accounted for their ease as performers.

I entertained the sisters with the saga of silk typewriter ribbons.

"Did the shipment from the States ever actually arrive?" Paule asked.

I told them that I waited for several weeks then telephoned the office supply store to find out what had happened," I said.

"Oh," a representative had told me. "United Parcel said it couldn't ship to Canada, and I didn't know whether we could mail them."

"So you just did nothing? You didn't write or phone to let me know one way or the other?"

"I think you'd better talk to someone else."

I talked to three other people and finally got someone who promised to help. "You mean I can just put them in the mail and they'll go to a foreign country? That doesn't sound so difficult."

More weeks passed, and then I received a yellow card form the Customs Bureau saying that they had impounded a box of silk typewriter ribbons until I paid duty on them. The woman in charge demanded to know why I had bought American typewriter ribbons—weren't Canadian ribbons good enough for me, or did I have some prejudice against Canada, and what kind of name was Crochet, anyway? I explained that I had tried every store in Rochambeau and all they had was nylon ribbons. She said that in any case, they were going to charge me 25% duty. I protested that this wasn't even an item produced in Canada. She said, "Our policy is to protect domestic industry whether it exists or not. And then you have to pay a 9% Federal sales tax."

"But the ribbons weren't bought here."

"That's beside the point," she explained.

Finally the ribbons arrived but then my electric typewriter went on the blink. Nothing major—just a slipped widget. I asked the department secretary whether the university had a technician who could fix it, to save me lugging the machine all the way downtown. She said I'd be better off going to the Olympia store, even if it meant taking a taxi. The university technician charged $20 just to answer the phone, and the fees mounted rapidly from there.

When I tried to turn the conversation to the question of the "posse" both girls blushed. "How did you hear about that?" Isabelle wanted to know. I didn't want to talk about the death threat note unless I had to, so I just said that I'd been interested in my predecessor's activities and the word had turned up.

"I understand that Prof. Girard rubbed some students the wrong way," I said.

"You can say that again!" Paule exclaimed. "Some of us were ready to kill him." Then she received a significant look from Isabelle and tried to back-pedal. I just waited with a sympathetic look and finally Isabelle broke the silence.

"Look, it was all just a game."

"What kind of game?"

"Well, you talked about Prof. Girard rubbing people the wrong way. You remember the presentation that Paule and I did on the Mörike Lieder?"

"Indeed I do; I found the whole performance completely enchanting."

"Well I guess he's less easily enchanted because he would always grumble about our analytical remarks. He didn't like us to suggest how a composer interpreted a text with his music."

"A lot of musicologists share his prejudice. Happily I'm not one of them."

"And some people got really offended when he'd correct their French," Paule said. "And him an American!"

"I can see where that might be annoying," I said. "But what's this posse all about?"

The sisters exchanged a look and then Paule said, "You might as well tell him."

"Okay," Isabelle said. "A bunch of us were sitting around one evening complaining about our teachers in general and Prof. Girard in particular when someone suggested killing him."

"Surely you're joking," I said.

"But that's the whole point," Paule said. "It was just a joke."

"What did you have in mind?" I asked.

"That was the game," Isabelle said. "Each person tried to think of a more outrageous way of getting rid of Girard."

"One person wanted to put a bomb under his car," Paule said. "Then another person suggested taking his car completely apart—it was just a Volkswagen Beetle, after all—and reassembling it in the atrium of the École de Musique."

"Paule and I suggested that we wait until his birthday, then strap him to a lawn chair, attach dozens of helium balloons to the framework, and let him fly away," Isabelle said.

"So this murder game wasn't directly tied to the plan to transfer musicology from Arts to Letters?" I asked.

"No," Paule said. "We knew about that, of course. Everybody was talking about it, but it wouldn't have affected any of us personally and we didn't really care that much about the general principle of the thing."

"Well, that's something of a relief," I said. "So you didn't actually do anything?"

"I wouldn't say that exactly," Isabelle said.

"What do you mean?" I asked.

Paule gave her a sharp look and Isabelle said, "We've already told him this much."

"All right," Paule said. "Let's just say that we may have played a few minor tricks on Professor Girard."

I realized that I might have pushed the sisters too far and so asked them about their plans in Montréal.

"I'm going to keep studying with Madame Trebuchet," Isabelle said.

"She's taking a sabbatical semester before her retirement," Paule explained. "She won't have any regular students except for Isabelle."

"What's going to happen here?" I asked.

"I understand there's going to be a new voice teacher in January," Isabelle said.

We chatted a bit longer—I wished them well in their future careers, they thanked me for being an encouraging teacher—and I headed back to my apartment.

Chapter 7

A WEEK BEFORE THE END of the semester, the maintenance workers agreed to call off the work stoppages that had deprived us of secretaries, library, photocopy machines, pianos, sound systems and mail for twenty-nine days (up to two weeks at a stretch) during the latter part of the fall. Teaching continued, at least in the School of Music, during these work stoppages but the students, tired of being pawns in the struggle between the university and the union, thought up some counter-tactics of their own:

- Block the exits to the university so that the opposing parties would be compelled to negotiate.

- Boycott classes (any excuse would do to avoid coming to class).

- Seize the Dean's office (a favourite tactic borrowed from students in the States).

- Refuse to pay inscription fees for the second term.

The professors didn't exercise their right to strike, but talk grew more serious about a professors' strike in January. Informed sources reported that the university would resort to a lockout if the dispute with the maintenance workers had not been settled by January. Since we would not have access to our offices in this event, I planned to take home a box or two of organ music and research materials before departing for Christmas vacation.

For me the autumn work stoppages had been merely inconvenient. Students in other schools of the university, by contrast, had had as few as six class meetings with professors who declined to cross the picket lines, and these students were understandably unhappy with the uncertainty whether the spring term would actually take place or not. The university's refusal to accept tuition payments for the spring term suggested that we might be in for quite a siege.

The handwriting question continued to pique my curiosity, so on one of the days that the university was actually open I crossed the campus—using the subterranean tunnels provided to allow easy movement about the campus during winter months—to Pavillon Dorval, where Alain Valcartier taught a course in urban planning in addition to his duties as Dean of the Faculty of Arts.

The class took place in a large lecture hall with heavily-raked stadium seating and spotlights on the blackboard where Prof. Valcartier was writing his last notes as I slipped in by a door high at the rear of the hall. Students were conscientiously copying what they saw, displaying a good deal more energy than I commonly witnessed in my Methodology of Research class.

Prof. Valcartier affected a goatee and a moustache painstakingly shaved so that it covered only the top half of his upper lip. (I'd never seen anything like it and couldn't understand the point. I maintained a moustache and beard so that I had to shave only once a week to clear out the underbrush around my throat.) He had a thin face and spoke in brief, incisive sentences, as if catering to the short-term memory capacity of his students. At the end of the lecture he didn't pause for questions but disappeared abruptly through a door at the side of the blackboard. The students mounted the stairs and filed past me.

When the traffic had eased I descended the stairs and stood before the blackboard, comparing Valcartier's choppy writing with the meticulously connected, precisely elegant hand on the notepaper. Perhaps he just wrote fast at the blackboard. I tried to make allowances and began to compare individual letters. I noticed that he didn't lift the chalk when crossing his t's but simply continued the line from wherever the word ended. I also noticed that he often used printed capital letters at the beginning of a sentence before continuing on in cursive. It was always possible that he preserved a different style when applying pen to paper but it didn't seem likely, and so I tentatively crossed him off my list. But if neither he nor Madame Contretemps were responsible for the note—and my conversation with the Bascombe sisters made it seem unlikely that the "posse" had written it—who was the author?

My answer came unexpectedly. As I have mentioned, masters degree candidates in performance at Fleur de Lis University were required to write an essay, the purpose of which was to teach them the joys of logical thought applied to defining and solving a problem.

Before undertaking their essays the students had to submit a *projet d'essai* presenting the problem, defining their objectives and justifying their plan of attack. All of this was bewildering for performers, some of whom had gotten through university without having to write anything more demanding than circling the correct letters on multiple-choice tests. The Methodology of Research was a course designed to help them, over the course of a semester, write their *projets d'essai*, the essay itself occupying six credits of the following semester.

For the first several weeks I waxed eloquent about the joys of logical thought applied to defining and solving a problem. The trouble started when it came time for the students to begin the actual process of writing. One afternoon I received a visit from Jeanne-Françoise Trébuchet, the most redoubtable of the voice professors, who sailed into my office in response to her students' complaints about the course. An extraordinary tower-like coiffure must have added at least six inches to her height to the point that if you measured from the most elevated point of hair, her height exceeded mine. She wore a necklace consisting of a large sapphire-coloured stone from which a number of silver threads hung in echelon form. Her eyes gave the impression that she perceived not only every superficial detail but penetrated to the essence of everything she beheld.

When I tried to explain the joys of logical thought applied to defining and solving a problem, she cut me off with an imperious gesture and said, "I understand your position; I want you to understand mine. You speak of defining objectives. My objective is always the same: to produce better singers. Don't you agree?" She continued without waiting for a response.

"Take my little soprano Linda. The Fauré *Chansons d'Eve* suit her voice perfectly. Consider the opening song, an evocation of the dawn of paradise. The form is simplicity itself, but the music, so ineffably sublime," (she paused to brush away a tear) "embodies the very essence of divine creation." I protested that it is very difficult to judge essays written in this style. "I can judge," she intoned. "I know these songs to the depth of my inner fullness, and if the student knows what she's talking about, her words will strike a resonant chord here." (She firmly planted her fists against her capacious bosom.) "Think about it," she said, and swept grandly out of my office.

In despair, I went to see the oldest living inhabitant, a former

Director of the school and now head of music education. Completely bald on the top of his head, he cultivated a magnificent moustache that drew attention away from his shiny pate. His heavy eyebrows probably intimidated more than one student, but he welcomed me into his office with an avuncular smile. As I looked at the multiple mounds of neatly stacked papers on his desk, I reflected that I stood in the presence of a master of administration and academic politics.

"Axel," he said, "we all know that the voice teachers don't know anything about writing papers and that the students listen only to their teachers. But of course we can't say that out loud, so we ask students to call on a musicologist to be co-director of their essays. It's up to you to pull the chestnuts out of the fire." When I looked as if I might raise a protest, he simply sat back in his chair, opened his arms and raised his palms as if to indicate that he had said not only all that he had to say but all that could be said on the subject.

I wrote Madame Trébuchet a brief note indicating that I would exert every effort on behalf of Linda and her other voice students struggling with the requirements of the *projet d'essai*. The next day I received a handwritten message from the voice teacher expressing her admiration of my perspicacity in recognizing the role of musicology in the service of performance.

When I finished choking over this magnificently deliberate misconstruction of my words I looked past the message to the medium: the handwriting looked strangely familiar. Then I pulled the "death threat" note from my desk and held it beside the elegantly formed script of Madame Trébuchet. I had discovered the author!

Just before the completion of the fall term, just after the mid-morning coffee break in our three-hour graduate seminar on the methodology of research, Screaming Annie launched into a pre-holiday harangue that surpassed in eloquence and pathos all her previous efforts in this genre, a production that assumed the structure of a gospel song by wailing soloist and back-up choir.

Annie: "We've been talking, Prof. Crochet, and I speak for all the rest of the students when I say that we've got too much work."

Chorus: "Too much work, Lord, too much work."

Annie: "The final project you've assigned us, to write an outline for an imaginary master's thesis, employing the research tools that we've learned during the semester, is a waste of time since we're just going to have to do the same thing when we write our master's essay."

Chorus: "Tell it, sister, tell it."

Annie: "And the assignment for the last session, to read the book you put on reserve and write a book review on it, is impossible— nobody's started yet and there isn't enough time for the whole class to read that book just so we can discuss it in class."

Chorus: "Not enough time, Lordy lord, no time."

Annie: "Anyway, we've all worked hard during the term and you have enough material to assign us grades, which is the main reason for this course after all, and if the secretaries really had gone on strike and shut down the university and the term had ended the way they said we wouldn't have had to do any more assignments for the last two weeks and it isn't fair to make us do any more just because they didn't go on strike after all and there really are two weeks left."

Chorus: "Unfair, Lord, oh it's just too unfair."

Annie: "We've all got juries coming up and concerts and final exams and other courses and recitals and Christmas shopping and all the work we haven't done in our other courses because we've been spending hours, yes hours, every week doing the assignments for your class and it's just too much, you understand, too much, so what are you going to do about it anyway?"

Chorus, snapping fingers and advancing toward the front of the room: "Watcha gonna do, yeah, watcha gonna do?"

I was tempted to launch a counteroffensive of my own leaping up on a table and shouting: "All right, you snot-nosed, sniffling, whimper-faced, weak-minded, lacklustre bunch of key pushers! I've had enough of your complaining. You over there—the next time you raise your hand I'm going to take it off at the shoulder with this bull whip (crack) you got it? You miserable, lazy, scatterbrained, good-for-nothing lickspittles! You can't even tell a footnote from a grace-note. You listen and you listen up good while I tell you in revolting detail just what's going to happen if you don't get those assignments done in time!"

Lacking the vocabulary for this response I merely nodded and agreed to consider their arguments. But ultimately I was vindicated by Shy Colette. Have I not told you about Shy Colette? Two thirds of the way through the term she came to my office and said she felt uncomfortable talking in class about things she didn't completely understand. Book reviews were one thing, but now we were coming to palaeography and watermarks and iconography and style analysis. Couldn't she just turn in written reports instead of speaking in class? I observed that the other students were in the same situation—this was new material for everyone. She didn't say anything, but her eyes began to well up. I suggested that one of the purposes of the course was to give students practice in presenting the results of their research in a variety of forms. Now she was really weeping. Clearly this discussion wasn't leading anywhere. I asked whether she intended to continue attending class. Between sobs she explained that that wouldn't be fair to the others. Rather than attempt to play therapist in French I just handed her a Kleenex (one way or another a good deal of weeping seemed to go on in my office) and invited her to submit an independent plan for finishing the term. Nobody in the class bothered to tell her when we abandoned the final project and book review and reduced the last assignment to a choice of two out of four, so Shy Colette achieved, without apparent difficulty, what Screaming Annie had claimed was impossible.

Chapter 8

JUST BEFORE CHRISTMAS BREAK I asked for an appointment with Madame Trébuchet and presented myself at the hour she appointed. Her studio held the usual grand piano, its sound muffled by a thick carpet that extended nearly to the walls. In place of the usual self-glorifying photographs of a singer at earlier stages in her career, the walls bore portraits of the great Lieder composers—Schubert, Schumann, Brahms, Wolf—and their French counterparts—Duparc, Berlioz, Fauré, Chausson, Debussy.

Madame Trébuchet motioned me to an armchair beside her desk and she took a seat in a matching *fauteuil.* "I understand that it's considered impolite to read other people's mail," I began, "but in this case the letter in question more or less thrust itself upon me." She said nothing but cocked her head a fraction of an inch to the right. I continued. "The office I inhabit was previously occupied by my predecessor, Andrew Girard. One day last term I came across an unsigned note that had apparently escaped the notice of whoever cleaned the office after his departure. As I have said, it was not my place to read the note, but the morbid nature of its contents made it almost impossible to avoid doing so. Not to put too fine a point on the matter, I believe you to be its author."

Madame Trébuchet folded her hands, nodded slowly and seemed to gather her thoughts. "Andrew Girard was a menace to this school," she said. "The plan for which he fought would have utterly destroyed the École de Musique." I waited for her to continue. "Andrew was not alone in his delusion. I have read about similar misguided efforts in the United States, in Canada, and here in Québec. Well-wishing educators eager for excellence without the patience to achieve it through hard work think they can work magic by raising standards, as if by so doing they will suddenly transform the students in their charge."

I nodded, not so much to imply agreement as to indicate that I was following her words. "You earned your doctorate from a respected university, a document representing sustained intellectual effort applied to a chosen topic. Your job in a school of music, as opposed to a purely academic environment, is to offer performers the product of your labours. Yes, I know that not all of them will appreciate it, but you have seen among your students those who will be able to apply what they have learned from you to their performances."

I lifted a hand but when she raised her own I acquiesced and let her finish. "Andrew didn't just want to move the École de Musique: he wanted to destroy it. His vision of music as an academic discipline had no place in it for performance, which is music's only reason for being. He considered a musical score to be the equivalent of an historical document rather than a blueprint for beautiful sounds. He scorned performers because they weren't scholars." She shook her head sadly. "I thought my words might jar him out of his dream world. Unfortunately, I failed."

"Perhaps you succeeded," I said. "Nobody has been able to tell me exactly why he returned to Paris. It could be that he didn't want to face the possibility of defeat."

The woman's face brightened. "I never looked at it that way."

"But you never actually intended to …"

Madame Trébuchet's expression changed as she gathered herself together. "Really, young man!" She rose, perhaps regretful of her openness, and I took my leave.

Chapter 9

THE NEW YEAR BROUGHT A new face to the École de Musique: Colette Brevard, a professor of voice formerly at Rochambeau Conservatory. I caught a brief glimpse of her short blonde hair and trim figure as I was going into my music history class, made inquiries, checked her schedule at the secretary's office, and made my way to her studio when I knew she had finished teaching for the day.

Seen from the front, Colette displayed blue eyes and a face whose muscles had clearly been used for smiles more often than frowns. She expressed pleasure that someone, other than her voice students, had taken the trouble to welcome her. I noted that she had left Madame Trebuchet's decorations in place and Colette explained that this office would not officially become her own until the following year when her predecessor actually retired. After we had spent some time chatting I asked whether she would be interested in attending a concert with me and she cheerfully accepted.

The following night I escorted Colette to a symphony concert held in the kind of opera house found in many smaller cities toward the end of the nineteenth and beginning of the twentieth centuries but mostly destroyed in intervening years to make way for more modern structures. I had not encountered any black orchestral conductors in the States, but James DePriest had enjoyed a hero's welcome in Rochambeau, where he displayed an uncanny ability to elicit fine playing from a modestly-talented orchestra.

The program included Debussy's *Prélude à l'après-midi d'un faune* (Prelude to the afternoon of a faun), based on the poem by Stéphane Mallarmé evoking the languorous dreams of a cloven-footed satyr. I told Colette how my American students insisted on telling me how the music perfectly conveyed the graceful movement of a gentle *fawn* drinking from a babbling brook.

"But they have never read the Mallarmé?"

"I'm afraid that's not part of the curriculum."

During the intermission we chatted about how she came to be bilingual: her father, an American radio engineer seconded to the Canadian forces during the Second World War, had met her mother in Montréal and thereafter married her. Colette grew up speaking English to one parent and French to the other. She also turned out to be a runner, who the previous fall had placed third in a ten-kilometre race in Rochambeau, where she had been teaching at the conservatory before coming to Fleur de Lis.

After the concert as we walked to the parking lot I noticed that she was wearing flat shoes.

"A lot of men get nervous being around a woman who's taller than they are," Colette explained.

"What I like is that whether we agree or not, we're seeing eye to eye—I think we're almost exactly the same height." She just smiled; I liked that smile a lot.

Chapter 10

THE SECOND WEEK IN JANUARY the Director called me into his office. "Axel," he said, "We're sending you on the road. Have you ever been to Jonquière or Chicoutimi? I understand they can be bracing at this time of year." When I looked perplexed, he went on, "Don't worry about your classes. Your students have been notified that you'll be away for a few days. I understand that some of them are particularly keen to catch up on their work." The Director's dead-pan humour always got me. "You'll be travelling with Pierre Gagnon. He'll explain the routine to you." Evidently he had nothing further to say so I turned to leave, but just as I reached the door the Director added, "Of course, you will have written your will," employing that future anterior tense that always gave me such problems in French. I had to hope that he was just kidding.

Valéry assured me that I wasn't being punished, or at least not personally. The university, always eager to expand the student base on which its provincial funding was calculated, had established branch campuses in regions of Québec incapable of supporting independent institutions, including one campus just south of the Arctic Circle. In addition, the School of Music had entered into agreements with a number of schools in the region whereby university professors—in this case Pierre Gagnon and myself—would serve as adjudicators for students passing from one instructional level to another, insuring in principle some degree of quality control and the questionable cachet of the reputation of the École de Musique of Fleur de Lis University.

Pierre Gagnon, a short man with a squarish face, had evidently decided early in his career that the road to success in the École de Musique lay in keeping a low profile, and this strategy seemed to have informed his entire identity. He dressed modestly, one could say inconspicuously, wore his hair neither long nor short, and had a habit of dropping his gaze, a trait that might have been a sign of becoming modesty in the heroine of a nineteenth-century novel but which I found somewhat unnerving in an adult colleague.

For all that, Gagnon, an eighteen-year veteran of these visits to the hinterlands, filled our long drives with good conversation, in a friendly but guarded manner, and happily shared his knowledge of all the best restaurants. I had been interested in this quiet clarinet teacher but had never had occasion to make his acquaintance. He told me he felt the same way about me, and so we spent evening dinners getting better acquainted. The course of our days had already been prescribed.

I spent the first morning in Arvida, listening to fifteen piano students, eight to fifteen years of age, each of whom sang a solfège exercise, performed a sight-reading exercise at the keyboard, played several scales, and executed an etude and four pieces of a difficulty prescribed by his or her level. I calculated that running a marathon required less stamina than listening to these performers. I was impressed by the beginners, who executed their scales and pieces with mechanical perfection even as their feet dangled from the piano bench. The older students, on the other hand, played alarmingly badly, lacking both technical mastery and musicality. I wasn't sure what this said about their teachers, but fortunately I wasn't required to render such judgement—I merely recorded what I heard.

Robert Frost talks, in "Desert Places," of finding his own interior spaces more terrifying than any desolation here on earth or in outer space. Myself, I've always found the wilderness unnerving. It was one thing to drive a few hours from Boston and see Vermont countryside, dotted with dairy farms and country churches, and quite another to set out from Rochambeau past still-frozen lakes, fields of snow and no signs of habitation. I used to be afraid of being abandoned when I visited a distant outpost like eastern Washington or Wyoming, far from the safety of the city. I wasn't particularly afraid of being stranded in Chicoutimi, although I confess that when Pierre left the motor running when he went to ask for directions, I had to fight off a mad impulse to jump into the driver's seat and head for San Francisco.

We arrived at the Motel Richelieu, painted a hideous combination of orange and green, and shared a late lunch at Le Petit Café Parisien, a triumph of wishful thinking over reality, whose "Soupe andalouse" (tomato with rice) had no more to do with Spain than the restaurant itself with Paris. Benjamin Franklin used to be the envy of his travelling companions because he couldn't tell good cooking from bad. I thought of him at lunch.

The second day of adjudication took place in a bright friendly room with seven windows and a life-size statue of the Virgin peering down at me to implore pity for the students. We began with six- and seven-year-old beginners who played their scales mechanically but correctly. I mentally awarded a cuteness prize to the girl who would recite in a monotone "Key of D major, two sharps, F sharp and C sharp" before performing. Unfortunately we weren't permitted to give points for cuteness. We gave points for scales, etudes, and for pieces, as well as sight-reading and solfège. The first few levels got ten minutes apiece, increasing with higher levels to a full half hour for level eleven. Pierre told horror stories of sitting through programs of students who had been passed along from one level to another out of charity and who spent over an hour blundering their way through the required repertoire of advanced degrees.

By afternoon I had begun to mistrust my judgement. Shouldn't level six students be able to play with more musicality than this, and with a more agreeable tone quality? Then a ten-year-old came in and played circles around the others. The best came at the end of the afternoon. The teacher said, "You're going to see something you haven't seen before" as she ushered in a tiny seven-year-old who played concerto movements musically and almost flawlessly, all from memory. It's always a special treat to hear music well-played; even after nine hours, your ears prick up. But then to realize that this wonderful playing was coming from a mere child—I began to understand the furor that Mozart created as a child prodigy. Somehow the weariness fell away and I revelled in an agreeable auditory experience.

Out of curiosity I asked the girl, when she played by heart, whether she heard the music in her ears or saw the score in front of her eyes. She told me that she saw the score. This phenomenon of eidetic imagery, commonly known as photographic memory, occurs commonly among children, though it disappears in adolescence. Until sixth grade I could read through my textbooks at the beginning of September and would not have to open them again for the rest of the year. This practice didn't do much for subsequent study habits, but that was another story.

On the third day I saw the side effects of a system that operated on a thirty-week calendar, leaving the students to go to seed for nearly half a year. In the morning I listened to five students of advanced degree who couldn't play their scales and who attacked the piano as if it were a hated enemy. In the afternoon I listened to percussionists: twelve-year-old boys who loved making a racket. The first two kids were just hackers but the third really had it. Despite the noise it was downright exciting to hear complicated rhythmic patterns involving three instruments at once executed with precision. Then came some trumpeters and a passel of clarinettists whose occasional slips of register produced sounds akin to that of chalk squeaking on blackboard and made me forget the fourteen recorder players to whom I had been subjected the day before.

When all you've done for seventy-two hours is eat, sleep and listen to notes—thousands, yea tens of thousands of notes, with precious little music for all that—notes that assault you and, for all their individual minutia, defeat you as surely as the Lilliputians defeated Gulliver—you seek the respite of silence during meals. No such luck. The restaurant Muzak subjected us to the Beethoven Pathétique Sonata, orchestrated with a heavy disco beat, the master's tritone changed to perfect fifth and his audacious harmonies conventionalized.

On the afternoon of the fourth day I hid in the concert hall where Pierre was listening to the last of his pianists. I'd spent the morning listening to guitarists, an agreeable, unstressful exercise interrupted by a surprise attack by the piano teacher from Arvida whose students I had suffered through the day before. They were the ones who banged away unmercifully at the piano without betraying the slightest interest in or comprehension of the music, rushing as if in a futile race to get to the end of the piece before the notes did. I graded them accordingly and the teacher was out for my hide. I spent fifteen minutes of fruitless conversation with the woman and was not eager for more. Nobody likes Beckmesser—that cantankerous pedant in Wagner's *Die Meistersinger*—and I yearned to leave the Marker's booth.

I spent the fifth day in a studio high above the Saguenay River, judging the students of the good sisters of Chicoutimi. On the wall hung a picture of the Virgin playing at the piano while cherubim dropped rose petals on the keyboard. One girl of an extremely advanced level was so nervous that she couldn't play a single scale without breaking down. It threatened to be a very long and difficult session. So I asked her to stand up and come over to look out the window with me. I stood behind her, placed my hands gently on her shoulders and said, "See how calmly and quietly the river flows. It will continue flowing long after this exam is over. And you, who are infinitely more important than either the river or the exam, will continue to breathe when it is finished. Now sit down at the piano and try to let the calm, quiet flow of that river penetrate your playing." She sat down and played through her program without a hitch.

On the long drive back to Rochambeau I talked with Pierre about Andrew Girard's campaign, without disclosing the existence of the "death threat" note. "Such a move would have been disastrous for the École de Musique," Pierre told me.

"You mean because performers might have been less inclined to come to Fleur de Lis?"

"No, you don't understand," he said. "Provincial funding for the university depends not only on the number of full-time students attending the main campus. They also factor in students at branch campuses and pupils in the adjudication program to which you and I have just been subjected."

"So what does that have to do with Andrew Girard?" I asked.

"When word of the proposed change in faculties reached the schools, at least a few people understood the long-term implications of the move."

"Which were?"

"If the École de Musique allowed the importance of its performance division to diminish, the schools let it be known that they would turn to the conservatory to adjudicate its performers."

"I take it that this issue involves both money and prestige."

"Large quantities of each."

"So how did you get involved in it?"

"You need to understand that people outside the university take little or no interest in its internal affairs, so even though Girard's campaign tied up the university for the better part of a year, word didn't reach the far corners of the province until fairly late in the game."

"How late might that have been?"

"Early in December, not long before the Faculty Senate vote was scheduled to take place. Some of my colleagues in the schools got in touch with me as their regular liaison with the École de Musique, and I presented the case to the Director."

"What happened then?"

"Actually the Director found himself in a particularly awkward situation since he had supported Girard from the start—I think he considered that the École would enhance its prestige by belonging to the Faculty of Letters."

"He presumably didn't foresee the consequences with the schools."

"That's the way I read it."

"What did he do?"

"I'm really not sure. All I know is that Andrew Girard returned to Paris and the whole affair sort of fizzled out."

This was the first time that the Director had been mentioned in connection with Girard. Would he have gone so far as to manufacture the "family crisis" that summoned Girard to Paris at a critical moment? If so, would he have been bold enough to carry out such a plan without consulting the Rector? Then I thought of a new possible source of information.

Chapter 11

Shortly after my return from the hinterlands I visited the university accounting office where I found a single secretary working. In contrast to the filing cabinets in the Secretariat of the École de Musique, whose drawers when pulled out extended two feet into the room, the accounting office files opened sideways, evidently to keep them closer to the wall. Several imaginatively curved desks filled the remaining space but the chairs remained empty. Perhaps the others were at lunch. My luck, because in the presence of her co-workers the woman I encountered might have been more guarded. When I mentioned Andrew Girard her face lit up.

"I really liked him," she said. "He treated secretaries like real people, not like some around here." She cast a furtive glance toward the door leading, I imagined, to the office of her superior.

"I've been wondering," I said, "what happened to his pay cheques and pension payments."

"They sent them to his widow," she said, then blanched. "I mean…" I waited. "Maybe you'd better come back some other time."

"Nobody's here," I said. "You can tell me."

"But they made us promise not to say anything." She lowered her voice. "Actually I'm glad that you're trying to find out what's going on. It just doesn't seem right to me."

"So Andrew Girard is really dead."

"Yes," she practically whispered, "but we're not supposed to know it."

I paused for a moment, trying to make sense of this information. If Girard had died at home, or anywhere else in the city, the municipal authorities must have been involved and one would expect to have seen an obituary or at least some kind of death notice. In the absence of either, I had to conclude that he died on campus, the only way the death could have been covered up as "an urgent trip to Paris to deal with a family crisis." But such an eventuality must have involved the campus security force in one way or another. How could the death of a faculty member be so completely concealed? Then I thought of a way.

"I'm not going to ask you to disclose any confidential information," I told the woman, who immediately looked relieved by my words. "But I am going to ask you to look up a file. Could you go to the personnel files for the campus security force and tell me whether anyone left the employ of the university last January?"

The woman frowned for a moment, concluded that my request seemed in no way to compromise her position, and so walked over to the bank of filing cabinets, opened a drawer, fingered through the folders and then withdrew a single file. She looked at the information and frowned again, as if uncertain whether to respond to my question affirmatively or not. I tried to help her out. "Is there anyone who was transferred to another branch of the university, say, to the far North?" Her smile answered my question before her words, so I hastened to her defense. "No. Don't say anything. I want you to be able to say truthfully that you never spoke about the incident."

I went immediately to Valéry's office to tell him what I had found out. At first he seemed incredulous but then he began rearranging items in his memory in light of my news. "It did seem odd that he never got in touch with me," he said. "The Director gave me Andrew's grade book and asked me to fill out his report cards. It was a fair amount of work and I would have thought Andrew would thank me once his family crisis was over."

"Let's push this once step further," I said. "We know that Girard died last December, evidently on the day before the vote on a controversial campaign. Would the university have taken such extraordinary steps if, say, he'd just had a heart attack?"

"I can't imagine why."

"Suppose he had committed suicide."

Valéry shrugged. "Still doesn't make sense. It might have been thought slightly embarrassing, but these things happen."

"Which leaves only murder."

"Your powers of reasoning continually astound me, Axel."

"Can you help me pin down the time?"

"As it happens, I can. I saw Andrew just at six, as I was leaving to go home. He said that he was headed to the library, and joked that in twenty-four hours we would be 'men of letters,' his *jeu de mots* on our becoming part of the Faculty of Letters. Since he didn't turn up for his morning classes or the afternoon vote, his death must have occurred that night."

"And presumably on campus."

"On campus," Valéry repeated.

"So now I have to start from scratch to find a murderer."

"No. There I find a flaw with your logic. This whole thing started with your finding a note threatening Andrew with death. He evidently tried to think of who could have sent it and scribbled his guesses at the bottom of the note. You checked the handwriting and eliminated each of them. As it happened, the note was written by someone he hadn't even considered."

"Right. So where's the flaw in my logic?"

"The flaw is your assumption that just because the people Girard suspected didn't actually send a note, they couldn't still have murdered him. I admire good writing just as much as you do, but nowhere in the rules does it say you have to send somebody a note before you kill him."

"By golly, you're right, Dr. Watson!"

"That's enough ratiocination for one day. Let me give you a ride home."

And Valéry gave me a ride not to my apartment but to his home, where Ghislaine's cooking put murder out of my mind at least for a few hours.

Chapter 12

"I REALLY LIKE THIS WOMAN," I thought after a movie date with Colette, who turned out not only to be my height but within a few months of my age. We'd gone to the Cinéma Cartier for a Truffaut retrospective and had seen *"Baisers volés"* (Stolen Kisses). The film may have become a bit dated but I still enjoyed Truffaut's coy cinematic trickery in the scene where Christine breaks her television when her parents leave for the weekend so that she can summon Antoine, who has become a television repairman. Truffaut has the camera move up the stairs, acknowledging the stream of discarded clothing along the way, then down the hallway to Christine's bedroom, shown to be empty. Then the camera backs up along the same hallway and turns into the master bedroom, where the young people are seen sleeping in the parents' bed.

Colette pointed out that the stairway sequence mirrored an earlier scene in which Antoine, still in the army, becomes lost on the stairs in a brothel. I particularly admired the episode in which Antoine sends a message by *pneumatique* and Truffaut shows us in detail how the paper is placed into a metal roll that reaches its destination through a series of underground tubes. Colette mentioned the echo of this scene in the breakfast scene in which Antoine and Christine, rather than speaking, exchange written notes leading to Antoine placing a bottle opener around Christine's ring finger. A woman who not only liked movies, but *got* movies: a real find. Comparing notes we discovered that we'd spent a fair amount of time together at the Cinéma Cartier before we'd started dating: it turned out that we had both attended marathon showings of Hans-Jürgen Syberberg's *Hitler* (over seven hours) and Claude Lanzmann's *Shoah* (over nine hours). When I asked Colette whether she considered sexuality to involve the mind as much as the body, she winked and said "You'll find out soon enough." Her kiss when we parted stirred both mind and body.

My thoughts turned to "La Musique et les grandes époques de

l'art," the course I'd been assigned to teach during the winter term. According to the university catalogue, "*This course is an introduction to the great periods and the major lines of development of the history of music and its relations with the general evolution of the history of the arts. It seeks to sensitize the student to works which are the expression of an epoch (Middle Ages, Renaissance, Baroque, etc.) and seeks to demonstrate that each generation conceived music and the other arts according to identifiable underlying principles.*" The prerequisite was a two-semester survey of music history.

When I asked what text had been used previously for this course I discovered there was none. The instructor would flash slides on the screen and the students would take notes. I asked how music was related to literature in this course and learned that mostly it stuck to the visual arts. Well, for goodness sake, if we're going to do this at all—and I had certain misgivings about the underlying premise—let's do it right. I saw no point in just having students write down generalizations. They needed to study actual examples of music, painting, sculpture, architecture, poetry, drama, essays, etc. A number of English-language texts attempted to provide a survey of one sort or another, but nothing existed in French, I found after visiting a number of bookshops and the university library. Very well, I would make my own anthology. Nothing doing, I was told—the government interpreted copyright laws very strictly and no one seemed to have heard of public domain.

I telephoned a publisher in New York and asked them to send me a one-volume anthology of music. If there was no anthology of European literature available, French literature alone would at least illustrate the "spirit" of each epoch, but Wallace Fowlie's anthology had been allowed to go out of print when he retired from Duke University and the only anthology in the library cost $40 a set. Another telephone call to New York turned up a less expensive one-volume anthology. Could they tell me what it contained? No—all the copies were in the warehouse—but if I sent a request on departmental letterhead they'd be happy to mail me an examination copy. I tried without success to explain the problems of the Canadian postal system.

What about art? The only French histories devoted a separate volume to each epoch: too expensive again. Why not just show slides, my colleagues asked? No; I wanted to put something in the students' hands. Inspiration came: what was the biggest art education outfit I could think of? The education division of the Metropolitan Museum of Art in New York. I called them up and they promised to send out a catalogue listing all their available reproductions.

Of course, this account gives the illusory impression of a logical mind at work, when a more accurate image would be that of a deranged rat in a laboratory maze, battering the walls in a frenzy of frustration and stumbling on to the next stage more by chance than by intention. Make it an Anglophone rat in a Francophone laboratory, decorate the walls of the maze with bureaucratic conundrums, inform the rat at every turn that he's getting further and further behind, and you'll have a more realistic picture of a demented musicologist muddling through.

Still too uncertain of my French to deliver my lectures from notes, I typed out the presentations and hired a student editor to remove the most egregious solecisms. After the editor had covered each twenty-page manuscript with red marks I typed up the lecture and then entered each of the corrections in my own private dictionary in an effort to avoid making that particular mistake again. This might be called the brute force approach to written French, the theory being that if you kept making enough different mistakes, you'd eventually exhaust all the possibilities and thereafter know the language. The brute force method lends itself well to computers, who don't tire easily, but I occasionally wondered whether it was the most efficient method for greying musicologists. I sometimes became discouraged at the realization that after eight months in Rochambeau I still couldn't write or utter a paragraph without making grammatical errors, even if they were new and different errors.

The university put other obstacles in my way. Before I arrived they kept a Xerox machine in the office of the School of Music but everyone kept using it so they moved the machine a quarter of a mile away and found the meanest man in the city to run it. Every week, when I delivered the handouts to be copied for my courses, I had to work myself up for a confrontation with the ogre of Pavillon Desjardins, an ornery, cantankerous, grumpy, churlish, mean son-of-a-bitch. After Christmas the administration added one more layer of paperwork—we had to fill out a requisition form, in the presence of the curmudgeon, every time we wanted to have something copied. He loved to pretend that he couldn't read the form.

"What's that, a three?"

"No, it's an eight."

"Looks like a three to me—look, there's a gap in the loop."

"No really, it's a three."

"Can't make twenty copies of that—against the rules."

"The rule says that *more* than twenty copies have to be approved by the Director. I've asked for just twenty copies—I have twenty students."

"Too busy."

"You were just sitting here doing a crossword puzzle. There's nobody else here."

"I won't be able to finish this before lunch. You'll have to come back this afternoon."

"Shall I leave it off for tomorrow?"

"No work on Thursday. New policy." (This may sound mundane in English: *nouvelle réglementation* better conveys the disdainful tone of French bureaucratic jargon.)

"Why don't you just do it now and get it over with?"

"Aha! There's a grammatical error on the first page. No copies made of grammatical errors. New policy."

"I'd like that collated, please."

"No collating. Too busy."

"You don't have to do yourself—you just punch the collate button on the machine."

"Sorry. Lunch hour. Come back tomorrow."

Gradually I began to achieve a mastery of argumentative French.

Chapter 13

TOWARD THE END OF JANUARY I received a telephone call from a woman with the appropriate name of LaCharité, representing the Ministry of Cultural Affairs, Division of Assistance to Musical Publication, asking whether I'd be willing to serve on a three-member adjudication board. "Sure thing," I said. The next day she arrived at my office with a huge box full of scores and grant proposals and said, "If you are able to spin this dross into gold before the setting of the sun, the Minister of Cultural Affairs will reward you with 100 ducats. If not," she warned grimly, "you will never see your children alive again."

So I sat down at my desk and pulled out the first proposal, an educational method for secondary schools called "Music is Fun," consisting of workbooks, scores, student guides, teacher guides and a bunch of cassette tapes. They wanted thousands of dollars to publish Volume Two of the teachers guide for *"the only musical instructional program approved by the Ministry of Education,"* a recurring leitmotif that added an element of unity to an otherwise sprawling, incoherent document. "Music is Fun" looked like one small good idea—teaching music using French and Québecois folksongs—run completely amok. After singing "Au clair de la lune," for example, the schoolchildren were supposed to write a dramatization following guidelines given in the manual, then paint a series of posters on the theme. *"The program features a wholly-integrated approach to the musical, dramatic and plastic arts."* The teacher was also provided with a grid for evaluating each child's work according to graded criteria, weighted quality points, peer comparison and general comportment. After memorizing the little tune, whose original simple charm had long since been smothered by an elephantine pedagogical apparatus, students were supposed to be rewarded by getting to sing it against a rock-style accompaniment recorded by professional studio musicians and packaged in handy cassette form as part of the wholly-integrated approach. After listening to this last item I scrawled "unconditionally unacceptable" across the application and turned to the next proposal.

Québec-for-Québeckers Publishers wanted $30,000 to publish arrangements of pop tunes for high school stage band. I reread the guidelines, discovered a clause saying that Ministry funds could not be used for the publication of pop tunes, and rejected the application on the grounds that a pop tune is a pop tune even when arranged for 76 trombones, or whatever they put into high school stage bands in the 80s.

The next application came from a publisher of organ music who wanted to disseminate a procession written for the Pope's last visit to the city. Really wretched music. I looked in the guidelines, found nothing banning wretchedness *per se*, and wrote "marginally acceptable for possible historical interest."

Finally I hit pay dirt—esoteric music by serious contemporary Canadian composers, works that would never be performed after their premieres, if they even managed to get a premiere. Four stars, I wrote on the application (14 years or older, parental guidance recommended, possible violence, nudity, and explicit serialism).

A week later the committee convened with Madame LaCharité to discuss its findings: one opera conductor, one public school music teacher and a bearded musicologist. The opera conductor questioned the use of public funds to publish works of contemporary music that no one would ever buy or perform and which would most likely remain on the publisher's shelves until they yellowed. Everyone looked askance at "Music is Fun." Madame LaCharité had done some checking and discovered that the Minister of Education, far from recommending the system, had simply given permission for it to be published (though one questioned the source of his authority—wasn't this a free country in which you could publish anything you wanted except for pornography and anti-Semitic literature?). We managed to wind up our deliberations and recommendations in four hours and left it to the Minister of Cultural Affairs to send the good or bad news to the applicants.

February began with an unlimited general strike by members of several consolidated unions, starting with government workers and moving—in a carefully orchestrated sequence—to schoolteachers, maintenance workers and doctors and nurses. I asked whether the School of Music was going to be shut down and learned that all the doors of the university would be locked on March 1. Evidently someone had calculated exactly how many days the university must be allowed to function before the entire term had to be abandoned. At the same time, truckloads of snow were being brought into the city for the international snow sculpting competition associated with the Winter Carnival, which started the following week. The unions appeared to be masters of timing, if nothing else. At least mail was still being delivered.

During a break from preparing the next lecture for "La Musique et les grandes époques de l'art" I wandered into Valéry's office.

"Hey, man," he said in English, his habitual greeting. I complained about the threatened strikes and he gave a familiar shrug. Then I returned to the subject of Andrew Girard and his mysterious disappearance.

"There's no point in talking with anyone in authority: they've perfected the art of stonewalling even better than Nixon's associates after Watergate. But I've been wondering whether there was anyplace else at the university that Andrew might have used as a work space?"

"Sure. He had a carrel at the library."

"You mean one of those little desks with shelves that the graduate students use?"

"I guess carrel may not be the right word. The library has a dozen or so locked rooms."

"You mean offices?"

"Cubby-holes would be more like it. They assign them to professors who don't want to be troubled lugging books back and forth from the library to their academic offices."

"I can see where that would be helpful for Andrew. It's about a ten-minute walk to the library from here via the tunnels."

"Less if you go overland."

"Still. I guess it might be worth checking out." We chatted a bit about our students' performances in the school's recent production of *Dialogues des Carmélites* and had to admit that some of the performers, though not academically gifted, could really sing. After a few more minutes I let Valéry get back to his Frescobaldi edition and I headed to the library, still thinking about the Poulenc opera.

In an effort to make early music more accessible to students in my music history class, I encouraged live performance rather than recordings. To illustrate plainsong we learned to sing the *Kyrie Orbis factor* from memory, and the class had given an enthusiastic, if imprecise, rendering of the canon, *Sumer is icumen in*. When we came to conductus, a medieval processional song, I'd asked for a volunteer to lead a parade all around the lecture hall. Simone Couture, a slender, dark-haired girl, had raised her hand. I gave her a copy of Perotin's *Beata viscera* which she sightread brilliantly.

With the departure of Isabelle Bascombe, Simone had seemed like a logical choice for the lead in Poulenc's opera but when she told me that she had been chosen to sing the role of Blanche, I asked her whether she knew what she was getting into. "This role will change you," I warned. Simone seemed abashed; she had probably expected words of congratulation rather than admonition. "Did your voice teacher tell you what the story was about?" I asked.

"It's about a group of nuns during the period of the French Revolution," she said.

"It's also about loss and fear," I said. "Blanche's mother died bearing her and her father dies at the guillotine. The Mother Superior of the order that she joins dies more or less in welcoming her into the convent." Simone's face grew very serious. "When the nuns' safety is threatened, Blanche bails out and hides at home. Have you ever had an experience of moral cowardice?" I asked.

Simone gave me a funny look. "You ask hard questions," she said. "This isn't something I talk about much but somehow it feels as if it's all right to share with you." I waited for her to continue. "Before I came here I attended the University of Montréal. They had a required course in music history, the same as here. The teacher kept making a play for me, and one time in his office he became quite physical." I waited for the young woman to continue. "A few of the other female students told me that they had had similar experiences, but I never reported him. That was one of the reasons I came here—it was a convenient escape."

I nodded to acknowledge the gravity of what Simone had just told me, and then continued. "In the opera Blanche flees the other sisters at a crucial moment: they have taken a vow of martyrdom and she is afraid to stay."

"But she redeems herself?"

I nodded. "At the end a revolutionary tribunal has condemned the sisters to the guillotine. The little band of fourteen women enters the

Place de la Révolution singing the 'Salve Regina.' One by one their voices disappear, the music interrupted each time by the terrible sound of the falling blade. At the last moment Blanche enters and takes up the melody, then follows the others to her death. Even just listening to it on records I find it one of the most harrowing passages in all of opera."

Simone swallowed hard but said nothing. "You will experience much emotion preparing for this role," I said, "but you must strictly keep your feelings subdued in the performance or you'll never be able to sing that last solo." On the night of the production Simone offered a spectacular performance.

I rounded the corner of the subterranean corridor, entered the lower level of the library, and walked to the elevator. Claude Beaudoin greeted me when I entered his office at the Audio-Vidéothèque on the fourth floor. (The name had been assigned by library administrators under the impression that the joint collections consisted entirely of records and slides.) A gentle man, Claude had thinning hair and the sad expression of the French crooner Charles Azvenour. In place of the usual necktie he wore a dark cravat, and his soft brown velour jacket seemed much more comfortable than my Harris tweed.

Claude expressed regret at being separated geographically from the musicologists and shared his amusement at my students' puzzlement over the *chasse à l'énigme*. Evidently no one had ever presented them with a scavenger hunt before; certainly none of their professors.

"So I imagine you supported Andrew Girard's efforts to move the École de Musique into the Faculty of Letters—wouldn't that have brought the musicologists right into this building?"

"Ah, that was quite a kerfuffle," he said diplomatically.

"Valéry said that Andrew had a small office right here in the library."

"That's right. Would you like to see it? I've been meaning to ask you whether you wanted to use it yourself. If not, one of the linguistics professors has been eying it enviously."

Claude led me past the card catalogues and through the stacks to the far wall of the library, lined with half a dozen tiny offices. He took out a key from a large ring and opened the door. I could see why anyone would enjoy working here. Though the workspace was tiny, a window at eye level afforded a nice view of the quadrangle below, in contrast to the viewless apertures in our academic offices. Claude sensed my pleasure with the place and said, "I'll let you get a feel for it before you make your decision."

"What happened to Andrew's things? I understand he left in something of a hurry."

"We reshelved the library materials and I mailed his personal belongings to his address in Paris."

"So nobody has been in here since last December?"

"The maintenance people dust once in awhile, but otherwise it's been vacant." A student approached with a question and Claude excused himself, closing the door behind him.

I sat down at the small writing desk and imagined what it would be like to work here. The books in current use would lie immediately at hand in the two shelves at the back of the desk; other books would wait nearby on the bookcase against the wall. An old-fashioned coat rack and a waste basket constituted the room's only other furnishings. The cubicle really looked empty. Suppose Andrew had wanted to conceal some document. I knelt under the writing desk—nothing taped to its bottom surface. There weren't even any drawers. Just to be certain I looked underneath the waste basket; nothing there either. I was about to leave when I thought of one other possibility. I slid the free-standing bookcase away from the wall and discovered a manila envelope taped to the back.

I opened the envelope and removed its contents, several letters dated the previous fall and signed by the Vice-Rector of Academic Affairs, Marie-Claude Contretemps. I sat down and scanned the letters in order. They began by expressing disapproval for Girard's campaign to transfer the École de Musique from Arts to Letters and became more threatening with each letter. In the last epistle Madame Contretemps claimed to have consulted with the Rector to discover a loophole by which Andrew's tenure could be revoked. This was really incendiary material because it undermined the whole basis of faculty employment.

Under the tenure system, or what Fleur de Lis University called *permanence*, after serving for a probationary period a professor gained job security for life. In principle tenure served as a bastion of academic freedom, permitting faculty members to express ideas—preferably within their domains of expertise—which they might have been reluctant to put forth had their jobs been on the line every time they gave voice to an unpopular thought. In practice tenure clogged up the academic grove with dead wood, professors who hadn't published anything since gaining tenure and probably never would. Regardless of the system's merits, these were the rules by which we played, and any suspicion that the university planned to abrogate them would have brought down a firestorm from the union of professors. I suspected that Andrew had preserved the threatening letters not out of fear for his future but as potential weapons in his campaign.

What would have been the next step for Madame Contretemps if the most extreme warning had failed to deter Girard? According to the handwriting she had not composed the "death threat" note that I'd discovered beside Girard's desk, but I imagined the directive she might have received from the Rector: "Do whatever you need to do to put an end to this and I'll cover for you."

I didn't see that I had anything to fear from the Vice-Rector in broad daylight, so I took the manila envelope and headed to her office.

Chapter 14

MADAME CONTRETEMPS OCCUPIED A CORNER office toward the top of Pavillon Poulidor, one of the twin towers in the middle of the campus. One bank of windows afforded a view of the majestic, post-modern steeples of Pavillon Desjardins; the other overlooked the long promenade leading to the offices of the Presses de l'Université Fleur de Lis, the department of student services, and the university radio station. Not for her the banks of filing cabinets that filled the outer office, nearly crushing her secretary's desk; not for her the telephones or the new fax machine that covered most of the secretary's work table, rendering it virtually unusable. No, Madame Contretemps, the Vice-Rector of Academic Affairs, reigned, an activity supported not by equipment but by a small jungle of green plants in one corner of the room, a vast, expensive carpet, a huge, glass-topped desk, and the glorious views already mentioned.

She wore a dark-grey suit, nearly the same colour as her hair, tucked in a neat bun. A dark green pendant offered the only decoration in this rather severe outfit, and while she greeted me with a brief handshake and a fleeting smile, she clearly did not welcome this breach of academic etiquette: Vice-Rectors talked with Directors, not with untenured assistant professors. I told her that I was investigating the death of Andrew Girard.

"And this is the matter of life and death with which you bullied my secretary?"

"Andrew Girard is dead."

"Nonsense. He's been living in Paris since abruptly leaving us a year ago December."

"I'm sorry; I have evidence of his death, which apparently took place here on campus."

Madame Contretemps prepared to bluster on further, and rather than argue with her I withdrew the letters I had brought from their manila envelope. "Where did you get these?" she demanded.

"That doesn't matter. I'm sure the Syndicat des Professeurs will be interested in seeing them, especially the last one."

Her tone suddenly altered and she gestured me to sit in one of the comfortable chairs near the window. I continued, "Given the circumstances of Girard's death, which remain a bit clouded, these letters would seem to be incriminating evidence."

"Now really, Professor Crochet, you don't actually imagine that I …"

"All I know is that despite the somewhat esoteric nature of Andrew Girard's campaign, he died just before the crucial vote was to take place, and these letters seem to be directly connected to those events. I don't want to appear indelicate, but can you recollect what you were doing on the eve of the Faculty Senate vote?"

Now Madame Contretemps seemed eager to please and to appease. She withdrew her appointment book for the previous year from a drawer in the desk, turned to December, and brightened. "Ah, yes. I was meeting with Madame LaCharité, of the Ministry of Cultural Affairs. I understand that you've recently had dealings with her."

"Surely you weren't adjudicating candidates for musical publication!"

"No, we were making plans for the festival of the arts held here the spring before your arrival." She pointed to a bulletin board partially obscured by a rubber plant and I made out the main heading of the blue and white poster, "Les Arts—Notre Force."

"I'm sure she'll remember the evening in question," she went on. "The representative from the conservatory expressed himself rather forcefully to the effect that the event should be held there rather than here. He worked himself up into such a state that he actually collapsed and had to be assisted from the room. It's not the sort of thing you forget easily."

"Please forgive me for any suggestion that I might be impugning your honour."

She brushed the apology aside with a gracious wave of her hand. Then the smile disappeared and she said, "Now that we've cleared that little matter up, I'd like you to give me the letters."

I hesitated. Quite possibly Madame LaCharité would confirm the story, but if Andrew Girard really had been murdered, and I still felt uneasy using the word, I would be considered negligent—perhaps even criminally negligent—if I allowed potential evidence to go astray.

Madame Contretemps seemed to read my thoughts because her tone went icy. "I hardly need point out, Axel, that while Professor Girard had tenure at this university, you do not. Now I demand that you give me those letters."

I made up my mind quickly, respectfully refused her request, promised to keep the letters confidential, and bolted from the office.

Chapter 15

I CELEBRATED VALENTINE'S DAY WITH Colette seeing "La Guerre des Tuques" (which eventually appeared in English as "The Dog Who Stopped a War"), a charming tale of Christmas vacation in a small town in Québec. The schoolchildren have divided themselves into two teams, one of which would build a snow fort which the other would attack. The amicable rivalry eventually got out of hand and it wasn't until a portion of the structure collapsed on a Saint Bernard dog that the hostilities could be resolved. I told Colette I was touched by the scene in which a crowd of friends travels home, dropping members off one by one. I told her that I kept wondering at what point the gang stopped being "the gang." She recalled a similar incident from her own childhood. "But I always travelled with my brother," she said, "so we constituted our own gang." The warmth of our parting at evening's end might well have been described by the Québecois expression *chaleureux*.

Since the beginning of the second term I had been attending meetings of an emergency committee convened by the art department. It seemed that theft and vandalism were rapidly decimating the art, and to a lesser extent, music collections. Students would razor out illustrations from art periodicals, books and exposition catalogues or they would tear musical scores out of their cardboard wrappers, thereby evading detection by the electronic sensors. They would hide books required for courses in obscure corners of the library so that no one else could use them, or they would simply steal the books.

Francophone members of the library committee remarked on the lack of respect shown toward libraries and other institutions by people of Latin blood. (As the only Anglophone on the committee I maintained a discreet silence.) The problem was compounded by the attitude of the library administration, whose official policy was to tolerate losses of $5,000 or $6,000 a year in any given division rather than hire an additional part-time employee to assure adequate surveillance in the evening. The administration was also reluctant to spend any money on physical changes. But something clearly had to be done since the sum required to replace the currently missing books now exceeded the entire annual budget of the art/music division and the art collection had been so badly mutilated that certain topics and periods could no longer be taught.

Hence our committee. The chairman tried with the best will in the world to get us to address the problems at hand but every time we came up with a solution the art librarian would bring in a new horror story showing that the idea wouldn't work. After a number of weeks we became extremely discouraged (and begrudgingly appreciative of the ingenuity of library vandals).

Consider: each book contained a yellow card to be removed when the book was borrowed and stamped with the university number of the borrower. The book was then desensitized, the borrower could take it out, and a daily computer printout would list the book, its date borrowed and date due. Say you wanted to steal four books: A, B, C, and D. You would substitute the yellow cards from books W, X, Y, and Z, concealing the correct cards someplace in the library. You would take out books A, B, C, and D in the prescribed manner, then return to the library, retrieve the concealed cards for A, B, C and D, put them in the envelopes for W, X, Y, and Z and carry *these* books to the return counter without checking them out. The cards for A, B, C and D would clear the computer, making it think that the books had been returned, the system would shows that everything was in order, and you'd be home clear with the books A, B, C and D.

When I explained this to Valéry he said there was no need to go to such trouble – the guards left 20 minutes before the library closed, so you had only to arrive at 11:40 p.m. and you could cart off anything you liked (with the aid of an accomplice to bypass the sensor turnstile).

My first proposal was to coat the entire collection with epoxy and turn it into a solid sheet of plastic, and while that idea was rejected, along with the plan of putting the entire collection on non-circulating closed reserve (it would be too costly to hire enough people to hunt up the books), those appeared to be the only ways to control the situation. Depressing business.

I had naïvely imagined that we might be able to enjoy the spring term without a strike. No such luck. Isolated work stoppages having failed to move the university, in the second week of February the maintenance workers took to shutting down the university for several days running. Students and professors could still enter but there were no secretaries, no copy machines, and no access to the library. The School of Music, instead of furnishing each classroom with a piano and a sound system, employed two drones to shuttle pianos and sound systems from one room to another. During the strike there were no drones, thus no pianos. Fortunately I had already put my own system on a cart, which I dragged behind me to classes.

The worst was yet to come. The professors' union threatened to call a strike in order to put pressure on the university, which up to now had been using various delaying tactics to avoid negotiating. Prevailing opinion was that the university was deliberately attempting to provoke a strike in order to save money, the money it would otherwise be paying me, among others. While students found the idea of a strike annoying, I found it downright threatening. Valéry told me that the last time the professors went on strike the university was shut down for four months. If that happened I'd have to give up my apartment and move into a cubby-hole in the cathedral. You hear about organists being interred in organ pipes, but I've never heard of anyone actually living in one.

Chapter 16

IN THE THIRD WEEK OF February we were in the middle of a fairly dull student presentation when the drilling began. Not everyone can be as brilliant as the Bascombe sisters, after all, but I listened with mounting frustration as one student, evidently incapable of analyzing melody, harmony, tonality, phrase structure—the essential elements of a musical composition—chose to focus on dynamics. "In the second measure a *crescendo* reflects the rising emotion of the poem, culminating in a *forte* on the word *tears*. A few measures later the composer writes a *mezzo-piano* followed by a *diminuendo*, suggestive of the poet's sense of loss." It takes 12 seconds to say these words aloud (six seconds for a Québecois.) Imagine listening to this sort of thing for half an hour.

Then the drilling began, immediately beneath our classroom, a dull, low-frequency vibration that rendered conversation difficult and, after a short time, left one feeling extremely irritable. I went downstairs, informed the worker that he was disturbing our class, and asked him to desist. He shrugged his shoulders and kept on going. I sent a student to the Secretariat to complain—they said there was nothing to be done. So after class I made an appointment to talk to the Director.

The Director was sympathetic, and explained that this was the second time workers had invaded the building without his advance knowledge, the first being to drill holes in the walls of all the offices. It turned out that the Minister of Public Safety had ascertained that professors in their offices, with the doors closed, might have difficulty hearing fire alarms in the corridors and had ordered the school to install a system of flashing lights in each office as an auxiliary alarm system. Failure to complete the system by the beginning of March would result in the whole School of Music being shut down.

"This university has a certain penchant for drilling," the Director continued. "A few years back, when a new professor was named student advisor, he insisted, loudly, on having an intercom installed between his office on the ninth floor and the secretary's office on the fourth. The dean at that time was fairly inexperienced and acceded to the demand. The next day workers arrived to drill holes through all five stories and install a tube between the fourth floor and the ninth. The young professor wanted to protest the disfiguration of his floor, but he'd made such a public scene in the first place that it was too late to withdraw the demand. Eventually the tube was filled with wires, although the professor could as easily have communicated with the secretary by simply shouting down the tube."

In any event, the Director promised, he would write his own letter of protest—at least maintenance workers could give us notice and let us change classrooms if necessary—and promised to inform me of the administration's response, if any. With regard to the warning system, I asked facetiously, what would happen in the case of a blind professor. (It seemed we really did have a blind organ teacher.) The Director solemnly assured me that he intended to hire a team of graduate students to sit in the professor's office and watch for flashing lights.

One advantage of never teaching the same course twice was that you avoided the risk of excess baggage. Unfortunately, this term I was teaching "Music Since 1750," a course that I had taught twice in the past and which, worse yet, represented home territory for me, historically speaking. The first time I taught the course I generated a heavy set of course notes which I duplicated for the students the second time around, augmented with additional printed material. During this present term, I had been trying to translate the whole indigestible mess into French. Reading Week gave me a chance to consider the folly of my ways: if each time I taught the course, I wrote new lecture notes to supplement the printed material already in the students' hands, and if I subsequently printed out *these* notes and distributed them to the students, to be added to my lecture notes for the previous time, there was theoretically no limit to the amount of paper I could generate and impose upon the poor student who, after all, was encountering all this material for the first time.

Instead of constantly increasing the amount of material, enriching the course with yet more works and yet more composers, more detailed analytical sketches, and more comprehensive background information, I should rather be constantly reducing it, so that students might have some hope of retaining historical landmarks whereby to orient themselves in future study. The logical conclusion of this reductive process was that I would eventually be telling the students about nothing, and since this was what they really wanted to learn anyway (it being an obligatory course), I should get along much better henceforth than heretofore.

Chapter 17

I MAY HAVE WORKED AS hard as this at various points in my life but I could not recall ever having worked harder. Every Tuesday and Friday morning I met a class of twenty-three students to whom I explained, for an hour and a half, how everything fits together—history, geography, fine arts, French literature, and music—from the Stone Age to the present in thirteen unforgettable weeks. The rest of the time I spent finding out for myself so I could explain it to them. Each lecture required a full day of research and two full days of writing out the text in French to be submitted for editing. The students asked whether I would deposit two copies of each lecture in the library, a reasonable enough request under the circumstances, so after receiving the corrected text from my editor I would type it up for the class.

As a result I learned quite a bit about the arts and European civilization at the same time as undergoing an intensive course in French composition. My editor said I was getting better, which I found comforting.

One day I spent from 9 a.m. to 3 p.m. writing the final ten pages of a lecture in longhand and from 3:30 to 5:30 typing the first ten pages. Then Valéry asked whether I would look at a rather complicated article on Frescobaldi that he had to write in English for an edition he was publishing. I gave him my ten pages of unedited manuscript in exchange and we sat in his office for an hour, each one reading and correcting the other's work. Then Ghislaine picked us up and we went to their house for supper. Afterward Valéry and I continued at the kitchen table from 8 to 10, furiously marking each other's papers with red pencils and from time to time thrusting sheets of paper under each other's noses and demanding, "What's this supposed to mean?"

The next morning I typed from 8:00 to 9:30, met with a student until 10:30, delivered a lecture (the 15th century: decline of feudalism, rise of the New Monarchies, papal corruption, linear perspective,

Robert Campin, Guillaume Dufay, François Villon, all tied together, or less, by the theme of self-identity and individualism). In the afternoon I started all over again preparing the first of two lectures on the 16th century. I wasn't sure whether it would get easier or harder once I hit more familiar territory, but each lecture presented an interesting challenge.

By the end of February I had decided it was time to invite Colette to my apartment for dinner. In summer the apartment complex in which I dwelled overflowed with flowers, featuring streams of hanging nasturtiums. Now colour resided in the electric blue sky and the coruscating brilliance of sunlight on each day's fresh snowfall. Individual properties separated by chest-high fences turned in winter into a playground for cross-country skiers as the white accumulation easily surmounted the fences. At night the city's streetlights and other ambient illumination set the reflective surface aglow, while the muffling effect of the deep snow cast a protective spell.

The decoration of my one-bedroom apartment could have been described as minimalist. On the walls hung a few prints along with groups of 8 x 10 enlargements of photographs from my travels about the United States: a solitary barn on the Palouse of Eastern Washington; yellow flowers against the blue-green ocean of California's Big Sur; an explosion of radiating succulent leaves from a green Arizona cactus; orange-tinged limestone formations from Wyoming. Large windows looking out onto the tree-lined river helped to compensate for the absence of indoor plants.

On the appointed evening Colette arrived dressed in a cashmere sweater over a dark brown skirt covering, I eventually discovered, brown knee socks. I hate using words like mauve and taupe, but the sweater must have been one of those colours. ("What's the matter, Axel," she later teased me. "Did your parents give you the crayon box with only sixteen colours instead of sixty-four?")

I served her curried lamb stew, one of my favourite crock-pot recipes, and a green salad, with homemade brownies and lemon sherbet for dessert. After dinner I asked Colette whether she might be interested in singing with me. She gracefully accepted the invitation and proposed Schubert's "Heidenröslein." I had brought my song scores home over Christmas break, in anticipation of another strike, so was able to locate the appropriate volume.

Colette stood in the rounded crook of the piano and I sat down to accompany her. In the song a young lad sees a rosebud growing and threatens to pick it. The rosebud threatens to prick him, "so that you will always think of me," but the boy, undeterred, picks it anyway. Colette subtly brought out the sexual undercurrent in accenting "ich breche dich" (I'll break you) and "ich steche dich" (I'll prick you).

I asked whether among the Wolf Mörike songs she knew "Erstes Liebeslied eines Mädchens" (A maiden's first love-song) and happily she did. This was a virtuoso piece both for pianist and soprano, and we were both a bit giddy by the time we'd gotten through it. If the Schubert song was mildly suggestive, the Wolf was downright erotic, with the girl talking about holding an eel or a snake in her hands, then having it slip "creeping and winding" into her breast. Then it penetrates her skin, rushes to her heart and snaps inside her to form a ring, the first experience of love that "bites me blissfully and yet destroys me."

Once before I had enjoyed a musical experience such as this. On a visit home I spent an evening with a family that included a violist of whom I had always been fond. Prior attachments prevented any direct physical interaction between us but music offered an alternative expression for our feelings. When we played a Brahms sonata that each of us had performed with other people but never with each other, the inflection of each answering phrase provided another opportunity for intimate interplay.

Accompanying Colette felt even more exciting, for we entered the musical adventure without constraints and the vibrant, thrilling quality of her soprano voice affected me even more deeply than the rich, mellow tone of the viola. The off-beat rhythms of Wolf's song setting captured and magnified the breathless excitement of Mörike's text while the bold harmonies, moving ever further from the familiar, intensified the poem's theme of penetration into the forbidden.

We both found the experience a bit overwhelming. I told Colette I liked the way she nestled into the crook of the grand piano. Colette told me she'd rather nestle into the crook of my arm. I said that could be arranged and we curled up together on the sofa. One thing led to another and before long we were in my bedroom where I discovered behind her demure exterior an imaginative and audacious lover.

Chapter 18

ALAIN VALCARTIER, DEAN OF THE Faculty of Arts, occupied an office in Pavillon Dorval, one of the twin towers on campus. Like Madame Contretemps he enjoyed an excellent view but unlike her had windows on only one side of the office, the perquisites of the pecking order being as carefully observed in academia as in the business world. Like the Vice-Rector he banished the record-keeping aspects of his position to the outer office but unlike her was unabashed about showing that he actually worked as well as administrating. His modest desk stood in marked contrast to her ostentatious furnishings and he evidently spent most of his time at a long wooden worktable with adjustable crane lamps at either end. A single spider plant hanging near the window provided the only greenery, in contrast to Mme Contretemps' small jungle.

Unlike the Vice-Rector, Alain continued to teach, albeit a single course in urban planning. As I entered the room he gestured me to a seat, pushed back into his own semi-reclining chair, pointed to a pile of just-marked student papers on the worktable and said, "I've never talked with you before, but you're a welcome visitor. Reading student papers for a couple of hours is enough to make your head spin. What's on your mind?"

"My office in Pavillon Desjardins is the same one Andrew Girard used to have." Valcartier cocked his head but said nothing so I continued. "Recently I came across some forgotten papers having to do with the Arts/Letters dispute."

"He and I were on opposing sides of that one," Alain said.

"That's why I thought I'd talk with you—this all happened before my time, so I'm interested in hearing your perspective on the issue."

"Well it's over and done with now, thank goodness. Who'd have thought that a technical jurisdictional question could tie up an entire university for the better part of a year?"

"You opposed moving the School of Music to the Faculty of Letters."

"That's right, although with the passage of time I have to admit that I understand Girard's motivation. I don't see how a scholarly department can expect to be taken seriously if it spends the majority of its time engaged in non-scholarly activity."

"You're referring to the performers."

"Darn right. The previous Dean had some cockeyed notions about making the Faculty of Arts one big happy family rather than a bunch of departments under a single umbrella. Before I became Dean I sat on a committee that attended graduate oral exams in each department. I remember one trumpet player who seemed to have blown all his brains into his horn."

"But you opposed the move at the time."

"Perhaps I shouldn't have taken it so personally, but I resented Girard's attitude."

"The pushy American?" I asked.

"You're an American, aren't you?" Alain said. "Well, I don't want to generalize, but I can't help recalling the riddle that my kids keep telling over and over: 'Where does a 500-pound canary sit?'"

"Anywhere it wants."

"That's the whole point. You get Americans acting as if they can tell the whole rest of the world what to do just because they call themselves a superpower."

"And that's the way you felt about Andrew?"

"Yes. The way he went around with his punctiliously correct Parisian French telling us how a Québecois university should be run. It really ticked me off."

"So how did you engage in the battle?"

Valcartier sat forward on his chair and looked at me intently. The passage of a year seemed to disappear as he relived the campaign. "Do you know how the question was supposed to be decided?"

"I understand that in matters of this sort each of the twelve faculties was supposed to have one vote."

"That's right. The university split down the middle, along more or less predictable lines."

"Do you suppose that's what ended up making the conflict so intense, the fact that every vote counted?"

"That's an interesting way to look at it. You understand that according to Faculty Senate regulations, a tie vote would have meant that the proposal died—there was no intervention by the Rector to decide the issue, the way you have in the States."

"I didn't realize that."

"So it looked as though we would keep the École the Musique here in Arts."

"What happened?"

"Andrew made some sort of deal with the Dean of Theology."

"And that would have tipped the balance. What did you do?"

"I tried to persuade the Dean that departments depending on students at the margin should stick together."

"He didn't buy it?"

"I had logic on my side but Andrew appealed to his emotions."

"I have trouble seeing how you can get emotional about which faculty your department is in."

"That isn't it. You know the history of the building you inhabit."

"It wasn't originally intended to be a School of Music."

"That's putting it mildly. Look at it, with those towers and transepts: all it needed was flying buttresses! I know they called it a seminary, but it looked like a goddamn cathedral."

"I'm afraid I'm not following this."

"That cathedral was going to become the domain of the Dean of Theology, his personal fiefdom."

"But what does that have to do with you?"

"You still don't get it. Ever since that time the Dean has carried a grudge against the Faculty of Arts for seizing *his* building."

"And unfortunately you personify the Faculty of Arts."

"Now you see."

"But that's irrational."

"Emotions tend to be that way, Axel."

"So he wouldn't even listen to your arguments."

"He may have listened, but let's just say he wasn't persuaded."

"So what happened next?"

A strange look went across Alain's face, as though he were wondering whether he hadn't been too open with someone he scarcely knew. Evidently he decided this was just past history because then he relaxed and continued.

"If Theology defected, then it looked as if Girard's proposal would pass. But if he failed to show up for the vote, I could move to table the proposal and I knew that others would back me up on it."

"But why would Girard miss such a crucial occasion?"

Alain gave a guilty smile. "Only through a dirty trick, I'm afraid. I'd heard rumours about a group of music students who had it in for Girard. I don't know whether they really had much interest one way or the other in his campaign, but they felt he was giving them a hard time."

"So you enlisted their aid?"

"I arranged for them to 'kidnap' Girard by taking him out to lunch—he was a celebrated gourmand—and holding him long enough to miss the vote. This was just at the end of term, mind you, and if the vote got postponed I figured that by the time the Faculty Senate got around to reconsidering the issue I might be able to persuade one of Girard's supporters to defect."

"So the trick worked."

"Not exactly. Girard didn't show up for the lunch. A family emergency took him back to Paris, permanently, as it turned out."

"Alain, I need to tell you that Andrew never went to Paris, at least not the way you mean."

"But ..."

"Andrew died here the night before the vote."

"That's a pretty amazing coincidence."

"It wasn't a coincidence." Alain was sitting upright now, his hands moving back and forth as he tried to make sense of what I was saying. "Somebody killed him."

"Come on! Surely you're on the wrong track," he said. "We Québecois may take politics more seriously than you Americans, but nobody at this university would have resorted to murder over the transfer of a department from one faculty to another."

"That's what I've been telling myself, but one way or the other Girard is dead."

"I know the timing looks awfully suspicious, but I still think you've been watching too many television shows if you think this vote would have been motive for murder."

"I tend to agree with you, and I appreciate your talking with me. The higher authorities at the university seem to have covered the matter up almost completely. But I'll let you know when I get to the bottom of it."

Valcartier escorted me from his office and I returned to Pavillon Desjardins by way of the tunnel.

Chapter 19

IT'S GENERALLY CONSIDERED CHURLISH FOR a professor to complain about his students. Still, the music history survey proved to be a particularly difficult class. It wasn't just students who arrived late (up to 45 minutes late) or left early. Aside from making my displeasure known, I wasn't sure what other steps I could take to discourage students from getting up and walking out in the middle of my lectures. It wasn't even that they were a lot less well-prepared than my previous history students at Frangipani University. Rather I found it ultimately demoralizing that non-music history majors, mostly performers, suffered the required history course with such ill grace.

Their only questions had to do with exams; their only comments concerned what they saw as the gross imbalance between the amount of work I imposed on them and the number of credits they received for the course. They visited my office only to protest the grading of their exams or now, just before term's end, to ask what they could do to pass the course even though they had failed all the tests up to this point.

One poor chap was taking this course for the third time and had yet to pass it. He was well on his way to failing it for the third time and feared that he would have to register again next year just for this one course, but this was the first time he'd mentioned the situation to me. One third of the class attended only for quizzes and tests and left the room as soon as they were over, a bit disconcerting, that.

In mid-March a delegation of five large students arrived at my door to demand that the essay portion of the final exam consist of a choice of two out of four questions. I readily acceded (they were all bigger than I) but considered that since I had already given them a list of a dozen questions from which those on the exam would be selected, the burden hardly seemed onerous. I could easily justify the course requirement in terms of the preparation of a well-rounded performer, but they weren't interested in becoming well-rounded performers—they just wanted to get their degrees. Fortunately we taught the course in rotation. Next year would be Valéry's turn.

When I brought these and other complaints to him, he would sigh sympathetically and say, "Le pauvre." At first I thought this to be French for "Poor you!" but as time went on I suspected it really meant "You wretched, miserable sod," and that he looked upon me with amusement. I wondered whether he was thinking, "The American just can't cut it." On the other hand, he once told me that the duty he disliked the most at the École de Musique was teaching music history to non-history majors.

At the beginning of the term my name was put into nomination as the representative of the Arts Faculty to the University Research Council for a term beginning 1 March and, there being no other candidates, I was duly elected. Onwards and upwards in the deliberative councils of Fleur de Lis University.

Madame Contretemps had mentioned her participation in a program celebrating "The Arts, Our Strength." Since January the university billboards had bragged "Technology, Our Strength." I found out how all this strength business translated into physical reality thanks to my membership on the University Research Council. The single meeting that I attended was the most crushingly, grindingly, evisceratingly dull morning I'd ever spent, as I told Claude Beaudoin as soon as it was over. Since serving with the music librarian on the emergency library committee I had detected in him a kindred spirit, though he managed to keep his opinions to himself.

"Could it have really been as dull as all that?" he asked as I took a seat in his office, really more of a glass cage forcibly inserted into the middle of the Audio-Vidéothèque

"Yes," I said. "Worse. It was astonishingly, colossally, stupefyingly dull. This was the Two Hundred and Twenty-First Reunion of the University Research Council—they actually printed this information on the agenda and the minutes."

"I suppose you had a 'mission,'" Claude said with a wry smile.

"Oh yes. We were supposedly evaluating a report on a university center for the study of the economic effects of energy policies according to a list of criteria each of which was broken down into multiple subheadings."

"It's always nice to have subheadings—keeps things straight."

"I don't know. They've had more than two hundred meetings already. I'm not at all confident that the evaluation will ever end. I'm afraid it may end up like the case of Jarndyce vs. Jarndyce in Dickens' *Bleak House*, simply dragging on for year after year."

"That's the way this university operates: eventually the costs of running the commission will exceed the budget of the center it is evaluating, but that never seems to bother anybody."

"Am I the only person to find these things boring?"

"Axel, think of it as a sanity test."

"How so?"

"If you're bored, then consider that you're still sane. What I worry about are the people who find these meetings interesting. Though I have to say I did attend one memorable meeting of such a commission. It was two years before you came. The theme that year was 'French—Our Strength' and they chose Robert Montrachet to chair it."

"The Dean of the Faculty of Letters?"

"That's right. Well Montrachet didn't always take his meds, complained they interfered with his sex life."

"He talked about this in public?"

"When he was up you could never tell what he might say. Anyway, he was up that day. He started off reading the commission's mandate at a mile a minute. Then that reminded him of a funny story, which he told, and the laughter, which started out nervously—as you can imagine, these have traditionally been pretty humourless affairs—grew in volume. That encouraged him to tell another funny story which apparently reminded him of some other story which even he couldn't bring himself to tell in public, so he just went into a fit of giggles. Finally the Vice-Rector of Research had to take over the meeting. The commission probably considered the day a disaster but I thought it was one of the best meetings I've ever attended."

"Funny I haven't heard about him."

"A year or so ago he went into rehab—he really had a pretty serious gambling problem—and I guess the doctors managed to get his manic/depressive problem under control at the same time."

I left Claude's office feeling better than I had when I arrived and went back to work with renewed vigour.

All subsequent meetings of the council fell, happily for me, on a day when I had a class to teach, and I offered, yea begged, to have the Vice-

Rector replace me, but Madame Contretemps instructed me to offer my excuses to the committee for the rest of the semester and to change my class schedule for the fall term. Meanwhile, every week I received piles of printed matter several inches thick from the research council and it began to clog up my office. I couldn't throw it away, I had no intention of ever reading it, but it continued to arrive in great indigestible hunks, a never-ending reminder of the university's strength.

Just when I thought that every possible group that could hold a strike had done so there came news of a possible police strike. Last fall when negotiations became deadlocked, the province called for arbitration, thereby buying several months of tranquility. The arbiter made a lengthy report, including a recommendation for a 4.5% salary increase. Parliament accepted the other provisions of the report but offered the police only a 3% hike in line with other salary increases for government employees. The policeman's union cried foul—you have to accept the arbiter's decision. No we don't, replied Parliament—the fine print says that the arbiter's recommendations aren't binding. Both sides refused to budge and the policeman's union declared war, saying that it would announce its pressure tactics. I envisioned a reign of terror.

The letters-to-the-editor column in *Le Soleil* published a communication from a woman who started off by declaring her sympathy with the police's cause, defending their right to the salary increase recommended by the arbiter and excoriating the provincial government. This same government, she reminded us, arbitrarily cut all the teachers salaries by 20% in 1982, thus breaking the terms of their contracts, imposed a year's freeze, and rolled back the salary ladder by several steps so that now in 1984 there were still teachers who had not yet returned to the 1982 level. It was you same policemen, the writer went on, who enforced the injunctions breaking the ensuing strike. You beat a few heads while you were at it, she added. The medicine doesn't taste as good when you're taking it rather than administering it, eh?

The policemen's union announced its strategy. Henceforth, except for flagrant cases, when automobile drivers committed traffic violations, the friendly policemen would stop them, issue a warning, and say please don't do it again. The province stood to lose some $78 million in revenue ordinarily generated by traffic tickets. The police also planned to take their duties seriously, sending out twice as many patrol cars as usual. Moreover, policeman would freely leave their districts if necessary to follow up on a case. The resulting mileage increases would cost the province a bundle. My sojourn in Québec was many things, but never boring. I still hadn't figured out whether I could ever fit into this strange place or whether I should just give up and accept permanent status as an outsider.

Visits from Colette helped me to forget the frustrations of tedious meetings, querulous students, and disruptive labour disputes. Frequently she would spend the evening at my apartment working, though seldom at a chair or desk, preferring to unroll my exercise mat and stretch out on it under the grand piano. While she reviewed her students' repertoire sheets I continued working on a new book for the music history course, "An Outline of Musical Thought" (which I thought sounded less pretentious in French, *Une esquisse de la pensée musicale*). Then I would look up to find her wearing nothing except one of my shirts and a come-hither look that announced the end of work for the evening.

One night I told Colette the story of discovering the "death threat" letter in my office, and the various conversations that had taken place as a result. "Why are you doing this, Axel?" she asked.

"At first I just felt curious about the previous occupant of my office, and what he could have been doing to provoke such a message. When I found out that he had died, my curiosity increased but along with it a sense of outrage."

"How do you mean?"

"We spend most of our time with students, and that gives us a sense of this being a teaching institution, but more and more it feels to me as if the energy of the university goes into feeding a faceless, mindless bureaucracy."

"Isn't that pretty much what happens at any university?"

"Sure, but wouldn't you expect the death of a professor to bring out the human side? Instead, it's been completely covered up, obliterated as if it never happened. I never knew Andrew Girard, but the same thing could happen to you or me. If you died, wouldn't you want people to know about it?"

"I see what you mean. But how far are you going to follow this thing?"

"I think I can give you a more specific answer than you might have been expecting. Do you have plans for March Break?"

"None in particular. I thought it would be nice to go someplace warm."

"That's not exactly what I had in mind. How would you feel about coming with me to Kuujjuaq?"

"You couldn't have picked anyplace closer to the North Pole?"

I told Colette about my return visit to the university accounting office where I had hung around until everyone had gone to lunch except the secretary who had assisted me earlier. Having checked the locations of the extension branches of Fleur de Lis University, I was certain that I knew where they'd sent the security officer who had seen Girard's body. So I asked the secretary to tell me, if I were planning a trip to Kuujjuaq to hunt caribou, might there be anyone from the Rochambeau vicinity who could give me information once I got there. She thought about the question, understood how carefully it had been crafted, opened a file cabinet, and gave me the name I needed, Serge Landry.

"You're not really thinking about hunting caribou, I hope," Colette said.

"No; I thought snowmobiling might be more appealing."

"Count me in," she said, "but the next trip we take together has got to be in the opposite direction."

"Agreed," I said.

Chapter 20

"I HOPE YOU BROUGHT YOUR ticket this time, Monsieur," said the agent at the Air Québec ticket counter, recalling my problem in November.

"Ticket, suitcase—everything I need," I said.

Happily the provincial government subsidized air travel to remote locations inaccessible by car, and a telephone call to the Fort Chimo Hotel revealed no sudden surge in reservations as a result of March Break.

As we travelled the eight hundred miles from Rochambeau to Kuujjuaq I told Colette my suspicions about Girard's death and she asked me an unexpected question. "What do you know about Madame Contretemps?"

"What did you have in mind?" I said.

"Isn't she the Director's boss?" Colette asked.

"I'm not sure," I said. "I would have thought that he would answer first to the Dean of the Faculty of Arts, Alain Valcartier. Why do you ask?"

"Yesterday I saw her come out of the bank and hand an envelope to a man in a parked car."

"You found that suspicious?"

"Well, after coming out of the bank she looked up and down the street before walking to the car."

"And the man in the car?"

"Was the Director."

I told Colette I had no idea what the exchange could signify but promised to follow up on it when we returned. We spent the rest of the flight discussing the relative advantages of warmer destinations for future excursions.

The plane circled over the several dozen buildings of the remote village then came to a gentle landing. We checked into the Fort Chimo Hotel, whose three floors made it the only multi-story structure in town, and then set out on foot to the small group of buildings that constituted the furthest extension of Fleur de Lis University.

"This is just the way my father described it," Colette said.

"You mean he's been here?"

"Yes. The U.S. Army operated a base here from 1941 to 1944 and then turned it over to the Canadian government after the war. My dad came up here twice to help set up a radar network."

I wore ski garb, which kept me warm enough, but I marvelled at how attractive Colette looked in the heavy fur-collared parka that one associates with the Far North. It didn't take us long to reach the squat buildings, identified by the university emblem flying from a flagpole just beneath the Québec provincial (or as the Québecois would say, national) flag.

I wanted to avoid any contact with Fleur de Lis officialdom, lest my visit prove embarrassing, or even dangerous, for the man I hoped could help me. Rather than enter the main building we walked around the perimeter until we came to a small hut marked Security.

"Serge Landry?" we inquired of the building's single occupant.

"That's me," he said. "What can I do for you?" Evidently they didn't place a lot of emphasis on uniforms in this part of the world. With his long underwear visible beneath a heavy plaid shirt this could have been a trapper or hunting guide, but Landry's penetrating glance and wary expression seemed to have come from the city.

I explained that I had been visiting various schools as a music adjudicator from Fleur de Lis, and learning that a former employee from the Rochambeau campus worked here, thought I would look him up.

"Mr. Crochet," he said, looking first at me, then at Colette, then back at me. "You seem like a nice enough fellow, but you are a terrible liar."

"And you are a very discerning security officer."

He smiled. "I used to be a detective in the Montréal police force."

"But no longer."

"No. They said I had a problem with authority." The passage of time had not completely erased the bitterness conveyed in his tone.

"Then we're kindred spirits," I said. "I've gotten the same comments everywhere I've worked."

"So why are you really here?" he asked, apparently taking an interest in any diversion from the monotony of this isolated outpost.

I recounted the story of Andrew Girard's death as far as I understood it. He nodded and said, "I guess you understand why I'm here. When you walk out of this building, this conversation never took place and we never met. Understood?" I nodded. He looked at Colette and received her assenting nod, then gestured for us to sit down in the two available chairs while he opened a folding chair for himself. Outside the snow blew around in a light wind under a cloudy sky. As far as the eye could see there appeared only shades of white and off-white: no trees, no bushes, no fences.

"You've come an awful long way to get very little, I'm afraid," Serge said. "I was making my rounds in the tunnels that night—they gave us a little golf cart to make it easier. I came around a corner and turned toward Pavillon Desjardins when I saw the body. There was no question that he was dead—there was blood everywhere."

"What did you do then?" Colette asked.

"In the case of an injury I would ordinarily have called right away for an ambulance," Serge said, "but this was so unusual I thought I'd better talk to the Rector first. I reached him directly and told him I would summon medical assistance, but he told me to leave that to him. The Rector turned up in less than five minutes later, along with a couple of guys in white jackets. But I remember noticing that they weren't wearing the usual outfit for St. Jean Ambulance."

"Then what happened?" I asked.

"The men in white disappeared with the body—they'd brought along a stretcher for the purpose. The Rector told me that I'd done the right thing to inform him. Then he told me to take the rest of the night off and not to mention anything I'd seen until he'd had a chance to notify the next of kin. That seemed reasonable enough to me, so I went out and downed a few beers."

"When did you start to get suspicious about what had gone on?"

"It seemed all right that evening. I asked the Rector if he wanted me to get in touch with the city police and he said he'd take care of that. I imagined he didn't want a lot of photographers and news people coming around the campus until he'd had a chance to get in touch with this man's people. But the next morning when the Rector appeared at my apartment I knew something wasn't right about this. And I really got worried when he had me pack my things, drove me to the airport himself, and put me on a plane for this godforsaken place." His gesture encompassed the room.

"You weren't married?"

"No. I lived alone in a furnished apartment—I guess he must have already known that—so there wasn't really much for me to bring."

"I take it you didn't have a lot of choice in the matter," Colette said.

"Not what you'd call a choice," Serge said. "The Rector explained that I'd be getting a considerable raise, as well as what he called 'hardship compensation' for living up here. But he also indicated—none too subtly—that if I turned down the offer, he had sufficient political connections to insure that I wouldn't work anywhere else in the province."

"Do you think he could really do that?" I asked.

"Do you think I was going to try to find out?" he countered.

"I suppose he forbade you to discuss the incident," I said.

"That part he made very clear," Serge said.

"So are you stuck here forever?" Colette asked.

"I think that was the general plan," Serge said.

"I take it that you have something else in mind," I said.

"Damn straight. It turns out that between the courses they actually offer here and correspondence courses I can complete a degree in criminal justice—how's that for irony?—without having to pay tuition. When I finish I have a friend in Winnipeg who thinks he can get me a job with the force there."

I couldn't think of any other questions to ask, so I thanked Serge for his assistance and prepared to leave.

"What do you folks plan on doing until you can get a flight south?" he asked.

"Perhaps you could tell us where we can go snowmobiling."

"That I can," he said. "I'll recommend a restaurant, too." He scribbled the information on a slip of paper. "I'd join you except this is such a small place I'm afraid word would get to one of the others," he gestured toward the main building, "and back to Rochambeau. I don't think the Rector's arm really extends this far, but I'm not interested in finding out."

I thanked Serge again, and he reminded me, "You've never been here."

Snowmobiling near civilization carries many risks, most of them the fault of snowmobilers who go out at night, often intoxicated, and fail to negotiate turns or spot chains blocking trails. Or they may set out onto a frozen lake and foolishly try to investigate "that dark patch up ahead."

Colette and I confined our explorations to the remaining hours of daylight and followed the operator's directions to remain on marked paths. Never having tried this sport before, I experienced a certain adolescent thrill at travelling at a reasonably fast pace across the snow, a beautiful woman sitting behind me, her gloved hands around my waist. But fairness dictated that we change places for the return trip. I wrapped my arms around her waist for awhile, and then moved my hands higher. Colette, an experienced snowmobiler, made no protest but simply increased our speed, reducing the time before we reached the privacy of our hotel room.

On the first afternoon after March Break the Director asked me to come to his office.

"I believe you have something belonging to Madame Contretemps," he began.

"After a letter is delivered, doesn't it belong to its recipient?" I asked.

"But after the recipient's death, ownership would revert to the sender."

"Not if the letter's contents contained evidence of a possible crime."

"No," he conceded. "In that case, the letter should be turned over to the proper authorities; in this situation, that would be me."

"With all due respect, what if I had reason to believe that the authority in question might be involved in the crime?"

The Director looked uncomfortable for a brief moment; then he suddenly laughed, somewhat artificially I later considered, and said, "You're thinking of my role in Girard's so-called kidnapping." I continued to look at him without saying anything, partly because I didn't know what he was talking about. "We are neither of us lawyers," the Director went on. "Perhaps I came at this subject badly. I am prepared to pay you for the return of those letters," he said, naming a figure that took me by surprise.

"I think I was more comfortable with the legal approach," I said. "I'm prepared to give you the letters if you promise that they be delivered to the Rector for final disposition."

"I believe that arrangement would be satisfactory," he said with an evident expression of relief.

Chapter 21

"I THINK I MAY HAVE been on the wrong track," I told Valéry during our daily get-together in his office. I told him about my conversation with Madame Contretemps, but not my meeting with the Director.

Valéry smiled. "You might want to hold onto those letters as a back-up plan when you come up for tenure. Did you check out her alibi?"

"Yes. Madame LaCharité confirmed her story about the choking conservatory representative. Québeckers really take politics seriously." Then I recounted my conversation with Alain Valcartier and Valéry chuckled at the thought of Andrew Girard, whose reputation as a lover of fine food had extended across the university, being held captive by graduate students in a restaurant.

"On the basis of that conversation I wondered whether Girard's death really could have been a coincidence."

"Now really," Valéry protested.

"Perhaps not the way you mean, but suppose there had been something else going on at the same time as the Faculty Senate vote, something else that might have precipitated Girard's death."

"Go on."

"Since I wasn't around then I thought the logical place to look was in the University Bulletin. I tried the library but Claude Beaudoin told me that the archives were kept at the history department."

"Did he tell you why?"

"I didn't think to ask."

"That's so typical of this place. The current Rector wasn't installed by God, contrary to what he may tell you. There was a vote in the University Senate."

"Not the Faculty Senate?"

"No, this was big-time stuff. You know, with proportionate representation from students, secretaries, migrant workers and the curmudgeon who runs the photocopier."

"Okay."

"The students opposed the man who was eventually elected and since he'd been fairly outspoken as Vice-Rector for Academic Affairs—the post that Madame Contretemps holds now—they thought they could make a case against him by tracking down public statements from an earlier era that he might regret now."

"Sounds like a plan."

"A very good plan, as it happened, because in earlier days the Rector, who now considers himself something of a sage, had been a real firebrand, whose public statements could hardly have been called judicious, or even temperate."

"So why didn't they succeed?"

"He just buried the archive where nobody could find it—in the office of his brother-in-law in the history department."

"Doesn't the university library keep a copy of all the bulletins?"

"They did until the Rector removed them. I have to hand it to the fellow—he certainly knows how to cover his tracks. But you were saying ..."

"So someone in the history department helped me locate the bulletins published around the time of the vote."

"And did you hit pay dirt?"

"I think so. It turns out that the Girard dispute was taking place at around the same time as the backlash from the Thibaut scandal."

"Wasn't that the minister who was taking kickbacks from a construction company?"

"That was just the tip of the iceberg. So many accusations of corruption emerged that it nearly brought down the government."

"But not quite?"

"No. The government immediately ordered an audit not only of the ministry in question but of every organization supported by the government. And just to show that they'd really gotten religion, they quoted Scripture. 'If thy right eye offend thee, pluck it out; if thy right hand offend this, cut it off.'"

"But hold on. Virtually every large agency in the province is supported by the government. This university, for example. It would be totally impractical."

"Right. So they did what people always do in cases like this. They pretended."

"You mean they didn't audit anybody?"

"Oh they held audits, all right—they needed numbers to publish in the newspapers—but selectively. According to the University Bulletin, they were planning to audit the largest faculty at Fleur de Lis University. And that's where I need your help. Which one is the largest?"

Valéry went to his shelf and pulled out the same three-ring binder I'd seen when I'd started. He opened to one of the first pages and displayed a list of university faculties and their subsidiary schools or departments. I scanned the list and began counting. "Let's see, that makes four departments for the Faculty of Arts, five for Engineering, three for Education, one each for Nursing, Law, and Theology, and six each for Letters, Medicine, Administration, Food and Agriculture, Science, and Social Sciences."

"So where does that get you?" Valéry asked.

"I'm not sure," I said. "I'll get back to you."

Chapter 22

I WAS STILL WORKING IN my office when Colette came by to pick me up for dinner and a movie. I embraced her warmly.

"You look excited," she said.

"I think I've finally gotten to the bottom of the Girard matter. After talking with Valéry Turgeon this afternoon I worked it out. The University Bulletin said there were plans to audit the "largest faculty" at Fleur de Lis. If Girard's proposal went through, moving the School of Music from the Faculty of Arts to the Faculty of Letters, that would make Letters the largest faculty, based on the number of its departments." Next door Valéry Turgeon locked his office and departed for the day.

"What's wrong with that?"

"Last fall Valéry told me that the Dean of the Faculty of Letters had embezzled funds and would never be able to withstand an audit. If the government had audited the Faculty of Letters he would have gone to jail. So the Dean had to prevent the Faculty Senate from voting on Girard's proposal and he did that by taking Girard out of the picture. The murderer was the Dean of Letters, Robert Montrachet."

"I think I may have met him when I came here for my interview in October: a kind of barrel-chested guy with no ear lobes. I know it sounds silly but I remember wondering at the time if a person without ear lobes could listen to music."

"Uh oh," I said.

"What's the matter?"

"That's the man who helped me find the university bulletins this morning."

"And I suppose you told him all about your investigation."

"Not exactly, but I think he knows that I've made the connection between Girard's death and the threatening audit."

New Quarter Note Tales

"Axel, you're entirely too trusting of people to be getting involved in this kind of thing."

"You may be right, but I don't think we should stay here any longer."

A knock at the door made both of us jump, but it turned out to be one of Colette's students with a question about her repertoire list. "I'll be with you in a moment," Colette told me. "I'll meet you out by the atrium."

I locked the double doors of the office and walked down the dimly-lit corridor to the atrium, an open area at the entrance of Pavillon Desjardins extending five stories between two towers containing stairways giving access to each floor.

I leaned against the railing and looked down at the fleur de lis composed of mosaic tiles in the floor at ground level. This building, with its post-modern spires and towers, must have looked pretty bizarre even as a seminary. I heard footsteps approach and turned with a smile to greet Colette but saw instead a heavy-set man with no ear lobes. He pressed me hard against the railing and I detected the smell of alcohol on his breath as he growled at me, "You had to stick your nose in where it wasn't wanted. You're as bad as the other one. Now you're going to die the same way."

I reckoned he planned to toss me over the railing. The pressure of his body prevented me from sliding off to either side, but if he intended to catapult me over the barrier he would have to reach down to grab my legs, and that would give me an opportunity to escape one way or another. I even envisioned leap-frogging over him. Then I saw the knife.

I instinctively grabbed his arm to keep the blade from its intended destination in my side, but he was stronger than I and the upward direction of his thrust, with his arm close to his body, gave him better leverage than my downward pull on the outside of his arm. I could feel my heart racing but he hardly seemed to be exerting himself. Even in the reduced lighting I could see the shininess of the blade. Was this the last thing that Andrew Girard had seen?

I felt Montrachet's arm lower. Was I succeeding? Maybe I was stronger than I thought. I felt momentarily exhilarated. I was going to get out of this after all. Then I realized that he had merely pulled back momentarily in order to get a better arc for the fatal thrust. I involuntarily pulled my chest in as though to distance myself, even slightly, from the metal about to enter my flesh. For a fleeting moment I recalled the lyrics of the song Colette had sung with me: "*With creeping and winding it slips into my breast. Amazing, it dares to bite me right through the skin and rushes to my heart. Oh love, I am afraid!*"

Suddenly Montrachet disappeared from view and a moment later I felt Colette in my arms. "It's all right now, Axel," she said, "but I think we ought to call the university police."

Chapter 23

We never got to the movies, or even dinner. Colette insisted we go back to her apartment, where she heated up some soup and turned on the gas fireplace, which seemed comforting despite its artificiality.

"So tell me again," Colette asked, "why Montrachet needed money so badly?"

"He was a compulsive gambler," I said. "Apparently he couldn't help himself."

"I imagine he must have gotten a thrill from living on the edge," Colette speculated, "always knowing that he might be caught. It seems he enjoyed taking risks."

"That was a risky strategy, following Andrew Girard to the library and from there into the tunnels to kill him," I said. "He apparently followed the same procedure again, trailing me from his office and waiting for an opportunity. Just what happened there at the end, anyway?"

Colette smiled. "You understand that you're not the first person I've gone out with. Well, other guys like other kinds of movies. In the case of the last man I was with, it was American action films."

I felt an involuntary pang of jealousy that I tried to keep from showing on my face. I just nodded and waited for her to continue.

"I remember being particularly impressed with a scene in which one man is standing at a urinal—is that really what those things look like?—and another man pulls his feet out from under him," Colette said. "With his hands occupied he can't even break his fall—he just goes chin first into the porcelain."

"Montrachet had a knife in his hands," I said.

"Facing upward," said Colette.

"So when you grabbed his ankles he fell on his knife," I said.

"That seems to be what happened," she said. "But how did he get away with it the first time?"

"The Rector is his brother-in-law," I said. "I imagine that his rehab treatment was part of the deal: the Rector simply got tired of having him raid the faculty budget to cover his gambling losses."

"What's going to happen now?" Colette asked. "Is the Rector going to cover up this death too?"

"Not likely," I said. "He might not get such a cooperative security guard this time around, but just to be sure, on our way out of the building I pulled the fire alarm. Dozens of people will have seen the body. There's no way they can keep it a secret."

"What about Madame Contretemps?" Colette asked, thinking of our conversation on the plane.

I explained about the political significance of the letters she had written to Andrew Girard. "She was evidently willing to go to some lengths to get them back—even to the point of trying to buy them."

"So which did you choose," Colette asked, "the money or the letters?"

"Neither one," I said. "I gave the letters to the Director."

"But couldn't you have used them to your advantage later on?" she asked.

"I'm out of my depth when it comes to political intrigue," I said. "I just wanted to be done with it."

"So the Director wasn't really involved at all?" she asked.

"I think he knew about the posse, and when Valcartier came to him with a plan for keeping Girard from attending the University Senate meeting, he arranged for the posse to carry out the plan."

"Are you tired?" Colette asked me.

"I don't think I could sleep right now. I'm too excited and relieved."

"Me too," Colette said. "But I can think of something else to do." She took my hand and led me to the bedroom.

THE MUSIC MAN MYSTERY

Chapter 1

MIDWAY ALONG THE BALCONY OF the Anglican cathedral in Rochambeau, Québec sits the Royal Box, its brass railings continually maintained at a high polish in anticipation of a regal visit. The only time I ever saw that pew occupied was in 1983 during a Friday evensong service held in honour of the visit by Prince Charles and Lady Diana. From my vantage point at the organ console I had to crane my neck to catch a glimpse of the royal couple, a view seldom permitted by the complicated liturgy of the service, with choral response and organ interludes in addition to hymns, canticles and anthems.

For this unique occasion, in addition to the half-dozen voices of the barely-existent cathedral choir, I could draw on a dozen singers from the city's other two Anglican parishes, but lacking extended rehearsal time I had decided to play it safe with a unison anthem, "Let Us Now Praise Famous Men" by Ralph Vaughan Williams. (For state occasions, you can't go wrong with Vaughan Williams.)

At the front of the chancel the bishop, white-haired, beatific and months away from retirement, occupied his throne, having delegated the ecclesiastical heavy lifting to Gordon Tapley, a short, sandy-haired man with a florid complexion who considered that throne to be his rightful inheritance after years of toiling as dean of a cathedral that drew scarcely twenty worshipers a Sunday during most of the year but filled with tourists during summer months or on special occasions such as this.

As a kind of payoff for loyalty during hard times, the dean had invited the city's five other Protestant men of the cloth—not excluding the Commanding General of the Salvation Army in full military regalia—to assist in the celebration. Having been through a similar exercise in ecumenism at Good Friday I knew what to expect: passages from Scripture arranged into a kind of dramatic reading to permit the participation of the entire corps of clergymen, each of whom felt compelled to give full weight to every syllable in order to demonstrate that he, at least, knew how to reverence God's Holy Word. Prince Charles had undoubtedly suffered through far worse without even raising a royal eyebrow.

I noted that among the massed choir and congregation I could see virtually the entire cast of "The Music Man," the musical that the local Savoyards had recruited me to lead when their previous musical director had decamped to Ottawa. Perhaps it had been cruel to ask the dean of the cathedral to portray George Shinn, Mayor of River City, Iowa. Gordon Tapley, full of self-importance, played the role completely straight, to excruciatingly funny effect. His unwitting deadpan humour gave new meaning to the term "dramatic irony."

Casting his wife, petite, grey-haired Priscilla, to be Mrs. Paroo turned out to have been an act of genius by Agnes Lee, the stage director for the production. In real life Priscilla, dwelling in the shadow of her domineering husband, seemed incapable of saying "Boo," to anyone, but in the role of an outspoken Irish widow she showed her true colours as a talented, self-assured woman having the time of her life. Weekly rehearsals, she told me, had become the focus of her existence. Easily the most popular member of the cast, Priscilla so completely inhabited her character, easily mastering an Irish brogue, that the other actors unconsciously began to treat her as though she really were a Celtic mavourneen brimming with vitality and folksy wisdom. I had trouble imagining her, after the final performance three days hence, going back to being a church mouse.

At the edge of the choir I noticed Geoffrey Lambert, head of Rochambeau's English School Board, round-faced and a bit stout, whom I'd persuaded to join the barbershop quartet whose harmonies play such an important part in the musical. Ordered by Mayor Shinn to obtain the credentials of con man Harold Hill, the music man of the title, members of the quartet become easily distracted whenever he starts them off on some favourite refrain and then ducks out of sight while they concentrate on perfecting their vocal blend. Geoffrey, more than some English-speaking Québeckers, or Anglophones, made his peace with the Quiet Revolution in which, two decades earlier, the majority Francophone population had supplanted the minority English hegemony.

Among other things, all the English-language street signs overnight gave way to their French-language equivalents, so that Maple Street became Rue des Erables. Arriving in Rochambeau in 1982 I accepted the status quo, but more or less monolingual English-speakers, who had been able to enjoy a comfortable existence in the city prior to the transformation, found the climate much less habitable afterwards. In generations past, wealthy English families regarded the French as little more than peasants. There remained a fair number of older residents who had no intention of ever learning French and seemed to resent the very presence of French speakers in *their* city.

The general exodus of English-owned businesses, either to bilingual Montréal or out of the province altogether, had reduced the English-language community to a somewhat embattled enclave. The Savoyards' annual Gilbert & Sullivan productions served not only to entertain but also to "show the flag" with chauvinistic zeal. The choice of "The Music Man," an *American* musical comedy, had occasioned a fair amount of controversy. As an American ex-pat I felt relieved that such a politically-charged decision had occurred before I came on board.

Some Anglophones, like the members of the Rochambeau Historical Society, had actively resisted the domination of French, particularly the activities of the French Language Police, who enforced strict laws regulating the relative size of French- and English-language signs in shops and businesses. Others, like Geoffrey Lambert, got along by going along. The presence of asbestos in the insulation of the school in whose theatre we planned to present "The Music Man" had been common knowledge for years. The English School Board, with the diminished Anglophone population in the city, could not hope to remove the illegal substance properly so for years Lambert had been simply paying off the building inspector, like a bamboo tree that bends in the wind without breaking. Lambert had been reluctant to take on the role of Oliver Hix in the barbershop quartet, but when I explained that he would not have to speak any lines he agreed to serve, "standing up for the team" as he put it.

At the opposite end of the pew sat Paul Cochrane, owner and proprietor of Cochrane Printing, who supplied the needs of the entire Anglophone business community—including the insurance firm of Stanstead & Whately—in addition to printing bulletins for the Anglican congregations and programs for the Savoyards. A timid, fearful man, Paul maintained the hangdog expression of someone awaiting a reprimand. Since his wife's death Paul had raised his son Brad, now twenty-one, with the support of English-language companies who had written off his large mark-ups as a form of corporate charity on a personal level. In contrast to his craven demeanour in daily life, Paul shone as one of only two tenors in the St. Matthias Senior Choir, and I had encountered no resistance when I asked him to play the role of Jacey Squires, first tenor of the barbershop quartet in "The Music Man."

Just in front of him, in the soprano section, sat Agnes Lee, the stage director for this production as for its Gilbert & Sullivan predecessors. A short but wiry woman, Agnes was fiercely devoted to the theatre, and brooked no dissent. Agnes was the only person I had ever seen confront Dean Tapley directly. At an early rehearsal, when she had caught him giving contrary instructions to one of the other actors, Agnes declared in front of the entire company, "Dean Tapley, in the cathedral you are master of all you survey. The theatre is my cathedral. When you're in my cathedral, what I say goes. Is that clear?" Dean Tapley didn't mutter under his breath or offer excuses that he was just trying to help. To my astonishment he said meekly, "Yes, ma'am," and that was the end of it.

Agnes also served as president of the Rochambeau Historical Society, honouring not only her love of the past—as seen from an Anglophone perspective—but also the memory of her father, who had donated his entire collection of local memorabilia to the society. To both the theatre and the museum Agnes brought an almost religious zeal which tended to stifle demurral. After all, how could you argue with someone who eyes burned with a holy passion?

We had no difficulty casting Eulalie Mackechnie Shinn, the mayor's wife, leader of the Wa Tan Ye dancers and First Lady of River City. In the song "Pick-a little" she explains the contempt of River City ladies for the attempts of town librarian, Marian Paroo, to "improve" their minds. A wealthy benefactor built the River City library, "but he left all the books to her." Marian advocates dirty books, they complain, like Chaucer, Rabelais, and Balzac.

Miriam Whately, wife of the junior partner in the insurance firm of Stanstead & Whately, seemed a natural for the part. Bossy, opinionated, a handsome, hefty figure of a woman, she had fought the French Language Police to a standstill on more than one occasion as secretary of the Rochambeau Historical Society. Born in Connecticut, Miriam had come to the province during the era when English speakers still ran the show. In the manner of southern women in the decades immediately after the American Civil War, she considered the Quiet Revolution to have been a personal affront. Miriam led the alto section in our massed evensong choir but I was just as happy not to have her in the tiny cathedral choir. She sang loudly and enthusiastically but hated to be corrected for her frequent musical errors.

Miriam's husband Herbert worked quietly behind the scenes in the Savoyards productions as in his business and in his marriage. Never a "people person," Herbert devoted himself to the nuts and bolts of the insurance business. Formerly an avid golfer, he had had to give up the game after a heart attack, and had learned to control stress in his personal life to prevent a recurrence, no small task given the tempestuous temperament of his wife. When a local artist in the Anglophone community contributed a series of brilliant sketches for "The Music Man," Herbert had enlarged the designs and recruited the young people in the production to assist him in painting the sets. Prematurely hunched over, he gave the impression of a weather-beaten barn yielding to the elements, but no one ever questioned his judgement or competence.

Seated beside him in the congregation I saw Cathy Stanstead, his partner's wife, who also served the production in an off-stage capacity. When I had inquired who took care of the non-musical aspects of the show—publicity, photography, parking attendants, ushers, back of house management and so forth—I had consistently received Cathy's name in response. Was she some kind of hard-driven workaholic? I wondered. That hardly accorded with the relaxed, gracious woman whom I had met at a dinner party shortly after my arrival in the city. Eventually I figured it out: people found Cathy's quiet charm irresistible. When it came to finding volunteers, Cathy didn't even need to make telephone calls; people called her asking how they could help. Her subtle managerial style made each member of the crew feel as if he or she were indispensable to the show's success. Cathy kept track of all the details without apparent effort and elicited cooperation without ever raising her voice, to the envy of Miriam Whately, who barged through the world like a bulldozer.

Dean Tapley nodded at me with a slight frown and I introduced the next hymn, "O God, Our Help in Ages Past." Practicing the three-manual cathedral organ brought me considerable pleasure, in contrast to the frustration I experienced in actual services in which the dean seemed determined to manage every detail. No one could take exception to this majestic hymn, but in our collection of "Hymns Ancient and Modern" Dean Tapley seemed to prefer mawkish nineteenth-century compositions which displayed neither the straightforward workmanship of the ancient nor the sprightly inventiveness of the modern. For once he didn't "correct" the tempo I had set by loudly bleating the hymn at what he considered to be its proper pace.

As the hymn ended my eye caught a bit of movement in the tiny booth that had been added to the rear of the balcony to house the lighting and sound systems. While I couldn't actually see the occupants I had no doubt as to their identities. Francis Tapley, the dean's seventeen-year-old son, was a tall, skinny lad, soft-spoken and somewhat awkward, the model of a gangly youth who would go all the way through high school without ever getting up the nerve to ask a girl for a date. Francis had inherited his father's steely grey eyes but none of his intensity. Far from being master of all he surveyed, the boy seemed almost apologetic for taking up space.

When "The Music Man" ended, most of the cast would go back to whatever they had been doing. For Francis the production was likely to have a longer-lived effect. For want of other contenders, Agnes had cast him as Tommy Djilas, the River City equivalent of a juvenile delinquent whom Mayor Shinn tries to keep away from his daughter Zaneeta. Our Zaneeta was played by Lorna Lambert, a local beauty whose flirtatiousness bordered on promiscuity, the sort of girl with whom Francis would never have had anything to do, save a shy "hello" at the annual Christmas party. But once the two young people were thrown together at the start of rehearsals in the fall, it didn't take long for a romance to develop, and far from Tommy corrupting Zaneeta, it was clearly Lorna who had taken the lead in initiating Francis so that now, at the end of May, giggles coming from any slight corner of privacy could have only one source. I imagined that Dean Tapley took a dim view of these goings-on, but until the end of the production he had no practical way of keeping the two young people apart. Geoffrey Lambert seemed long ago to have abandoned any hope of controlling the wanton ways of his only daughter.

Marie Dufresne, director of the St. Matthias Senior Choir, served as Marian Paroo, the female lead in "The Music Man." Typecasting, she had observed, seeing that both Marie and Marian were librarians. When the congregation of St. Barnabas had dwindled to the point that they could no longer afford to maintain their own church, the bishop had put the building up for sale. Not surprisingly, there had not been much of a market for a deconsecrated parish church. Marie's father had picked the place up for a song and left it to her when he died.

When the city of Rochambeau determined that the building would make an admirable municipal library, Marie declined to sell but worked out an arrangement whereby she would lease the building to the city for a nominal fee and the city would engage her as chief librarian. Some Savoyard traditionalists had complained that Marie, offspring of an English Protestant father and a French Roman Catholic mother, wasn't really "one of us," but nobody could fault her clear, vibrant voice or her ease onstage. In fact, with her father's Irish heritage on his mother's side, she made an extremely convincing daughter for Priscilla Tapley's Widow Paroo. Nonetheless, the head of costuming insisted that Marian had to be a blonde, bringing out movie posters of Shirley Jones in support of her argument, so Marie's jet-black hair had to be covered by a wig.

Mark Stanstead, president of the Savoyards, had exercised the rights of office to take the musical's leading role of Harold Hill, the amiable con man who persuades the good citizens of River City, Iowa to invest in instruments and uniforms for a boys' band. This was not Mark's first invocation of the *droit du seigneur*. The previous year he had insisted on playing Captain Corcoran in "H.M.S. Pinafore," and his wooden delivery and mediocre voice had led the stage director and the musical director to commiserate in common frustration.

Mark inherited the firm of Stanstead & Whately from his father, who had founded the business with Herbert Whately's father during the era when English speakers ran the city. He learned to adapt when, in the aftermath of the Quiet Revolution, all contracts had to be produced in both official languages. Having resisted the general Anglophone exodus, Mark found himself senior partner of the oldest English-owned business in the city. Though minimally talented as a musician, Stanstead displayed considerable acumen as a businessman: versatile, knowledgeable, capable of seeing the big picture, and canny enough to have built bridges into the Francophone business community.

Mark Stanstead should have been sitting in the tenor section of our "massed choir." But we were going to have to find another Harold Hill for "The Music Man" because on Thursday night, following choir practice at St. Matthias Church, Mark had walked in front of a truck and been killed instantly.

During the singing of the final hymn, "Now the Day Is Over," Prince Charles and Lady Diana made a discreet departure, followed by a parade of participating clergymen led by the bishop. The choir sang a seven-fold Amen, I launched into an organ postlude, and the service came to a close.

Chapter 2

ON SATURDAY MORNING I RECEIVED a telephone call from Benoit Chanson, music editor for *Le Soleil*, Rochambeau's French-language newspaper. Ordinarily *Le Soleil* would not have deigned to publicize a production by the Savoyards, but the death of such an important figure in the business community must have turned it into a news story that Benoit felt compelled to cover.

"What is this 'Music Man' that you're putting on?" he asked me.

"The action takes place on the Fourth of July, 1912, sort of the American equivalent of St. Jean Baptiste, Québec's Fête Nationale."

"Go on."

"Harold Hill—that's the character Mark Stanstead was supposed to play—is a con man pretending to be a salesman, who travels from town to town persuading the citizens to order instruments and uniforms for a boys' band. He hangs around long enough for the stuff to arrive, then takes the money and runs, leaving the people with a leaderless band and instruments no one knows how to play."

"I gather something different happens in River City."

"That's right. This time Harold Hill falls in love with the town librarian, a music teacher who immediately sees that he's a fraud but doesn't turn him in because he manages to persuade her younger brother, a stutterer, to come out of his shell and begin talking."

"So the smooth-talking con man is left speechless by the librarian and the mute brother gains the gift of speech."

"You should be our publicist!"

"So what are you going to do without a leading man?"

"When they asked me to direct the show I insisted that we double-cast the leads, so young Brad Cochrane will have to carry on in Mark's place. We'll see how he manages at the dress rehearsal this evening."

"Is that Paul Cochrane's boy?"

"Uh huh."

"So this is your first year with the Savoyards?"

"That's right."

"How's it working out?"

"I heard from one of the parents after our first rehearsal. Their daughter reported, 'He didn't scream at us.' Actually, it might be better if you didn't print that. My predecessor still has a lot of loyal followers here. We've been practicing since September and I'm pleased with the way the chorus has mastered the music."

"What about the librarian? I take it she's the female lead?"

"That's right. Marie Dufresne plays the librarian/music teacher. Perhaps you've heard her.:"

"Yeah. Her ex-husband works here at the paper."

"The biggest challenge was recruiting a barbershop quartet."

"What do they do in the show?"

"The mayor of River City is suspicious of Harold Hill from the outset, and keeps asking the four members of the school board to get his credentials. Professor Hill succeeds in persuading four men who can't stand each other that they have the perfect voices for a barbershop quartet. Pretty soon they're inseparable."

"That sounds easier to execute on paper than to put into practice."

"That's for sure. I've spent more hours trying to get these guys to sing in tune than on any other part of the production."

"Let me get this straight. For years, the librarian has been trying to bring some cultural life to the town but fails. Then this fake music professor arrives and the women start practicing classic dance and the school board starts singing barbershop quartets. But she's supposedly a real music teacher and he's supposedly a fraud."

"I guess I never looked at it that way before."

"Your shows usually take place in April. Did you move the production to coincide with the royal visit?"

"That was the idea, but evidently Prince Charles and Lady Diana have already left for Montréal, so they won't get to see the show."

"I heard something about seventy-six trombones associated with this production. How is that possible?"

"They're imaginary."

"Imaginary?"

"It's part of Harold Hill's con. Actually he doesn't know one note from another, but he captivates the townspeople with his account of the occasion that Gilmore, Liberatti, Pat Conway, The Great Creatore, W.C. Handy, and John Philip Sousa, all came to town on the very same historic day. Then he sings the song you've heard:

Seventy-six trombones caught the morning sun
With a hundred and ten cornets right behind,
There were more than a thousand reeds
Springing up like weeds,
There were horns of every shape and kind.

"Purely imaginary, you say?"

"That's right."

"But in the movie, I thought they were all there?"

"That's one of several problems with the movie version. In Hollywood's view of things, if an audience expects seventy-six trombones, you have to deliver them."

"Even if they're imaginary, it paints a pretty picture. How're you going to evoke all that with a piano?"

"Actually the board sprung for a few instruments."

"I'm glad to hear it. Now this musical comedy is a departure from the Savoyard's annual Gilbert & Sullivan production."

"That right. Their choice of that particular show is what made me accept the invitation to direct it."

"Is there some hidden political agenda here?"

"How do you mean?"

"Well, last year's show was sheer propaganda."

"You mean 'H.M.S. Pinafore'?"

"That's right. 'In spite of all temptations to belong to other nations, he remains an Englishman!' Not too subtle if you ask me."

"I'm sure it was meant to be a parody of English jingoism."

"It's all in the way it's spoken and all in the way it's heard."

"Perhaps you're right."

"So about these Iowans. Aren't they pretty stupid to be gulled by this ersatz music man? And isn't this a thinly-veiled attack on the Francophone community?"

"More stubborn than stupid, I would say. In fact, the show opens with a song about stubbornness:

We can be cold
As our falling thermometers in December

If you ask about our weather in July.
And we're so by God stubborn
We could stand touchin' noses
For a week at a time
And never see eye-to-eye."

"My point exactly. This is the way the English view French Québeckers."

"But it goes on to say:
But we'll give you our shirt
And a back to go with it
If your crops should happen to die.
I don't think you can find any malice hidden in the show."

"I heard that there was something about language."

"Perhaps you mean when Harold Hill asks, 'Are certain words creeping into his vocabulary? Words like "Swell," and "So's your old man"?'"

"That's just what I'm talking about—making fun of attempts to maintain the purity of one's language. You don't consider all this talk about forbidden language a thinly-veiled attack on the *Commission de Protection de la langue française?*"

"You mean the Language Police?"

"We don't call it that."

"I think that's a bit of a stretch. It's just a comedy, after all."

"Many a message can be carried in a witticism, Monsieur."

"I'll bear that in mind."

"You mentioned a stutterer. As a professor of music history you are surely aware of the political overtones of that choice."

"I hadn't really thought about it."

"Think of Valsek, the stutterer in 'The Bartered Bride' who personifies the Czech people subjugated by their oppressive German masters."

"Actually, in 'The Music Man' the little boy lisps."

"What happens to him?"

"A little girl named Amaryllis makes fun of him because he can't pronounce her name."

"Aha!"

"What do you mean, 'Aha!'"

"The directrice of the *Commission de Protection de la langue française* is named Amarante. I rest my case."

"I'm sure it's just a coincidence."

"I think I have enough for my story."

"I suppose it's going to be headed, 'English Community Prepares Annual Assault on Francophonie'?"

"Your words, Monsieur; not mine."

I hung up the telephone and thought about the day that lay ahead. I had a wedding to play at the cathedral at four and I thought I'd practice the organ before that since the evening would be devoted to the dress rehearsal for the show. My thoughts were interrupted by the telephone—Cathy Stanstead inviting me to lunch. Something in her voice suggested that this was not simply a social occasion. I looked at my watch, then through the window to see the clouds clearing after an early-morning drizzle. I calculated that I'd just have time for a short run, and headed to a nearby park that had a running track a metric mile in length. As I ran around the track I recalled my astonishment at seeing an announcement the year before for a 350 kilometre race at the site. Surely there had been an error—even a marathon was only 42 kilometres.

But I was mistaken. They really held a 350 kilometre endurance race to celebrate Rochambeau's 350th anniversary as the third oldest city in the province. Who would participate in such an event, I wondered? I found out during a summer French immersion course when Phil Latulippe, the pride of Québec and one of Canada's most renowned athletes, presented an inspirational talk in a disarmingly modest style. He had obviously given this presentation many times before and he spoke with the practiced ease of an experienced raconteur.

Twenty years before Phil, as he insisted on being called, presented himself to his doctor. Then in his forties, fifty pounds overweight, a three-pack-a-day smoker and heavy drinker, Phil wanted to know if there was any reason why he shouldn't take up long-distance running. The doctor laughed at him and advised him only not to go too fast. Since Phil found even mild exertion taxing, that advice didn't seem hard to follow. Next Phil went to a running expert and asked him to prescribe a training program so that he would be able to run a hundred miles without stopping. The fellow eventually subdued his mirth, then seeing that Phil was in earnest, wrote out a conditioning program. At the end of six weeks of intense work, Phil was able to run one mile without stopping.

He kept at it. The weight fell, he gave up drinking, though it took two years to give up smoking, and eventually he was able to achieve his goal of running a hundred miles without stopping. (That "eventually" must have covered a lot of territory. I knew what I felt like at the end of a 26-mile marathon; one hundred miles seemed unimaginable.) He told this story because he considered that anybody could duplicate his feats if they wanted to—he seemed absolutely convinced that he was nothing out of the ordinary. He was not a particularly fast runner—his best marathon time was slower than mine, for example—but he ran extraordinary distances.

After doing the hundred miles, Phil was approached by a group of friends who said, "Listen, Phil; the world record is only 220 miles— you're practically halfway there. Why don't you train a little more and go for it?" So he did, and made his way into the record book. As his fame began to spread, folks would ask him to come dedicate their running facilities with some long run. Eventually he got the idea of running across Canada, followed a few years later by a run all around Québec province, and more recently, a run from Alaska to his home in Loretteville. All these exploits took place while he was in his sixties.

Phil won the 350-kilometer ultramarathon race of which I spoke. But he concluded his talk by saying that he didn't want us to go out telling people we'd heard about a man who ran 2500 miles, but that we'd a met a man who had saved himself. It occurred to me that I was indirectly indebted to Geoffrey Lambert for this inspirational message, since the French immersion program I attended fell under the auspices of the Rochambeau English School Board. I also left thinking that marathons didn't seem too long any more. The thought carried me one more time around the track, then back to my apartment. I showered and biked to the Stanstead residence.

Chapter 3

THE STANSTEAD HOUSE, THOUGH NOT large, had been artfully contrived to take full advantage of its splendid location overlooking the river. The living room, the largest space in the house, took the form of an outsized bay window, with three walls affording fine views. Cathy had intentionally avoided adding curtains in order to preserve as wide a perspective as possible.

I added my personal condolences to the written messages that seemed to have arrived from the entire English-speaking community, judging from the number of cards poised on the grand piano and letters overflowing a basket in the hallway. Cathy told me that her friends had provided enormous support in these days following Mark's death but made it clear that her summons to me had a different purpose.

During lunch we talked about Mark's funeral. Anglicans from all three congregations had shown up, along with a fair representation from the Francophone community, filling St. Matthias' Church to capacity. Occupied with a wedding on Saturday afternoon, Dean Tapley and I were virtually the only people associated with the production who hadn't been able to attend. Cathy had been particularly touched by the collection of wildflowers that the children in the production had gathered for her. I asked how she was holding up and Cathy mentioned a number of close friends who had been in and out of the house since Saturday to help out. I thanked Cathy for her efforts in coordinating virtually every non-musical aspect of the production. I also imagined that a simple shibboleth like "The show must go on" could have helped to sustain her by focussing energy and attention on an activity outside herself.

Afterwards, as we sat in the living room, Cathy came to the point of her invitation. "Francis came over this morning with some disturbing news." Francis Tapley had adopted the Stanstead's as a home away from home. Mark's open generosity contrasted with the strict Scottish parsimony of Francis's controlling father. During the winter Mark frequently took the boy skiing. They would return home to hot chocolate and home-made cookies prepared by Cathy, whose easy confidence contrasted with Mrs. Tapley's timidity, making Cathy the mother he always wished he'd had.

"What did Francis have to say?"

"This takes a bit of explaining. You know how close he and Lorna have grown."

"That's a nice way to put it. Physically inseparable might also describe the situation."

"Yes. Well, it appears that with the warmer weather they've started using the bit of remaining woods around St. Matthias for their trysts."

"How does that work?"

"I keep forgetting that you're at the cathedral rather than the church. Choir practices take place on Thursday evenings, same as anywhere else. In order to deal with the transportation problem, the church holds Teen Canteen on the same night."

"Providing Francis and Lorna an opportunity to slip away unnoticed?"

"I wouldn't say unnoticed—let's just say a blind eye is turned appropriately."

"Okay."

"On Thursday, about the time that the choir rehearsal was letting out, Francis and Lorna were in the woods, being physically inseparable, as you put it. Francis reports that a stranger came into the bushes near them. They heard the choir members coming down the steps toward the parking lot and realized they'd better rejoin the youth group to preserve their cover, so to speak, so they didn't see what happened next."

"Uh oh; I think I see where this is leading."

"Francis didn't think any more about it until he heard about Mark's death. Then he started replaying the scene in his mind and decided he needed to talk with me."

"So you're suggesting that Mark's death may not have been accidental."

"Nobody ever thought it was accidental. Don't be squeamish on my account, Axel. People think Mark killed himself, even if they're too polite to say so." I thought I detected a note of bitterness in Cathy's voice. The same well-wishers who had come to her assistance after her husband's death still belonged to a small community whose favourite topic of conversation was the personal life of anyone not present.

"But this stranger in the bushes casts a new light on the situation."

"It's hard to consider it a coincidence. I mean, what would anyone have been doing there?"

"Well, the first thought that comes to mind is that a man was emptying his bladder."

"I thought of that, but Francis said no—the stranger was completely still, as if lying in wait."

"So this stranger could have rushed out of the bushes and pushed Mark into the path of an oncoming truck?"

"That's what Francis suggested."

"But that's murder!"

"Axel, sometimes you have an uncomfortable way of stating the obvious."

"You've had some time to think about this but I'm just getting up to speed. This must make a great difference for you."

"Axel, I really need to know."

"I can understand that. I take it you're assuming that this stranger, whoever it is, must have known Mark's routine pretty well. That would limit the number of people who could have been involved."

"Suspects, Axel. Stop beating around the bush."

"You've clearly been thinking this through."

"I don't know, Axel. Why is it that men get all namby-pamby when discussing death with a woman? Are you afraid I'm going to faint or something?"

"Well …"

"Axel, I've gone through a lot in these past few days but I haven't collapsed yet. I've had plenty of women friends who've helped me with my grief, and Lord knows the pain isn't going to go away any time soon. I'm still getting used to the idea of Mark not being around any more. It isn't easy. But that's not why I asked you here. Axel, I consider you a friend. I'm asking you as a friend to find out how Mark died."

"Isn't this a job for the police?"

"Axel, you sound just like one of those mystery novels. The police have already marked it down as an accidental death, even though they think it was suicide."

"But with the stranger in the bushes …"

"Axel, I'm fairly self-confident but I don't like to be humiliated. Can you imagine the response if I, an Anglophone woman, were to telephone the Francophone chief of police and request that his force reopen their investigation because a friend thinks he heard a stranger in the bushes?"

"Well, when you put it that way …"

"How else could you put it? Will you do this for me, Axel? As music director, at the moment you have access to virtually everyone who had anything to do with Mark. You're ideally situated for the job, aside from an unaccountable unwillingness to call a spade a spade."

Under the circumstances, how could I refuse? My leading man dies; his wife asks me to investigate. I didn't see that I had much of a choice. I promised Cathy I'd do my best, but as I pedalled my bicycle up the Stanstead driveway I reflected that this was the last thing I wanted to undertake one day before the opening of the show.

I also reflected that I had a fair amount in common with Harold Hill. He had arrived in River City on July 4, 1912. I had arrived in Rochambeau on July 4, 1982. He sized up the situation with a view of selling the idea of a boys' band. I surveyed the lay of the land in the interest of founding an *a cappella* choir—the first in Rochambeau— and had engaged the efforts of Benoit Chanson to that end. The story he published about my intentions led to a flurry of phone calls and made it relatively easy to recruit singers. Mark Stanstead had sung in my *a cappella* choir as well as taking the role of Harold Hill. I guessed I owed his widow whatever assistance I could offer.

On the other hand, Mark had been born and bred in Rochambeau, knew the community intimately, and had successfully navigated the changing political course associated with the reversal of fortunes of Anglophones and Francophones. I was an outsider only beginning to get an idea of the situation. From all accounts, and from my own experience, Mark had been master of dealing with people, learning what made them tick, and had used this skill to build a highly successful business. I was a scholar, more comfortable in libraries than in social situations, happier reading and writing books than dealing with people directly. This was going to be a bit of a stretch.

As Sherlock Holmes would have put it, the game was afoot.

Chapter 4

THE ANGLICAN CATHEDRAL BOASTED A three-manual Hook & Hastings organ, the largest I had ever enjoyed as my regular instrument. A funny thing happened the week before my arrival in Rochambeau, however: an unsuspected pipe (water, not musical) had burst, flooding the instrument and causing severe damage. When I began my job as organist, three-fifths of the instrument was away being repaired and the remainder was under attack by a cipher.

Those who understand organs from the inside talk about ciphers as malfunctions of electrical connections and wind flow. I preferred to think of them as furry varmints who invade the instrument to make life miserable for the organist. From the congregation's vantage point, the explanation didn't matter much—the result was a sustained note that you couldn't get rid of short of shutting the instrument down. I had been using the piano to accompany church services for two weeks when the organ repairman turned up and chased the cipher away. When I berated him for not actually exterminating the varmint, he smiled calmly and said that perhaps the furry critter would find a home in the organ at the United Church up the street. "You mean the church that hired your competitor to do their organ restoration?" I inquired. He just winked and went back to his work.

A few weeks later the repairman returned with all the ranks we'd been doing without all year—the entire Swell manual, the Positive organ, and several ranks on the Great. At the same time, he carted off all of the currently operating pipes for releathering and revoicing. He thought that the complete organ, which I'd never heard, might or might not be restored by fall.

I had been practicing for an hour or so when Francis Tapley came up to the console. "Cathy suggested I might find you here," he said.

I turned off the organ and gave the young man my full attention. "She told me your story, but I'd rather hear it from you first hand."

"There isn't an awful lot to tell. Lorna and I were in the woods when the stranger came into the bushes near the path."

"You didn't go to investigate?"

"I guess you could say I was otherwise occupied."

"How exactly?"

"Lorna was giving me a bj. Do you know what a bj is?"

"Yes, Francis." Ah, the innocent arrogance of adolescents who, having just discovered sex, imagine that no one before them has ever thought of it.

"So I couldn't tell what was going on. I just know what I heard."

"Tell you what. I'm not all that familiar with the layout at St. Matthias. Suppose we try to recreate the situation here. I understand there are steps leading from the church down to the parking lot."

"Right. Let's move over to the chancel steps." I left the console and joined Francis at the front of the cathedral. "Okay. Now say this is the church. The pews can be the parking lot. Over here by the organ console are the trees."

"That would put the highway on the opposite side of the steps by the lectern. That's one thing I haven't been able to understand. How could someone go from the parking lot steps right to the highway? Is it really that close with no barrier?"

"You have to remember the peculiar relationship between Church and State in this province, Axel. Church property—even if it's owned by Anglicans—is considered sacred. On the other hand, if the government wants to build a highway, it just builds it. In this case, the parking lot extended to the edge of the church property, so the province built the highway right beside it. The church wouldn't let the province take any of its property for a fence and the province wasn't going to give up any of its right-of-way, so the highway goes right up to the property line. There's just a single line of shrubs between the path and the road."

"I suppose they might have been more concerned for safety if there were French-speaking church people to protect."

"Perhaps so."

"But Mark Stanstead was a very large man. Are you telling me that this so-called stranger could have knocked him off the path and through the bushes right into traffic?"

"I'll show you. You be Mark standing on the steps and I'll be the stranger."

"Okay. I'll tell you when I'm …" Francis threw himself across the steps and hurled his weight against my knees. I went flying off the steps and crashed into the lectern. "I wasn't ready!"

"Exactly."

"But how could an assailant count on there being a truck at the right time?"

"Have you ever travelled on that highway at night?"

I recalled the evening, shortly after my arrival in Rochambeau when I still had the use of a rental car, that I'd driven to my office at the university to unpack my books. Even making allowances for the terror of unfamiliarity—an unknown road and a frightened American trying to deal with French-only traffic signs—the flow of truck traffic on that stretch of highway had been pretty intense. It may have been just the way Francis described it, but I couldn't make all the pieces fit.

"This still doesn't make sense. There are, what, a dozen people in the choir? If this happened the way you're suggesting, how come no one saw Mark die?"

"What did the newspaper say?"

"It didn't report any witnesses."

"Mark wasn't just the president of the Senior Choir; he was Rector's Warden for the church. Every Thursday he had to be sure all the lights were off and the doors locked after the Teen Canteen. He was always the last one down the steps to the parking lot."

"This is beginning to get clearer." Suicide seemed like a strange occurrence when Mark's death was first announced—it just didn't go with what I knew of him—and when I talked with Cathy earlier that day she confirmed that the idea of Mark taking his own life just didn't add up. "But then …"

"I know. Who did it?"

The arrival of a woman bringing flowers to the chancel signalled the end of detective work and the beginning of the wedding ceremony. I thanked Francis for his information and began putting my music in order.

Chapter 5

WHEN YOU'VE BEEN PLAYING WEDDINGS for twenty-five years, one more ceremony isn't anything to write home about. Then you hit a wedding like the one I played for in June, which smashed the existing endurance record at an enervating 1 ¾ hours. The bride was a member of my *a cappella* choir, the kind of sweet, unassuming girl whose modest requests eventually accumulate into major commitments. Would I be willing to direct members of the chorus in a couple of numbers? Sure, happy to help out. Oh, and could I play the organ to accompany them? Yeah, I reckon. And there'll be a few solos—could I accompany them, too? I suppose so. Oh, and could I play the Mendelssohn Wedding March as we're going out? Aw, why not?

So she got the music together—really wretched singing-commercial stuff for the most part—and I spent two evenings rehearsing the choir in their ooh's and ah's accompanying the soloists. Then she wanted us to make a recording—not during the wedding itself, but the night before. It seems she had a friend with professional recording equipment. You know what taping is like: we were there for three hours immortalizing this awful tripe.

Come the day of the wedding, I became aware that our efforts were but a small part of the master plan that this woman had assembled in her quiet, unassuming way. The church was a hypermodern circular structure built along the lines of the Houston Astrodome. From our seats in the upper grandstand behind center field we listened to a choir of cherubs singing a saccharine tune to the accompaniment of a kind of giant electronic harmonica playing do-dee-dee-dee-dee-dee, do-dee-dee-dee-dee-dee.

The prescribed sacramental rites were enhanced by a homily delivered by the priest and an informal sermon preached by somebody's brother, a lay counsellor. Even the prayers were orchestrated: after reading a seemingly endless succession of benedictions, the priest invited members of the congregation to add their own spontaneous thoughts, and one by one cousins and in-laws pulled out and read aloud their extra-liturgical "spontaneous" contributions.

I'd been asked to diddle quietly during communion, and obediently added a bit of ecclesiastical Muzak to the proceedings. Evidently the wedding dinner was no less elephantine, because the postprandial dance didn't get underway until 11 p.m. (We musicians, our job accomplished, gathered to enjoy a potluck supper closer to home.)

We didn't get many weddings at the cathedral—not surprising given the advanced age of the parishioners—but I still had more than my share of nuptial celebrations. One morning just before Christmas an organist friend telephoned to ask whether I could play a wedding that day: it seems he had inadvertently scheduled two obligations at the same time. So I picked out some music, went to the cathedral to fetch my shoes, and installed myself at the console of the recently restored organ of Chalmers Wesley Church. Restored, maybe, but tuned, no. The Great trumpet, in particular, was so out of tune as to be practically unusable. It sounded like a bagpipe, and I would simply have avoided using the stop except that the bride had specifically requested the Purcell Trumpet Tune to process and the Jeremiah Clarke Trumpet Voluntary for the recessional, so I had no choice. (Afterwards I learned that the bride's mother particularly liked the trumpet: she said it sounded like a bagpipe.)

The service was conducted in French, which would have posed no problems at the cathedral since the dean was bilingual, but the minister here sounded like an aged French bishop who had lost his dentures and was in any event more accustomed to reading the service in Latin. I knew the text well enough in English to be able to follow, but it was tricky. At any rate, the organist's fee paid for an unexpected day of skiing.

Today's wedding at the cathedral involved a bride who had once visited Rochambeau on a grade school field trip and fallen in love with the city. The straightforward ceremony—the dean bleating the prescribed liturgy—gave me an opportunity to reflect on the strange state of Anglicanism in this city. The passage of Bill 101, forbidding the education of children in a language other than French, had precipitated a general flight of Anglophones from the province, with a devastating effect on the Anglican Church.

Trinity Cathedral, the oldest Anglican cathedral outside Great Britain, had a couple of dozen communicants on a good Sunday, and often had too few to support hymn-singing. St. Barnabas had closed its building and now shared quarters with St. Matthias but because of doctrinal differences the two congregations refused to meet together for services.

I was not the only one to see that all the city's Anglicans joined together might make up enough souls for one small church. The problem lay in the joining. In his Easter message, the bishop, calling for an end to Anglican separatism in Rochambeau, announced a program of reconciliation and invited each of the member congregations to submit a plan of action.

To launch the campaign the bishop announced a march for Anglican unity, later turned into a caravan for logistical reasons, with parts of the ceremony to be held at each parish. In the event, the bishop and the dean were the only marchers, led by the Major General of the Salvation Army, all the other Anglicans having decided to remain on home ground as part of the "welcoming committees."

In his Pentecost message, the bishop disclosed the merger plans submitted by the congregations: St. Matthias proposed to merge with the Salvation Army; St. Barnabas proposed to reconvert the municipal library for use by the combined congregations (the cathedral would be razed in order to provide expanded parking facilities for the Hotel Clarendon); the cathedral congregation extended a warm welcome to Anglicans of whatever belief to worship at the cathedral. The bishop called for further deliberations.

Nothing ever happens in churches between Victoria Day and Labour Day, but by the first week in October all three congregations had submitted their revised unification plans: St. Matthias proposed to merge with the Port Chaplain's trailer; St. Barnabas offered to set aside several clearly designated pews for visiting Anglicans of other faiths; the cathedral congregation pledged an "open parking lot" policy for visiting Anglicans and volunteered to give up the new red hymnal as a goodwill gesture (reverting to the beloved *Hymns Ancient and Modern*.). Having failed to reach an accord on a joint thanksgiving service, the three parishes each sent representatives to a celebration of American Thanksgiving sponsored by the colony of American expatriates.

Last fall we had a meeting to plan an ecumenical Christmas service.

One might think that the hardest task would be recruiting a choir, but it turned out that overcoming institutional and personal prejudice was far more difficult. If we invited the Roman Catholic Church, the Methodists wouldn't attend, and if we included Francophones there were certain English churches that wouldn't come. Even within the tiny Anglican community there was one rector who didn't want to have anything to do with the others. The only thing you could count on was the participation of the Salvation Army, who offered to furnish tuba, horn, and trumpet to accompany carol-singing.

The bride and groom exchanged vows and rings and then the dean launched into a homily that I suspected would be recycled as Sunday's sermon. Despite the absence of a viable congregation, the dean soldiered on just as if the church celebrations still formed the centre of daily existence for the city's faithful. At the beginning of May he had sent me a characteristically terse memo.

"Can you play an evensong service for the installation of a Canon? Dinner afterwards." Sure thing.

Dinner afterwards turned out to be the annual meeting of The Church Society, held at the Garrison Club, the oldest private club in North America, which two years ago took the revolutionary step of permitting women to enter by the main door. The club was all wood and leather, with paper towels in the men's rooms of a higher quality than the napkins most people use at a fancy dinner. The lobby boasted two enormous moose heads, presumably bagged by members, and the walls of the private rooms were lined with portraits of prime ministers of Canada, Governors-General and Lieutenant-Governors of Canada and Québec, and group portraits of infantry brigades and naval crews.

Before dinner began, the bishop recounted a tale of a Christian in Roman times, thrown to the lions. As he saw the fearsome beast approach, the Christian fell to his knees in prayer. Several moments passed and he still hadn't been attacked. Slowly he looked around and saw the lion on its knees beside him. Addressing the lion, he said, "What are *you* praying for?" "I'm not praying," replied the beast. "I'm merely saying grace."

The dean's autocratic manner—particularly his habit of changing the tempo of a hymn after I had played it through—led me to submit a letter of resignation. At that point, but never before, the dean proposed a monthly staff meeting at which the two of us could discuss issues before they got out of hand (his choice of words). News of my resignation travelled faster than the subsequent reconciliation and before long word going around the university had it that I had given up the Cathedral organ job because of the ghost.

This fascinated me, so when the occasion presented itself I asked one of the organ students at the university for more information. As it happens, she herself had seen the ghost one time when she was practicing late at night at the cathedral, so had no reason to doubt the validity of the rumour. At first she had thought it might have been a burglar or a vagrant, but as she looked more closely the human figure wandering about the choir loft was definitely spectral in origin.

When I mentioned this story to the dean at our next staff meeting he said that he wasn't at all surprised. The cathedral was full of spirits, mostly benign, including that of a former bishop buried in the edifice, which the dean himself had often heard walking about even when he was alone in the building with all the doors securely fastened. As for other organists, one of my predecessors had once burst out of the cathedral at midnight, his hair standing on end, claiming to have seen the ghost, but the dean considered this organist somewhat high-strung and wasn't much impressed by the report. The sister of my immediate predecessor, known to be sensitive to otherworldly manifestations had, while practicing for a guest recital, seen the spirit of the old bishop, sitting in the Bishop's Throne, smiling beatifically, evidently enjoying the music.

At last the wedding came to a close. I launched into the Mendelssohn Wedding March, and then rode my bike back home for a bit of peace and quiet before the evening's dress rehearsal.

Chapter 6

LESTER B. PEARSON SCHOOL HAD been built just before the Quiet Revolution sent the Anglophone population into a state of decline, hastened by the passage of Bill 101. The school's state-of-the-art theatre included not only a well-equipped stage and lighting facilities but even a row of private dressing rooms for the performers. Marie Dufresne, an experienced trouper, was already costumed, made up and bewigged when I knocked on her door, and she seemed eager to talk with me about the demise of the person intended to be her leading man in the production. I explained Francis's theory about Mark's death and she confirmed the description of Mark's Thursday night routine.

"You see what this means, Marie," I said. "It isn't enough for a murderer to have known only that Mark attended choir rehearsal on Thursday evenings. He had to know that Mark would be the last person to walk down the steps to the parking lot. Surely that reduces the list of suspects to those in the choir, if you rule out members of the Teen Canteen."

"It shouldn't be too hard to check on the young people," Marie said. "Their parents would have been waiting for them in the parking lot. It's just a matter of finding out the order in which people left."

"Perhaps you could make me a list of Senior Choir members when you get a chance."

"No time like the present," she said. "We still have a little while before the rehearsal." She took a pad from her purse and wrote out a list of names.

St. Matthias Senior Choir

12 singers (night that Mark died)

Soprano
Agnes Lee
Dorothy Metcalfe
Bonnie Sewall
Helen Reisbacher
Emily Winthrop

Tenor
Mark Stanstead
Paul Cochrane

Alto
Miriam Whately
Connie Sewall

Bass
Geoffrey Lambert
Brian Metcalfe
Henry Reisbacher

Although the ensemble bore the name of the church in which the choir rehearsed, the actual situation was more complicated than that, Marie explained. The St. Barnabas congregation, which worshipped in the same building since giving up its church—but not actually worshipping *with* the St. Matthias parishioners—contributed five of the twelve choir members. The Senior Choir alternated between the two congregations week by week, providing, along with the organist and choir director, the only formal links between them.

Marie held her pencil in the air as she recalled the rehearsal in question. "Let's see," she said. "Emily Winthrop was sick that night, so we don't have to keep her name. I saw the Sewall sisters go out together. The Reisbachers left together and so did the Metcalfes. If we assume that they all went home, that reduces the number a bit." Marie crossed out a few names and then showed me the revised list.

Soprano
Agnes Lee
~~Dorothy Metcalfe~~
~~Bonnie Sewall~~
~~Helen Reisbacher~~
~~Emily Winthrop~~

Tenor
Mark Stanstead
Paul Cochrane

Alto
Miriam Whately
~~Connie Sewall~~

Bass
Geoffrey Lambert
~~Brian Metcalfe~~
~~Henry Reisbacher~~

"May I take this with me?" I asked.

"That's the reason I wrote it," she said. I put the slip of paper in my pocket and went to see whether all the instrumentalists had arrived.

Chapter 7

THE RUN-THROUGH OF THE FIRST act went better than I had anticipated. Brad Cochrane, our replacement for Harold Hill, got through the tongue-twisting patter of "Ya Got Trouble" with only a few minor mishaps. The "Wells Fargo Wagon" number had always given the company problems since so many individual people had to make themselves heard, at just the right moment, announcing their orders: "I got some salmon from Seattle last September," then "And I expect a new rockin' chair," and then "I hope I get my raisins from Fresno." For once they all came in on cue. I felt as if our weeks of preparation were paying off.

Of course, the firecracker that Tommy Djilas was supposed to set off just behind Mrs. Shinn's bustle actually set the dress on fire and it was only alert thinking by one of the Wa Tan Ye dancers, who smothered the flames with her Indian blanket, that prevented the incident from becoming serious rather than just a source of merriment at Mrs. Shinn's expense. That's why we have dress rehearsals.

During the break before the second act I found Herbert Whately sitting down just offstage and decided to join him. He looked tired—evidently painting the scenery had taken a lot out of him even though the young people had done much of the physical labour. I complimented him on how realistic the sets looked and how tricky it must have been to manage all the detailed work. As usual Herbert was quick to deflect praise.

"Really more like paint-by-numbers than anything else," he said. "The genius lies in the design, not the execution."

"So you may say, but I can imagine that transferring small sketches to full-scale sets involved a good deal more effort than you're willing to take credit for."

"Could be," Herbert said, "but the youngsters were a great help."

"And I don't know what we would have done if you hadn't drawn on your connections to get us that scrim. In the second act having Marian sing from her bedroom behind the scrim while the barbershop quartet croons in front of it creates a great effect."

"Well you did your best to help, Axel." Learning that the School of Music had an enormous gauze cloth, I had asked to borrow it for the production. When it came out that the production in question belonged to the (Anglophone) Savoyards, the question of a loan from the (Francophone) School of Music turned cloudy. Permission would have to be obtained from the Director. I was prepared to seek permission. It would require considerable manpower to transport the bulky scrim from the theatre to an appropriate vehicle. I was prepared to supply the manpower and the vehicle. Forms would have to be completed covering jurisdiction and liability. I was prepared to fill out forms. In any event, came the clincher, they've already cut up the scrim to make costumes.

"Why do you think there's so much ill will between the French and English, Herbert?"

"To understand that you have to go back a bit in history."

"You mean the Plains of Abraham?"

"I was thinking of the Roman Empire. How do you suppose they maintained their rule for so many centuries?"

"I haven't really given it a great deal of thought. Brutal repression, I imagine."

"On the contrary—the Romans posted only modest garrisons at their outposts. But they brought roads, canals, and with them better transportation and communication—improvements to the infrastructure, we'd say nowadays. But more than that, they mostly left the conquered people alone—let them keep their customs, religion, way of life."

"I take it the English didn't learn that lesson in Québec."

"Axel, until the Quiet Revolution the French did all the work but English ran the businesses and insisted that their employees 'speak white.'"

"You mean English?"

Herbert nodded. "Have you any idea how humiliating that was? This was racism pure and simple, as bad as anything you had in the South."

I wasn't sure about that. I hadn't heard about any lynchings in

Québec Province nor cases of English Québeckers burning down French churches, but I let it pass.

"You've driven in Montréal, haven't you?" I nodded. "You know that sign on the Pont Champlain?"

"You mean that scary one that says 'Beware of Oncoming Buses in Your Lane'?"

"That's the one. Have you ever thought about why the warning appears only in French? 'Ill will' doesn't begin to describe the antagonism between the two cultures."

I returned to the question at hand. "You may have heard that Cathy Stanstead asked me to do a little digging with respect to Mark's death."

"Murder, you mean."

"Well, it does look as if that may be the case. I was wondering if your firm has done any business lately that might have given someone a reason for wanting to get Mark out of the way."

"Kill him, you mean."

"Well, yes."

"I've been thinking about that since I talked with Cathy. There's one obvious answer to your question, but the problem is that the Anglophone community is so small and close-knit that anything I tell you is going to cause trouble."

"You're probably right. The police have no reason to inquire further, so I guess I'll repeat the words Bogie said in *The Maltese Falcon*: 'When your partner gets killed, you gotta do something about it.'"

"I remember the film and the line. Fact of the matter is I'd already made up my mind to tell you what I knew. I just wanted to be sure you understood the problem."

"I do. I respect your dilemma and I'm grateful for your help."

"In a way, you're looking at the problem."

"How do you mean?"

"I presume you know the situation with the asbestos in this school." I nodded. "For years Geoffrey Lambert has been paying off the building inspector and nobody has cared very much. Asbestos doesn't actually cause any problems so long as it's contained behind walls so there hasn't been any real cause for concern."

"I take it that something has changed."

"Right you are. A lot of insurance companies have moved out of province and a lot of others have amalgamated. We're one of the last independent outfits left. There's been some pressure on the government to control the industry, so last year they passed new regulations. I won't bore you with all the details, but there were two provisions that have a direct bearing on the situation at hand."

"Go on."

"First off, insurance for public buildings, such as this school, was thrown open to competitive bidding, so naturally we made an offer."

"You mean Stanstead & Whately didn't insure the English-language school?"

"No. I told you that the English community is close-knit but the French community is even more so. The building inspector in question has a brother-in-law in the insurance business."

"So naturally …"

"Naturally. As my late partner was so fond of saying, as he betrayed a friend, 'Business is business.'"

"So you bid on the contract …"

"And won it. The new law specified not only open competition but closed bids, so nobody knew which bid to favour."

"Well that was good for you, wasn't it?"

"Depends on how you look at it. This brings us to the second provision I mentioned."

"Which is?"

"Starting July 1, the insurance company is legally responsible for enforcement of code regulations in the buildings it insures. In other words, all previously grandfathered relationships are null and void."

"Putting you on the hook for the asbestos."

"Precisely."

"No more paying off the building inspector?"

"You got it. This caused no small amount of consternation on the part of the inspector—you can imagine that this wasn't his only source of supplemental income—but somebody with more political clout than he had insisted on inserting that clause into the regulations."

"So this presumably caused some conflict between Mark and Geoffrey."

"That's putting it mildly. All during rehearsals Mark has been after Geoffrey to bring the building up to code, and he finally gave him an ultimatum that it had to be done by the time the production was over."

"By this coming Tuesday, in other words."

"That's right."

"But with Mark gone, what's going to happen?"

"I'm going to cancel the contract. I don't think Geoffrey Lambert has a hope in hell of getting the asbestos removed from this school. I also know that our competitors in the French community would like nothing better than to catch us covering up for a colleague. The whole situation is common knowledge and you can be sure that once the deadline arrives, someone is just waiting to report us."

"So it's really just a business decision: the loss of the contract is less damaging than the fine for not observing the regulations."

"That's why I get paid for keeping the books."

"Unfortunately that gives Geoffrey Lambert an excellent motive for killing Mark."

"You see the problem."

I thanked Herbert for his help and turned to look for the barbershop quartet when Lorna Lambert pulled me aside. She was tall, full-figured, the kind of girl for which the expression "seventeen going on twenty-seven" had been invented. Personally I thought she would have looked prettier without quite so much eye makeup. I considered her basically a good kid, but I would hate to have been her father.

"Axel, I heard what Mr. Whately told you."

"You've been eavesdropping."

"I just like to know what's going on."

"But still …"

"My father didn't kill Mr. Stanstead, but I know who did. It was Agnes Lee!"

"What gives you that idea?"

"She's always hated the way Mr. Stanstead would insist on taking leading roles. You know he couldn't act."

"Well …"

"She thought he was ruining the show."

"But that doesn't seem cause for …"

"Oh yeah? Agnes Lee is a nut about the theatre. It's her whole life."

I had to admit that Lorna had a point. I had never seen anything like the single-minded intensity that Agnes brought to the production.

She hadn't been able to conceal her irritation with Mark Stanstead's inability to take direction, and I could imagine that her frustration in this show would have been magnified by her experiences with Stanstead in previous productions. But I tried to deflect Lorna's accusation.

"That still seems like an awfully big step to take just out of irritation with his acting."

"It's not just that. Agnes Lee has hated Mr. Stanstead for years."

"Really?"

"It goes back to her father. He had started a small insurance agency and when Mark Stanstead's father was looking for a partner, he'd hoped to be the one. When Mr. Stanstead Sr. teamed up with Mr. Whately's father instead, it dashed his hopes. And his business went under, too. Agnes Lee grew up hating the Stanstead family. And now Mark Stanstead has been causing difficulties in the theatre, the thing she loves most."

I recalled Agnes' "this is my cathedral" speech when she put Gordon Tapley in his place, and had to concede that Lorna might have a point. I promised to think about what she'd said, then told the girl to find her place for Act II.

Chapter 8

THE SECOND ACT WENT EVEN better than the first. For the "Lida Rose" number the barbershop quartet managed to walk across the stage, perfectly in step, while synchronizing their singing with that of Marian Paroo, whose voice came from a second-story bedroom on the opposite side of the scrim. The square dancers in "Shipoopi" succeeded, for once, in coordinating their steps with the music and the finale came off without a hitch.

I was feeling exultant when I was brought down to earth by the stentorian voice of Eulalie Mackechnie Shinn, *aka* Miriam Whately. It was probably a common enough situation—people empowered by life's circumstances in only one small domain, who resolved that in that domain, by God, things would be done properly. Perhaps it was just my imagination that the Anglican Church seemed to provide a home for a disproportionate number of such people, usually in the guise of Head of the Altar Guild. But they somehow managed to impose this mentality of correctness at all costs upon everyone in their charge. A friend came with me to an Anglican service one Sunday, and while I was practicing with the choir she tried to make herself useful in the kitchen putting away cups. But when a regular member of the congregation explained, not unkindly but in no uncertain terms, that the cup handles were supposed to go to the right, not the left, my friend left the kitchen and never crossed the threshold of the church again.

"Axel, I've heard about your so-called investigation."

"But I ..."

"Word travels fast among the cast of a show."

"I suppose you have something to contribute."

"Axel, I've been one of your admirers since you came to Rochambeau. I like the way you started the city's first *a cappella* choir and the way you dare to argue with Dean Tapley."

"I sense a 'but' coming."

"No, it's a 'so.' So I don't want to see you making a fool of yourself."

"And that's what you think I'm doing?"

"You're organist at the cathedral. You can't be expected to know the history of St. Matthias."

"I have a feeling you're going to fill me in."

Miriam didn't miss a beat. "This story is right up your alley. A few years ago a member of the Altar Guild—a *former* member, I should say—forgot to put the lid on the garbage pail in the church kitchen. A family of raccoons managed to find an entrance into the basement, came upstairs and scattered garbage all over the kitchen."

"I don't see …"

"Wait; it gets better. One of the rodents found its way into the sanctuary. The organ tuner—the *former* organ tuner, I should say— had left the chamber open. The raccoon entered and discovered the exquisite taste of leather."

"Oh no!"

"Oh yes. Fortunately he was discovered before he'd done too much damage, and in less than a week the organ had been repaired and wire barriers placed over all the basement windows lest the varmints be tempted to return, but you have only to mention the word 'raccoon' at that church to provoke a chorus of groans."

"This is all very interesting, but …"

"So far, no ring-tailed creature has made it back into the building, but we see their eyes glowing in the headlights of our cars every Thursday evening after choir rehearsal. The woods around the church are infested."

"So you mean …"

"That so-called 'stranger' that Francis Tapley supposedly heard in the bushes that night was just a raccoon."

"But he said …"

"Axel, the woods are dark. He never told you he saw anything."

"That may be, but …"

"And he and Lorna weren't exactly concentrating on woodland sounds, I'll reckon."

"Probably not."

"Okay. Now let's look at it the other way. No woman likes to think her husband is capable of suicide, but you have to admit, Mark has been acting strange recently."

"How do you mean?"

"Come on, Axel. Surely you heard about the 'I love you all' speech."

That I had. In the middle of one rehearsal Mark had called for attention, thanked the company for their efforts—individually and collectively—observed what it meant to him to be associated with such a fine group of people, recalled the service their parents had rendered his father, assured the company that he loved them all, and then burst into tears. Agnes called for a five-minute break then put her arm around the big man and led him out of the room. The pair returned after a short time and the rehearsal proceeded as if nothing had happened: you can't beat the English for ignoring what's under their noses.

"I take your point," I told Miriam.

"For all their protestations, nobody was really surprised when the police announced Mark's suicide."

"I thought they called it an accident."

"It's a euphemism, Axel. Grow up. I know it's not as satisfying to your imagination as murder, but that's the way it is."

"But Francis seemed so sure."

"Weren't you ever young, Axel? Think of the effect of hormones on the brain, especially the brain of Francis Tapley, lovestruck for the first time in his short, overprotected life. It's one thing for an addled adolescent to be bamboozled by a raccoon, but in a grown man it's unseemly, not to say embarrassing."

"So you're suggesting ..."

"That you give it up before you completely destroy your credibility as an intelligent musician."

"Well, you've given me a lot to think about. I'm grateful for that."

"Think nothing of it."

I went home thinking that perhaps I should stick to what I knew and leave the detective work to the detectives.

Chapter 9

THE NEARLY-EMPTY CATHEDRAL FOR SUNDAY'S service made a sorry contrast with the panoply of Friday's evensong before royalty. I still hadn't decided what constituted "reality" for the Anglican cathedral.

When I learned the previous September that the weekly CBC church program, broadcast all across Canada on the French television network, was going to televise a service at the cathedral to kick off the Week of Christian Unity, I had my doubts: who wants to look at an empty sanctuary and listen to a broken-down organ? I underestimated the power of television.

On the last Saturday afternoon in September, the time chosen to tape the service to be broadcast Sunday morning, the cathedral was full, the choir stalls packed with clergy and combined choirs, which spilled over into the first few pews of the congregation, my *a cappella* choir performing from the balcony, and upstairs, next to the organ pipes, a technician who came all the way from Toronto to restore the high A that I hadn't heard since my arrival in Rochambeau.

All this took a mite of planning, yea even finagling. My *a cappella* choir, for example, included two union members and two apprentices in its ranks. Union rules say that you can't appear on television unless you're paid nor sing in a choir that doesn't pay all its members. When the CBC program originated from St. Dominique's, which has one of the finest choirs in the city, the televised service remained choir-less because two members belonged to the union and CBC wasn't about to pay all twenty singers at union rates. After a lot of hemming and hawing, they negotiated a deal for the service at the cathedral whereby the union members and apprentices would receive regular union rates and CBC would pay a penalty to the union for not paying the others.

What an experience it was to hear a whole cathedral full of people singing hymns (in French, for the benefit of Francophone viewers) and to think that it used to be like that every Sunday (though of course without all the bright lights, cameras, and a service carefully tailored to fit the 56-minute limits of the program).

Wouldn't you know that our pet cipher wouldn't be able to resist the lure of national television any more than the rest of us—he made an unscheduled appearance during the last hymn and had to be rudely stifled before the postlude. The next day the organ technician captured the little critter, transported him one hundred and fifty miles north to a provincial forest, and released him. (Who said organ technicians don't have a heart?)

My *a cappella* choir, meanwhile, continued working on a program of musical settings of the Song of Songs, featuring such haunting erotic texts as "Stay me with flagons, comfort me with cabbages, gag me with a spoon, for I am sick of love."

I greeted the dean before going to the organ console to set up my music for the service. I commented on the cover for the Sunday bulletin.

"That's nothing compared with what we would have had if Mark Stanstead hadn't shuffled off this mortal coil so precipitately."

"How do you mean?"

"Something in the new insurance regulations required reprinting all the contracts with English on one side of the page and French on the other, instead of separate French- and English-language contracts the way they've done up to now."

"And so?"

"And so Mark decided it was time to stop subsidizing Paul Cochrane's overpriced print shop and go for something more efficient. 'Business is business,' I think he said."

"What does that have to do with our bulletins?"

"Mark planned to negotiate a single contract that would cover his insurance business, the Savoyards, and all the Anglican churches. We would have been able to have real colour bulletin covers every Sunday.'

"What would have happened to Paul Cochrane?"

"I can't imagine that our bulletins made up much of his business."

I wasn't sure how accurate that was, but let it pass. I went to the organ and looked over the Dean's choices of hymns for the day. More Victorian tripe.

The Christian Church, as even non-believers acknowledge, embraces within its heritage some of the greatest works of literature and music ever conceived, notably the King James translation of the Bible and the liturgical works of Palestrina and Bach. Unfortunately, the church also preserves, notably in the Anglican hymnal, works of literature and music whose artistic quality lies somewhat beneath that of a Hallmark greeting card. My greatest satisfaction in serving as organist of the Anglican cathedral was the opportunity to perform, Sunday after Sunday, masterpieces from the organ literature. My greatest trial was the obligation to play, Sunday after Sunday, monstrosities of hymns chosen by the dean.

The period of Lent, still within recent memory, is a penitential season for organists because the proportion of tolerable hymns appropriate to the season is so minuscule. At the Anglican cathedral the act of penitence takes on proportions suitable to the grandeur of the building, so wretched are the hymns one is compelled to play. One wonders, blasphemously I suppose, what Our Lord would have done in the wilderness if, instead of having to withstand the blandishments of Satan, He was obliged to listen to Anglican Lenten hymns for forty days and forty nights. When I mentioned the dean's taste in hymns, Miriam Whately said, in an acid tone, "The dean's only taste is in his mouth."

I don't know why hymns matter so much to me. At one staff luncheon I complained about the way the dean constantly reset the tempo of the hymns, and he told me, "You're a marvellous organist, Axel, don't get me wrong, but your hymn-playing is erratic." I must have looked shocked because he continued, "Don't take my word for it. You know the Wollensak in the office—record the next service and judge for yourself." I did so and was dumbfounded: the introduction wasn't the same tempo as the hymn-playing and I cut short measures at the ends of lines, leaving everyone breathless. I felt chastened by the experience. Then I recalled my organ teacher's secret for maintaining a rock-solid tempo for playing Bach, and began vocalizing "duh duh duh duh" to mark the eighth-notes. The next Sunday the dean didn't exactly favour me with a smile, but his almost imperceptible nod indicated that I'd corrected the problem.

But the dean got under my skin in so many ways. At Halloween he preached a sermon on the text, "Be ye therefore pumpkins of the Lord." (Give an enormous grin of human gladness and let your little candle shine forth, etc., etc.) Lord spare us.

Chapter 10

THE AIR OF EXCITEMENT AND nervousness Sunday afternoon before our first performance expressed itself in giggles and loud, rapid conversation. The children in the chorus ran on and off stage, townspeople unaccustomed to wearing makeup posed for each other, and the members of the barbershop quartet tried not to show how spiffy they felt in their matching outfits.

Early on I had suggested that it would be fun to provide the quartet with more and more elaborate dress as the evening progressed. They started off in shopkeepers' garb, then turned up in red-and-white striped jackets, next time in straw hats, and finally strolled onstage carrying canes. They nearly stole the show.

I saw Priscilla Tapley standing by the piano, muttering her lines, and wished her luck.

"It's a regular shame that Mark isn't around to see this," she said. "He put so much of himself into this company."

"That he did," I said, recalling the dozens of ways in which Mark's way with people had guided the production past the myriad tiny disagreements or petty jealousies that could have sunk it. "I understand he was almost a second father to Francis."

"Ah, I shouldn't be saying it, but with Gordon working so hard sometimes it seemed as if Mark were his first father."

"So what do you make of his death?"

A cautious expression came over Priscilla's face. "It isn't fitting for me to speak too freely, Axel, but let me say this. Sometimes it's difficult for the stronger member of a couple to accept her husband's ways."

"You're thinking of Miriam," I guessed.

"A woman who isn't afraid to speak her mind and push her weight around sometimes becomes impatient with a man who seems to lack ambition, particularly when she thinks other people are getting the credit that he deserves."

Though I hadn't thought about it until now, Herbert Whately stood to inherit the insurance company, assuming it had been set up as a partnership. Could Miriam have taken it upon herself to advance her husband's career with one bold stroke? It bore thinking about. I admired Priscilla's circumspect refusal even to mention an actual name.

Judging by the audience's reaction to the first act, Mark Stanstead's efforts had paid off, but I was no less impressed by the evidence of Cathy's quiet handiwork even before the curtain went up. A team of high school students supervised the parking, 8 x 10 photographs of every cast member appeared in the lobby, other teens sold refreshments, took tickets, showed patrons to their seats, and handed them impressive looking programs produced by Cochrane Printing.

The audience, accustomed to years of Gilbert & Sullivan operettas accompanied by a solitary piano, sat up in surprise when the overture showed off the added instruments I'd persuaded the company to engage: three trumpets, trombone, bass and percussion.

The opening Rock Island number whose rhythms had given us such trouble through eight months of rehearsals finally came together. Harold Hill arrives in town by train, whose physical presence is suggested by a large cardboard cut-out, with windows through which the passengers' heads can be seen, and whose characteristic sounds are conveyed by the accents and complicated cross-rhythms of a speaking chorus.

The train starts up slowly with repetitions of the word "Cash" suggesting the gradual engagement of the pistons. "Cash for the merchandise, cash for the button hooks, cash for the cotton goods, cash for the hard goods, cash for the fancy goods, cash for the noggins and the piggins and the firkins, cash for the hogshead, cask and demijohn, cash for the crackers and the pickles and the flypaper."

Eventually the train reaches full speed, with the repetitions of the word "gone" setting the tempo: "Gone, gone, gone with the hogshead, cask and demijohn, gone with the sugar barrel, pickle barrel, milk pan, gone with the tub and the pail and tierce."

Just as the train arrives at River City the traveling salesmen on board begin comparing notes about one Harold Hill, whose chicanery has been spoiling their livelihood. You could almost hear the escaping steam in the second salesman's sibilant consonants:

I don't know how he does it but he lives like a king and he dallies and he gathers and he plucks and he shines, and when the man dances Certainly, boys, what else? The piper pays him! Yes sir, yes sir, yes sir, yes sir, when the man dances, certainly, boys, what else? The piper pays him! Yesssir, Yessssir.

Brad Cochrane outdid himself as Professor Hill. He had an enviable no-lose situation: anything he did wrong would be forgiven; anything he did right would be doubly applauded. I had lent Agnes Lee a copy of Meredith Willson's novelization of his play, and she had adopted his suggestions in blocking Brad's moments on stage. I had emphasized to Brad that he was not supposed to be performing but improvising, as he judged the effect of his oratory on the townspeople. *"Harold's dramatic sense now urged movement,"* Willson wrote. *"He started across the street, his climactic objective the center of the park and the statue of Henry Madison—deceased local philanthropist. What a spot for a finish. If he could only time it right in the shadow of the great man's likeness!"*

Agnes seemed ecstatic as the curtain fell at the end of the first act. I had kept my eyes riveted on Brad, mouthing every word he sang, trusting the professional instrumentalists to keep track of the music on their own. But aside from a few minor errors Brad had done a superb job, bounding about the stage with a youthful agility far beyond the capabilities of the more mechanical Mark Stanstead. But surely Agnes would not have committed murder just to bring about this result.

I particularly liked the moment when Harold Hill recruits Mrs. Shinn to his cause. Seeing her move her foot, he interrupts his patter with a panegyric on her grace. 'What natural flow of rhythm,' he says. 'Every move you make, Mrs. Shinn, bespeaks Del Sarte.' Encouraged by the praise, she agrees to accept the chairmanship of the Ladies Auxiliary for the Classic Dance. As the young Brad Cochrane went through this smooth act of seduction I thought for a moment that Miriam Whately was experiencing vicarious pleasure at being treated, even in pretence, as an attractive woman rather than as a bossy old battleaxe.

Not long thereafter Marie Dufresne sang my favourite song from the show, "My White Knight," a number that composer Meredith Willson replaced in the movie version of the musical, ostensibly because he thought it too closely resembled the music of Lerner and Lowe, a decision I was never able to understand. Throughout our production

Agnes and I had to ward off suggestions from cast members who had seen only the film version and thought we needed to follow it exactly. "That's not the way they did it in the movie" seemed to be a constant refrain. One person even volunteered to furnish a pair of horses for the Wells Fargo number until Agnes Lee sensibly put the kibosh on the idea. Another woman offered her dog for the show. In the movie Winthrop Paroo had a black-and-white terrier, just like her Fifi. "She wouldn't have to have any lines or anything, and she's really well trained." No dogs. No thank you. Forget about it.

Chapter 11

MARIE DUFRESNE BECKONED ME INTO her dressing room during the intermission to inquire about the progress of my investigation. I congratulated her on "My White Knight" and she told me that one of her biggest challenges in the show was to avoid giggling when Harold Hill threatens to dump a bag of marbles onto the library floor. As an actual librarian, she had never been able to maintain the absolute silence associated with the River City library. She said she considered herself lucky if she could keep the kids from playing their boom boxes while in the building.

Marian dismissed the raccoon theory with a snort, saying that she hadn't seen one of the animals anywhere near the church in more than a year.

"If we're going to assume it was murder," I said, "I've heard about three candidates so far." I explained the arguments in favour of Agnes Lee, Miriam Whately and Geoffrey Lambert."

"Geoffrey's your man," Marie said. "And it isn't just a matter of asbestos."

"What's the story?"

"It's actually a bit funny, considering the situation," she said. "You know how in the show Geoffrey, as a member of the school board, keeps asking Mark, as Harold Hill, to provide proper credentials for his claim to be a professor of music. But actually Geoffrey's the one with the credentials problem."

"How do you mean?"

"What are his qualifications to be head of the Rochambeau English School Board?"

"I understood he has a master's degree in educational engineering."

"Uh huh. Have you ever heard of a master's degree in educational engineering?"

"Now that you mention it, no."

"It doesn't exist. As a matter of fact, Geoffrey doesn't have a university degree of any sort."

"How do you know this?"

"You keep forgetting that I'm a librarian in real life as well as on the stage."

"I reckon you don't have many patrons like Eulalie Mackechnie Shinn."

Marie grinned. "I love that scene," she said. "Mrs. Shinn storms up to the desk, thrusts a copy of *The Rubaiyat of Omar Khayyam* in my face, and demands 'Who is responsible for this racy literature getting into my daughter's hands?'" Marie impersonated the overbearing mayor's wife so well that I almost wished we'd cast her for the part.

"'I recommended it,' I said, filling in Marian's line. 'It's beautiful Persian poetry.'"

"'It's *dirty* Persian poetry!' Marie continued reciting Eulalie's lines. 'People lying out in the woods, eating sandwiches and getting drunk … with pitfalls and with gin! Drinking directly out of jugs! With innocent young girls! No daughter of mine—'"

"'Mrs. Shinn,' I substituted for the librarian. 'It's a classic.'"

"'It's a *smutty* book,' Marie recited, 'like most of the others you keep here, I daresay.'" Marie couldn't remain in character any longer but just laughed in satisfaction at Meredith Willson's witty dialogue.

"But what made you start looking into Lambert's credentials, or lack thereof?" I returned to the point of my visit.

"Your investigation, of course. We librarians love a challenge."

"Do you think Mark knew?"

"If he didn't, he was bound to find out eventually. He took the liability issue very seriously. At one choir rehearsal I'd made a crack about the precarious situation of a church musician—you know, we serve 'at the pleasure of the rector'—compared with the security of the insurance business."

"What did Mark say?"

"He told me that it would take only one case of improper oversight and his firm could be destroyed."

"Surely he was exaggerating. Insurance companies and banks seem immune to the usual problems of business."

"That may be true for the big companies, but I imagine that for a small concern like Stanstead & Whately, he could be describing the situation accurately."

"So you think Geoffrey was afraid of losing his job if the truth ever came out?"

"Jobs in the English community are scarcer than hen's teeth these days, Axel. I imagine Geoffrey collects a comfortable salary. If the credentials question ever came to light he'd be ruined."

"But I don't really have anything to go on. What should I do?"

"I think you might start by having a bit of a chat with Geoffrey Lambert."

I told her I would do just that and wished her well for my second favourite number in the show, the song in which Marian sings "Dream of Now" simultaneously with the barbershop quartet rendering "Lida Rose."

Chapter 12

WHEN I MET WITH THE Savoyards board in the summer to discuss mounting "The Music Man," I pointed out that the production demanded a huge cast and, given the continuing decline of the Anglophone population, we would do well to advertise widely for interested amateur singers, dancers and set painters. "Fine, fine," everybody said. I volunteered to write recruiting announcements in both languages and to lend the mailing list from my *a cappella* choir to the chair of the publicity committee in order to reach as large a population as possible. "Fine, fine." So when I got back from vacation in August, I naïvely assumed that there would have been public service announcements in all the newspapers. Nary a word. I called the president of the company, who assured me that it would be taken care of by the following week. A week passed; still nothing. By the time we started rehearsals, every old member of the company had been contacted, but there was still no recruitment for new members. Finally I got to the bottom of it. One of the board members told me, "We decided it would cost too much money. Besides, we wanted to give our people first chance." So Rochambeau xenophobia works both ways.

Act II came off nearly as smoothly as Act I, a result that could not have been predicted from the chaos attending our first rehearsal in the actual theatre, six weeks earlier. "Waltzers, waltzers!" Agnes had called. "Would somebody go find the waltzers? And where's the barbershop quartet?" ("I think they're out in the hall practicing.") "Well, somebody call them. And Marcellus, there was a piano there that you just ran into. Oh, excuse me; that was the footbridge. Okay. Who's the first waltzing couple? Where's your partner?" ("He couldn't make it today.") "No, Winthrop, the live frog was in the previous scene. Thank you, dear. Everybody offstage—we'll run it again."

"Dancers, please. Line up behind the scrim—you get just six measures of trill, then go into the dance: one, two, three, one two, three." The choreographer counted measures aloud—27, 28, 29. "Can you arrange the music to give us 32 bars?"

"Listen, everybody! You're not going to be able to gather behind the scrim after all because we have to turn the backdrop around for the Madison High School Gymnasium. If we give you a blackout can you get onstage and find your places in *front* of the scrim without getting hurt? No! Quieter! On tiptoe! Lights up! Music!" (Miriam Whately, as Mrs. Shinn, directed the Del Sarte dancers. "Lovely, ladies; lovely. No turn. Take the body with you. Lovely. Now let's have a go at our Grecian Urns. One Grecian Urn. …Two Grecian Urns. … and a Fountain …trickle, trickle, trickle. Splendid, ladies. I predict that our Del Sarte display will be the highlight of the Ice Cream Sociable.")

"Sorry, Mayor Shinn," Agnes continued. "You can't walk in through the scrim. We're going to have to change your entrance. Who let that dog into the theatre? Will somebody please catch that animal and remove it?"

(Gordon Tapley did his best with the alliterative lines. "You gullible, green-grass goats! Can't you get it through your heads that's you're being swindled out of your eye teeth right now—this minute? There's a burglar in the parlor.")

"That's 'burglar in the bedroom'," Agnes corrected him. "'There's a burglar in the bedroom while you're fiddling in the parlor.'"

"Winthrop," Agnes called. "You're supposed to come on from stage left, not stage right. Run, ladies, run! All right, who's next? What happened to the Grecian ladies? No, you can't come on that way—there's a scrim there! Okay. Let's try the whole sequence again. Music!"

Given the tiny size of the Anglophone community I should not have been surprised to see these same townspeople turning up in the dean's Thanksgiving liturgy, which seemed to have been inspired by the show's Grecian Urns sequence. The dean preceded the Thanksgiving service by announcing that there would be no sermon. He then went on for ten minutes to explain how meaningful this service was going to be and how grateful we should all be to the Altar Guild for spreading cabbages and cauliflowers all about the church. After the reading of the Gospel came a procession of gifts, starting with donations of canned and dried goods, all carried to the front of the church in brown shopping bags. Then we sang a hymn. Next came "Gifts of Agriculture," young people carrying rakes, hoes and shovels which they brought to the front of the church, raised over their heads in imitation of the Elevation of the Host, and then deposited behind the altar.

The next hymn was one of the most offensive things I've ever seen in a church. The dean, anticipating that the text might raise a few eyebrows, explained to the congregation that the words had been composed by the 79-year-old widow of a police officer living in Jerusalem, as if that would somehow excuse the following lines:

Seeds of love and kindness bring forth good wholesome food;
Grains of joy and laughter grow into festive mood;
But unborn, helpless infants too often now have died;
And poisoned, deathly, harvests result from pesticide.
Whilst we make combustion fumes, and smoke our landscape mars,
Nations draft restrictions on cancer-making tars;
What will we do today, friends, our appetites to slake?
Let's think what seeds we're planting; humanity's at stake.

(Sung to the tune of "All Things Bright and Beautiful," if you can believe it.) Next came "Gifts of Family Life," with young people bearing stuffed animals, television sets, and an iron. Another hymn. Then "Gifts of Industry and Commerce," more young people, this time in hardhats, carrying a chain-saw, electrical cable, and a typewriter. Another hymn. "Gifts of Study, Art and Design" brought the young people down the aisle once more with a globe and what looked like a leftover Tall Ships poster from the ill-fated festival. Another hymn, remarkably phallic, a short of churchified Walt Whitman:

God of concrete, God of steel, God of piston and of wheel,
God of pylon, God of steam, God of girder and of beam,
God of atom, God of mine: all the world of power is thine.
Etc.

The 'Gifts of Faith" included, along with Bible, chalice and paten, a gallon jug of wine which the dean proceeded to pour, backwoods over-the-elbow style, into a chalice. After several more hymns we finally made it to the communion rite, which the dean intoned so that we might understand the familiar text *as if for the very first time.*

Lord, have mercy upon us.

No wonder Agnes had been pleased to cast Gordon Tapley as mayor of River City—he was born to play the part. His churchly officiousness just made the performance all the funnier because he understood the mayor as a serious rather than a comic figure. Geoffrey Lambert told me about one rehearsal of the scene where Mayor Shinn instructs the members of the school board to demand Professor Hill's credentials. According to the script he's supposed to say "That man's slipperier than a greased pig," but when Gordon Tapley delivered the line, it came out "slipperier than a greased prig." Everybody thought he'd done it on purpose and began to laugh. Tapley turned red and tried again. This time it came out "Slipperier than a priest gig." Naturally everyone laughed even harder. When he said "Slipperier than a pieced grig" some people actually rolled on the floor, and when he finally altered it to "slipperier than a Newfoundland codfish" the crowd just applauded. He tried to smile but he clearly felt flummoxed by the incident.

How I hated working for that man.

Chapter 13

AFTER THE PERFORMANCE I CALLED Geoffrey Lambert aside for a confidential word. He was justifiably proud of the barbershop quartet. "We finally got those tricky harmonies in 'Lida Rose.'" I assured him that the quartet had been one of the high points of the show. I felt reluctant to bring up the question of credentials, knowing that it would deflate Geoffrey's happy mood, but I was unprepared for the magnitude of the change. I had thought the expression 'his face fell' to be merely a figure of speech until I saw the transformation of Lambert's demeanour. The usually bright eyes turned to lifeless embers and the skin below them sagged. An extra chin seemed to materialize from nowhere and jowls descended from once-buoyant cheeks. "You mustn't tell anyone," Geoffrey whispered hoarsely.

"I wouldn't think of it," I said.

"Do you really think so badly of me?" he said in an imploring tone.

"You don't understand, Geoffrey," I said. "I've only had the greatest respect for you."

"But why ..."

"You need to understand that I'm not doing anything. I'm just trying to understand how Mark died."

"But I had nothing to do with that," he said in a confused tone.

"Fine; tell me about it."

"No; you tell me. How is Mark supposed to have died?"

I recounted the basic picture as I understood it so far, omitting only the raccoons, the names of the other possible suspects, and his daughter's fellationary activities.

"So it all hinges on the order of procession to the parking lot last Thursday," Geoffrey said after a moment of reflection.

"I suppose you could call that a particularly Anglican way of looking at the picture."

"Then I'm all right." Geoffrey looked visibly relieved. The colour began to return to his face and his posture, which had drooped noticeably during the past few minutes, now started to regain its normal state.

"Would you like to elaborate?" I asked.

"Every Thursday Lorna and I give Francis Tapley a ride home after Teen Canteen. I went to the car when the choir rehearsal ended and they met me there. Then Agnes Lee came over to the car to suggest an improvement to one of the scenes that the kids have together. So I couldn't have been the last one down the steps." Geoffrey gave the impression of a prisoner on death row learning that his sentence has been commuted.

At that moment Francis and Lorna appeared, arm in arm, grinning guiltily. Geoffrey silently nodded to me and I took the opportunity to confirm his story. I would have to speak with Agnes at some point, but the 'order of procession,' as Lambert put it, seemed to have provided him with a satisfactory alibi.

I put my arm around his shoulders and said, "I'm relieved."

"*You're* relieved!" he exclaimed.

"What's this about?" asked Lorna.

"Your father had one of the most musically challenging roles in the entire show," I said, "and he performed it admirably."

Geoffrey communicated his appreciation with a smile and shepherded the youngsters toward the parking lot. A knot of anxiety that I hadn't even been aware of released in my stomach and I found myself able to take a full breath again after several minutes in which oxygen had been a stranger to my lungs. I hate learning people's guilty secrets.

Chapter 14

I DECIDED THAT A NIGHT at the movies would relieve the responsibilities of musical comedy and murder, and settled on "Alice au pays des merveilles" as the perfect antidote to both River City and Rochambeau. Most film musicals, when presented in another language, offer subtitles or dubbing for the dialogue but leave the songs untranslated. Only Walt Disney cared enough to recruit not only French-speaking actors to recreate the familiar roles in "Alice in Wonderland" but French singers to perform artfully translated versions of favourite songs like "All in a Summer's Afternoon" and "A Very Merry Unbirthday." Seeing classic American films in French provided me with free language lessons. I'll never forget my delight at hearing Dorothy's words on returning to Kansas from Oz—"There's no place like home"—elegantly rendered as "Je rêve auprès de ceux qui j'aime."

Yet questions of language that I found fascinating struck others as merely frustrating. At a dinner party I attended early in the spring one chap, a piano student at the Conservatoire, recounted an experience he had had in Rochambeau on his seventeenth birthday. He was assisting some Italian and German tourists whose only common language was English, when a Québécois gentleman accosted him saying, "You are French—you should not be speaking English!" and struck him across the face. The young man retained his composure and responded, "Sir, I speak four languages; how many do you speak?" The monolingual critic offering no reply, he continued, "When you speak four languages, then you come and slap me."

My Anglophone host told about becoming acquainted with his Francophone neighbour, a building contractor. Once, in conversation, the man disclosed that he was French, not Québécois. Immediately regretting his remark, he begged my friend not to tell anyone, for were it to become generally known, he would lose a lot of his business. The

Québécois don't as a rule care much for the French, whom they feel have abandoned the province.

The son of another of my host's acquaintances was, in the 70's, a rabid separatist whose polemical extremism embarrassed his father. One time the young man visited friends in a Francophone community in Western Canada. In the course of his journey he became aware, for the first time in his life, that in terms of numbers at least, French was not, in fact, the dominant language of North America. The realization so affected him that on returning home he immediately set about trying to learn English, but despite a determined effort, he found that he was simply too old to master the language, and the combined impact of this defeat and the realization that had produced it, led him to a complete nervous breakdown from which he never fully recovered.

Other guests commented on the bitterness expressed by members of the English community who grew up in a genuinely bilingual Rochambeau, where one could get along with only rudimentary French, as they watched the city become more than 90% French. The language question remained a shock for the unprepared. The rector of one of the Anglican parishes in the city, recruited from Derry, New Hampshire, came to Rochambeau not knowing French, and after a year left in dismay and frustration.

During my first year teaching at the university, graduate students in my seminars regularly supplied words when I got stuck. The undergraduates, as a rule, could not: when I needed a word in French I had to describe it for them in French. This was all to the good, from the point of view of my own education, but it still surprised me that despite the influence of American television and movies, there remained a large, otherwise educated population on the North American continent that simply didn't know English.

I joked with friends about Rochambeau's Language Police, but shopkeepers who ran afoul of the language laws found nothing to laugh at. A few weeks before the opening of "The Music Man," just to show that Bill 101 was nothing to scoff at, the Language Police swooped down on a hotel keeper in St. Anne-de-Beaupré who dared to use, on a sign posted on the door of his establishment, Le Motel in Dublois, the word "office" in the sense of "bureau de réception" (reception counter).

I translate from *Le Soleil*: "In an extremely important judgment, since it creates jurisprudence, Judge Jean Drouin, of the Cours des sessions de la paix, declared that the word 'office' in the cited context is an Anglicism and thus violates the Charte de la langue française.

"The judge heard the testimony of Louis Dusseault, expert in linguistics and semantics of the Commission de protection de la langue française, who declared, 'the acceptance of "office" would present a danger for it would demonstrate a simplifying laxity which would reflect "déculturation." As language and thought are inseparable, every weakening of the language invariably translates into a decline in the intellectual level of the community.'"

The linguistics counsellor explained that the word "office" does exist in French, but absolutely not as a synonym for "bureau de réception." The term is used for institutions (Office de la language française, Office des autoroutes, etc.) or in the area of services (for example in the expression "vos bons offices" (your good offices).

According to Judge Drouin, Charles Gagnon knew the word "office" to be an Anglicism and he flouted the efforts of the Commission de protection de la langue française. The fact that the defendant preceded the word "office" by an "L" on the pretext that he wanted to Gallicize it, proves, the judge added, that he was conscious of having violated the law. So the Language Police swept him off to jail in a paddy wagon while his sobbing wife pleaded for mercy and their four children cried uncomprehendingly, "Papa! Papa!"

As a relative newcomer to Rochambeau I realized that the cultural division represented by the disputes over language went far deeper than I could readily comprehend. Perhaps I had been too eager to accept Marie Dufresne's list of choir members as a convenient way of making my quest more manageable. Was it not just as likely that in the course of carrying on an Anglophone business in a now predominantly Francophone environment Mark Stanstead had, perhaps without even knowing it, rubbed some people the wrong way? For all his jolly glad-handing, his fundamental principle remained "Business is business." He had shown no hesitation in taking a long-standing contract away from one of his Francophone competitors. Did his opponents regard this as just 'the breaks of the game' or might there have been a more serious price to pay? The stories I had heard about members of the English community suggested long-standing resentments that might have mortal consequences. Why should it be any different for *la communauté Francophone?*

Chapter 15

On Monday morning Agnes Lee called and we exchanged mutual congratulations on the successful opening of the show. Even the staunchest defenders of the British flag among the audience seemed to have accepted the production of an American musical after years of nothing but Gilbert and Sullivan.

Agnes warned me, on the basis of her previous experience with the Savoyards, that yesterday's nervousness would turn to overconfidence.

"For the first performance we just try to keep people from running into the scenery. By the second performance they think they're professionals."

"That's a bad thing?" I asked.

"Overconfidence leads to overacting," Agnes explained. "If some piece of stage business got an unexpected laugh at the first performance, people figure doing it more will produce an even bigger laugh."

"Whereas, in fact, less is more?"

"We'll make a stage director out of you yet, Axel."

"I have to hand it to you, Agnes: casting the Tapley's—all three of them—was brilliant."

"That's an interesting case, Axel. In Priscilla we have unexpected talents just waiting come out; in Francis we have a young lad transformed by opportunity put in his path."

"And in Gordon a man whose talents could be subverted without his even knowing it."

Agnes chuckled. "It's funny the way some people really take their characters very seriously."

"You mean Gordon?"

"Actually I was thinking of Miriam. It's that 'Head of the Altar Guild' mentality. 'Everything has to be exactly right and I'm the person to make sure it happens.'"

"I'm guessing you're referring to the Del Sarte dancers. Was there ever such a thing?"

"Darned if I know, but evidently there was a fad for forming human figures into artistic poses."

"In France they called it *tableaux vivants*. Debussy's friend Pierre Louÿs once wrote him to say that he'd just spent a delightful afternoon in the company of naked ladies, referring to that curious custom."

"In the show the women are supposed to represent Grecian urns— you know those statues with one leg raised, one arm extended, and water gushing out of the mouth."

"I can picture it, though it makes me shudder."

"Well, some of the women in the cast are getting on in age and asking them to balance on one foot is pushing it."

"Uh huh."

"So at one rehearsal, Miriam recited her lines, 'One Grecian urn, two Grecian urns, three Grecian urns,' as the women under her direction try to hold the appropriate pose. But at the climactic point one of the women fell over, her companion fell on her and the third woman toppled over the other two. Now these particular ladies being a bit broad in the beam, so to speak, all I could think of was 'One pachyderm, two pachyderms, three pachyderms.' Fortunately everyone else was already laughing so my mirth didn't cause offence."

"It's a shame Mark couldn't have been here to enjoy the performance."

"Yes, well …"

"You've probably heard that Cathy has asked me to try to figure out how he died."

"You don't think he just wandered accidentally off the path?"

"Doesn't seem too likely."

"I've heard about your 'line of procession' theory."

"I wanted to ask you about that Thursday night. I understand that after the rehearsal you spoke with Francis and Lorna."

"That's right. Funny how you can scarcely utter one name without the other these days."

"So you met them in the parking lot."

"Yes; then I drove Miriam home since her car was being repaired. We followed Geoffrey out of the parking lot, and I remember seeing

Marie's car in my rear-view mirror. She drives that import with the yellow running lights."

"You've got an eye for detail."

"That's what theatre is all about, Axel."

"How did you get into this business anyway?"

"The usual way, I suppose. I enjoyed acting and performed in a theatre group that used to exist among the English community."

"Back in the days when there were more people to draw on."

"That's right. One time we were rehearsing 'The Importance of Being Earnest'—I played Gwendolyn. The director really didn't seem to understand the play very well—it's not that easy to make Oscar Wilde's witticisms sound natural."

"But you had a better idea."

"Well, I had plenty of time offstage to think about alternate readings, but I didn't say anything. It just wouldn't have been right."

"Then what happened?"

"Worse luck, the director broke his leg and was laid up for the better part of a month. The cast didn't know what to do—they didn't want to give up on the production—so I volunteered to kind of hold things together until his return."

"But in fact you turned the show around so completely that by the time the director got back he scarcely recognized the production, and the cast liked your way of doing things so much better than his that they gently but firmly showed him to the exit."

"That's more or less the way it happened," Agnes said with no unseemly show of false modesty.

"And the rest, as they say, is history."

"I've been doing this for quite a long time, Axel."

So the theatre really was Agnes' cathedral. We wished each other good luck for the afternoon's performance and hung up. Two performances may have looked like small reward for eight months of preparation but nobody seemed to be complaining.

If Agnes had furnished both Geoffrey and Miriam with alibis I needed to look elsewhere on my list. I left early for the theatre in hope of finding Herbert Whately before the performance and saw him repairing a piece of scenery that had gotten banged up the afternoon before when the Wells Fargo wagon went off course.

"Hi, Axel," Herbert greeted me. "I'll bet you're pleased with the way the show went yesterday."

"It came off well," I said, "and your sets made me feel as if I were right back in 1912. Do you mind if I ask you a quick business question before we get started again?"

"Shoot."

"I understand the new insurance regulations that you explained to me on Saturday include a change in the way contracts are presented."

"It's more fallout from Bill 101. When you first came to Rochambeau, the red stop signs said 'Arrêt' and 'Stop,' right?"

"That's what I recall. Then the government replaced them all with signs that said only 'Arrêt.' It must have cost the taxpayers a pretty penny."

"And made a few bucks for the company that produced the signs."

"That's true, I guess."

"You can imagine that an insurance company will ordinarily have two sets of forms, one in French, one in English."

"Makes sense."

"You can also imagine that a company like ours, that does most of its business in the Anglophone community, is going to stock more English-language forms than French."

"Right."

"The new regulations say that French-only forms are just fine, but if you want to use English on one side of a form, the other side has to be in French."

"That'll cost you a lot of money printing up new forms."

"But not any of our Francophone competitors."

"Almost seems discriminatory."

"All part of the protection of the French language, Axel."

A similar regulation made it impossible for me to see Hollywood films in English until the French-dubbed version had appeared in theatres for at least a month.

"Paul Cochrane has done all your printing for years, hasn't he?"

"That's right."

"So reprinting contracts will be a real windfall for him."

"Yes and no. Mark kind of decided that we'd carried Paul long enough—he runs a pretty small outfit and, to tell the truth, he charges a lot more than the Francophone printers."

"He must have been upset at the prospect of losing that contract."

"I don't think he needs to worry, Axel."

"You mean you're going to keep on using him?"

"He's had to raise Brad all by himself, and he lives on a pretty thin profit margin. It doesn't seem fair to take that away from him."

"But that last time I talked with you it sounded as if business decisions were a matter of dollars and cents."

"Don't get me wrong, Axel. This is a hard business and I keep a pretty careful eye on the bottom line, but I'm no Scrooge."

"Like Mark?'

"Come on, Axel. *De mortuis nil nisi bonum.*"

"Right you are. Of the dead speak no evil."

I left Herbert and followed the sound of Paul Cochrane warming up. I don't think that the man had ever sung a warm-up note in his life before being asked to sing first tenor in the barbershop quartet, but during the winter months I noticed that he began wearing a scarf, even indoors, ("Can't risk catching a cold, Axel," he'd explained) and I observed that as he arrived at one rehearsal he was listening to a Placido Domingo recording on his car cassette player. I tracked the sound of cascading scales to a storeroom next to the loading dock.

"Hi, Axel," he greeted me. "How did you like the bit with the canes?"

At the curtain call of yesterday's performance the members of the barbershop quartet had managed to execute a simultaneous cane spin-and-catch in the air, to the delight of the audience. The maneuver must have taken hours of practice to perfect. I doffed an imaginary hat in tribute to his dexterity and realized that this was probably the first time I had ever seen Paul Cochrane smile. "You must be mighty proud of Brad, too," I said.

"I'll say. I was holding my breath during that long 'Ya Got Trouble' number, but he got through it with scarcely a flub. I guess you must be thanking your lucky stars that you insisted on double-casting the leads."

"Actually I was hoping I might have a word with you about Mark before we get started."

"What's up?"

As I explained the connection between Mark Stanstead and Cochrane Printing Paul's mouth tightened and his jaw set. His voice sounded bitter as he interrupted my account. "Do you know what that bastard had the nerve to say to me? 'I've known your family for a long time, Paul, but business is business.' I could have shot him."

"Or pushed him in front of a truck?"

"What are you talking about?"

I explained how the close link between his printing firm and Stanstead's insurance company gave him a motive for murder. A deep swallow made his Adam's apple rise and fall and Paul looked for a moment as if his entire world was about to collapse.

"I wouldn't do that, Axel. Surely you don't think so."

"I haven't made any judgment about you, Paul. The only thing I know about you is that you're one fine first tenor. I'm just following the leads wherever they take me."

"'Business is business,'" he said sardonically.

"You misunderstand, Paul. I'm not in a position to make any decisions. But it would help me to know what you did after choir rehearsal on Thursday night."

"I walked down the path with Marie. The Senior Choir is singing 'He watching over Israel' on Sunday and I was having a little trouble with the tenor line, so I stayed for a few minutes after rehearsal and she helped me out with it."

"I'd hate to say I'm glad for your difficulties, but a tricky tenor line in a Mendelssohn anthem seems to have given you an alibi."

"You can check with Marie. We were standing next to my car when Agnes came down the steps. She must have wanted to talk with Marie about the show."

"You mean she didn't come with Miriam?"

"No; she was alone. She gave me a suggestion to pass on to the rest of the quartet about how we should keep facing the audience while we were strolling across the stage in the 'Lida Rose' number."

Paul's account didn't jibe with what Agnes had told me so I made a note to check with her again. By now it was time to get the show started so I wished Paul luck—in everything—and headed to the orchestra pit.

Chapter 16

THE FIRST ACT OF "THE Music Man" includes a tongue-twisting chorus for the women of River City, who must keep repeating "Pick a little, talk a little, pick a little, talk a little, cheep cheep cheep, talk a lot, pick a little more"—evoking a band of chickens—while Maud tells Professor Hill that the librarian advocates dirty books. "Dirty books?" he rejoins, at which three of the other ladies recite a litany of literary atrocities: "Chaucer," "Rabelais," "Balzac."

The timing of Maud's speech is crucial, because the chorus is singing behind her and each item in the litany falls at a specific point in the music. The first several times we rehearsed the number, Maud fluffed the line, thereby ruining the entrances of the other ladies and killing a laugh, an unforgivable sin in musical comedy. We waited patiently for several weeks with no signs of improvement, at which point I suggested to Agnes Lee that perhaps it would be safer if someone else spoke the line in question. No—Agnes had faith in Maud, who would pull through in the end.

Three weeks before the show, when Maud still couldn't speak the line properly, I insisted to Mark Stanstead, the president of the company, that—this being a musical matter—as music director I wanted to make a substitution. Mark said he would get back to me. The next day Mark arrived at my apartment for an illuminating conversation.

"Axel," he said. "There are a few things you should know. First, Maud's daughter, the founder of this company, is intensely jealous of you."

"But that's irrational," I protested. "She lives 400 miles away and has nothing to do with the company any more."

"Axel, when you get older you will come to appreciate that there is precious little rationality in this world, least of all in personal relationships. Now if you'll permit me to continue without interruptions: this daughter, then, is jealous of you and the mother dislikes you as a result. Now I could ask Ethel, the most musical of the five ladies, to recite this one line. But Ethel hates Maud, and dropped out of the church choir that Maud's daughter directed. Maud is also co-chairman of costumes, the other co-chairman being Mrs. Shinn, the best friend of Maud's daughter. If we gave Maud's line to Ethel, Maud would quit the company, taking with her Mrs. Shinn and also the seamstress. Moreover, Maud would do her best to scuttle the publicity for the show among the English community. Finally, Agnes Lee, the dramatic director, who doesn't understand that this is essentially a musical matter, but who is a close friend of Maud's, would also quit the show. Now that you've heard this story, if you still want me to ask Ethel to read Maud's line, I'll do it. I leave the decision to you."

And this was why, whenever we came to that passage in the score, I simply smiled beatifically at Maud, and swore never to become involved with another amateur theatre company. But this afternoon, *mirabile dictu*, Maud actually got the line right for the very first time. I could have hugged her.

Our small orchestra executed the score with aplomb, although as we came to the end of the first act I realized that our drummer, a young Francophone woman, hadn't a clue about the production to which she was making such a valuable contribution. Her parents would have been perfectly bilingual but this girl belonged to a generation which, for political reasons, refused to learn English. Every drumbeat was precisely in place, but for all she knew about the story unfolding on the stage behind her, she could have been performing Gilbert and Sullivan.

This isn't to say that Anglophones had any reason to feel smug about their command of French. A friend of mine was reading a modern French play for a literature course. It was well after midnight and she may have been a bit less alert than usual. The stage directions called for a room with a large blank wall with a lizard on it. A boy and his mother enter. The woman complains about the lizard and asks her son to cover it with a picture. Shortly thereafter her husband comes home, criticizes the picture and removes it, exposing the lizard. He berates his wife, who explains that she has already twice summoned the plasterer but that the lizard keeps coming back. At this point my friend decided things were getting out of hand and had recourse to a dictionary, where she discovered an essential gender distinction: little boy lizards are indeed lizards, but little girl lizards (and in rechecking the text of the play she found that the lizard was unquestionably of the feminine gender) are cracks, or fissures.

I had heard of communications problems occurring even in a purely Anglophone environment. One of my colleagues at the university spent a year teaching high school in rural North Carolina. One day his students announced that they wouldn't be there the next day. There was going to be a big fire at the raceway, the students were all planning to go, and the school would be closed. My friend was confused., How did they know in advance that there would be a big fire, and if they knew, why couldn't they warn someone to prevent it? Finally one of the students was able to resolve the confusion. "No, Mr. Stillman, not a far, the country fire!"

Not all the instrumental music came from the orchestra. Little Amaryllis has to play a piece on the piano, complete with wrong notes that other members of the cast come to the instrument to correct. I imagined that Meredith Willson had had a merry time composing the "Piano Lesson" scene, in which Marian Paroo tries to keep track of her student's playing at the same time as warding off her mother's matchmaking efforts.

Priscilla had developed an almost maternal relationship with Marie Dufresne, to the point of asking the stage director whether she couldn't alter the line "If a woman has a husband and you've got none, why should she take advice from you, Even if you can quote Balzac and Shakespeare and all them other highfalutin' Greeks," to avoid causing possible offence to the recently-divorced Marie. "It's just a show, Priscilla," Marie tried to explain, but even so Priscilla drew on a special source of intensity when she sang, "I know all about your standards, and if you don't mind my sayin' so there's not a man alive who could hope to measure up to that blend of Paul Bunyan, Saint Pat and Noah Webster you've got concocted for yourself outta your Irish imagination, your Iowa stubbornness and your liberry fulla books!"

Not that Priscilla really wanted Marie to make a play for either Mark Stanstead (married) or Brad Cochrane (unmarried but too young). Rather I think her alter ego as a wise matchmaking Irishwoman allowed her such a congenial place for personal growth and self-fulfillment that she began to feel more comfortable as Mrs. Paroo than as Mrs. Tapley.

Priscilla seemed to have accepted the idea of Lorna as a companion for Francis, tutoring the boy in subjects that neither of his parents would have felt comfortable broaching. Indeed, she showed an almost protective attitude toward the teenagers. During one rehearsal, when Agnes called for the couple and one of the other kids said accurately, "Oh, they're making out in one of the dressing rooms," Priscilla valiantly lied and claimed to have seen Lorna helping the costume mistress while Francis was assisting the sound technician at the opposite end of the auditorium.

The first act came to a conclusion with the Wells Fargo number. Each of the tiny solos came in on cue: "It could be curtains ... or dishes ... or a double boiler," but Winthrop won the hearts of the audience. The boy's favourite moment in the show came not in his solo, "Gary, Indiana," but at his brief moment in the spotlight during the first act finale in which he got to sing

O-ho the Wellth Fargo Wagon ith a-comin' now,
I don't know how I can ever wait to thee.
It could be thumpin' for thumone who ith'
No relation but it could be thump'n thpetyul
Just for me!

Winthrop had perfected his lisp to the point that whenever we performed the number everybody around him got splattered with saliva. When they complained he just laughed. Bratty little kid!

Chapter 17

As soon as the first act ended Geoffrey Lambert and Paul Cochrane approached me and asked whether we could find a quiet place to talk. Their serious demeanour seemed incongruous with their garish garb which, combined with the stoutness of Lambert and the skinniness of Cochrane, made me think of Laurel and Hardy. I had to stifle a grin as I led them to the loading area that Paul had used for his vocal warm-ups.

The two men looked at each other and evidently decided that Geoffrey should begin. "Axel," he said, "Paul and I have been talking this over and we have an idea."

"I'm all ears," I said.

"We were so relieved to be off the hook as suspects for Mark's death that we didn't take the matter any further."

"But now we've decided we owe it to Mark to tell you what we think," Paul chimed in.

"As we figure it," Geoffrey said, "you've pretty much eliminated members of the St. Matthias choir as suspects, but obviously somebody killed Mark."

"Somebody who knew how Anglican churches work," said Paul.

"And who outside St. Matthias knows Anglican churches better than anybody?"

I wasn't sure this was meant to be a rhetorical question, so after an awkward pause I said, "I don't know; the Bishop?"

"Wrong answer, Axel," said Geoffrey. "Dean Tapley!"

"Surely you're joking," I said.

"No; think about it," said Paul. "Tapley would know that Mark had to be the last person out of that parish on a Thursday night. It would have been easy for him to wait in the bushes."

"But what possible reason would Dean Tapley have for wanting Mark dead?" I asked.

"Aha!" said Paul. "This is the good part. Last week Geoffrey's wife heard from one of the women in her ACW group who had been at Church House to ask the bishop to give a talk at the Anglican Church Women's annual meeting."

"The door to the bishop's office was open and she couldn't help hearing the conversation," Geoffrey said.

"I can just imagine," I said.

"Mark Stanstead was showing the bishop why the Cathedral should be shut down—it cost too much to heat in the winter when only a few souls attended services. He suggested that the tiny congregation come to St. Matthias and that the Cathedral be turned into a museum open to tourists in the summertime," Geoffrey said.

"I imagine the bishop took a dim view of the idea," I said.

"On the contrary," Paul said. "He told Mark to write up a financial analysis for him to study."

"Word got around," Geoffrey said, "as word will, and eventually reached Dean Tapley."

"Oh, and let me tell you," Paul pitched his already high voice up half an octave to mimic the eavesdropper, "was he ever furious!"

"You do that rather well," I said, having heard far too many churchwomen gossiping.

"So if he could get Mark out of the way before he delivered the financial report, he had a good chance that the bishop would retire before the matter came to a head," Paul said in his normal voice.

"He could hardly have refuted the idea on its merits," Geoffrey said.

Dean Tapley a murderer? The thought seemed preposterous on the face of it. On the other hand, all the other people I'd been considering were also good practicing Christians. And I had to admit that Tapley had a vindictive side to him. I had heard the story of how, some years back, when the wardens and the council defied the dean's wishes on some issue that he took seriously, he summarily dismissed them all. I wondered whether Mark Stanstead might have been involved in that fracas before joining the congregation at St. Matthias. I thanked the two singers for sharing their ideas with me and promised to give the matter serious thought. (Hang around institutions long enough and you begin to start sounding like one.)

I located Herbert Whately sitting on top of one of the trunks used for the "Wells Fargo Wagon" number toward the end of the second act. He looked exhausted and I realized what life must be like for a heart attack survivor who had to measure his every effort lest an injudicious expenditure of energy bring on a recurrence. He'd had to run the insurance company single-handedly since Mark Stanstead's death while supervising the construction and painting of sets, not by a professional crew but by a group of enthusiastic but inexperienced teenagers who had to be shown what to do in every detail and whose attention spans sometimes left something to be desired. And then there were my questions, but at this point I saw no alternative to following the story to its end.

I sat down on the trunk beside Herbert and said, "Before this whole thing started, I didn't give the insurance business much thought. I had no idea that a business could affect so many people."

"With all due respect, Axel, academics don't tend to be in touch with the real world."

"But I keep running into dead ends. I understand the importance of the asbestos question and printing contracts, but so far as I can see, neither Geoffrey Lambert nor Paul Cochrane was responsible for Mark's death. Still, I keep thinking that it must have been connected to something he was doing, or was about to do. Was Mark involved in some business decision or some investment that you haven't mentioned yet?"

Herbert gave a sudden start, as if something I'd said had jolted him out of his lethargy. He paused, as if considering his options, then said, "Mark had been planning to sell a business property in the city in order to buy a cottage. Cathy opposed the move—as far as she was concerned, it was enough trouble keeping up one house; she didn't want the responsibility for another. But Mark was evidently thinking about his retirement and figured that cottages were only going to go up in value."

"I can't imagine that the cottage would make much of a difference. How about the business property? Would anyone have been affected by its sale."

"Well, the Rochambeau Historical Society keeps its archives on one floor of the building."

"That probably wouldn't matter much."

"Maybe not to you, but it sure matters to Agnes Lee."

"Tell me more."

"The society rents the space for a dollar a year. You can imagine that they don't really have any resources. Agnes' father left them his collection of historical documents and artefacts and Agnes has spent her life as its custodian, as much in reverence for her father as out of devotion to the history of Rochambeau. If she lost a place for the archives, she'd have no choice but to sell her father's collection at auction."

"Did Mark know about all this?"

"Of course. He told Agnes that he had the greatest respect for the Rochambeau Historical Society but that business is business."

"Do you plan to sell the building now?"

"No need. I already have a cottage."

Herbert's story strengthened Agnes Lee's motive for murder. I had heard about single women who devoted their lives to preserving the memory of their fathers. Mark's business decisions seemed calculated and rational. To have an obsession threatened might lead one to take an action that seemed disproportionate to its cause. When Lorna Lambert had spoken of Agnes's preference for Brad over Mark for the lead in the musical, I had thought the girl was simply coming to her father's defense. Even given the passionate emotions of theatre people, it had seemed like a pretty slender motive. But the potential loss of the collection—Agnes's last physical tie with her father—might have led her to take extreme measures.

The bell announcing the end of intermission interrupted my rumination and I returned to the pit for the second act.

Chapter 18

THE SCRIPT OF "THE MUSIC Man" calls for several sound effects which, someone decided, fell within the domain of the music director, a train whistle being considered, one supposes, a member of the woodwind family. So one morning in March Mark Stanstead drove me out to a "Régional," an imposing educational complex once devoted to the education of Roman Catholic Anglophones (one elite minority!) then, after the Quiet Revolution—in which the Church lost control of secondary education and just about everything else—sold to the government as an educational administrative centre.

The audio-visual department stood at the end of a long corridor. The technician in charge, a rather impatient man surrounded by an array of electronic equipment, took the blank recording tape donated by a cast member and prepared to copy the effects we wanted. The following conversation ensued:

Axel: We need a train whistle.

Technician: Well, which recording do you want—we have 200 sound effects records here. How about this? (Whoo whoo)

Axel: No; that's a diesel engine—we need a steam engine.

Technician: All right. Try this. (Whoo whoo)

Axel: But that's the sound of a train stopping at a station. We need one whistling in the distance.

Technician: Listen, Mac. I ain't got all day.

Axel. Okay. We'll take the next one that turns up.

Which is why, when Marian Paroo tells Harold Hill at the end of Act II, "You'd better hurry, there's your train," it sounds as though the whole damn train is passing right through the audience.

Mark insisted that we make five repetitions of each sound effect, just to be sure. This included five peals of thunder, five train whistles, five train whistles accompanied by bells, and five angry crowds murmuring (Murmur, murmur, murmur). When we listened to the finished sound track, we discovered a mysterious bleep between each of the twenty selections. It turned out that the helpful cast member had supplied not a virgin tape but a recording of disco music, so that every time we stopped and restarted the tape, a tiny cacophonous fragment came through. The technician had to go back and erase each bleep, one by one, leaving it for me to put in leaders and deliver the tape to the stage manager. Chalk up another two hours to the credit of the Savoyards.

W. C. Fields once said that anyone who hated dogs and children couldn't be all bad. I had read that many actors hated to work with kids, and in the course of rehearsing "The Music Man" I came to understand why. A week before we opened, the boy playing Winthrop, the shy lisper whom Harold Hill persuades to come out of his shell, cornered me and said, "Axel, I don't think Amaryllis knows her lines."

"Is that right?"

"I've memorized all her lines."

"I see."

"So I was thinking I could play both parts, with quick costume changes the way they do on Broadway."

"Just keep practicing your part, Winthrop."

"But I know it by heart. Would you like to hear me singing 'Gary, Indiana' again?"

"Not right now, Winthrop."

I recalled Agnes Lee's observation about actors who identified too closely with the characters they portrayed. At the end of the piano lesson scene, Winthrop remains silent when Amaryllis invites him to her birthday party. "Say 'Thank you, Amaryllis,'" Mrs. Paroo prompted.

"He won't say my name because of the s's," Amaryllis explains condescendingly.

"Thank you, Amaryllith," says Winthrop.

"Amaryllith, Amaryllith! He said Amaryllith," chants the little girl. At this point, the first time they rehearsed the scene, Winthrop just hauled off and whacked her. He was evidently experiencing for the first time in his life what it felt like to be picked on for something he couldn't help, and he didn't like it one bit. Much as I considered the kid an obnoxious brat, I couldn't help sympathizing. In my case it was a combination of being the second shortest kid in the class and too mouthy for my own good. As the song says, "The world is a stage, the stage is a world of entertainment."

Winthrop wasn't the only actor who thought his role was too small. At our penultimate rehearsal Marjorie Northcote approached me.

"Axel, I'd like you to enlarge my part."

"How do you mean?"

"Well, that's the way it's supposed to happen. The prima donna makes demands and the music director gives her a larger part.

"Marjorie, you're not a prima donna. You're not even a seconda donna. You're just a member of the chorus."

"All the more reason why I should have a larger part."

Rather than refuse point blank, as I should have done, I told her to take it up with Agnes. My thoughts kept returning to our illustrious stage director, whom I sought out after the performance.

Chapter 19

I was standing in the lobby of the theatre, happily listening to words of congratulations from members of the audience, when Lorna approached me. "Axel," she said. "I need to talk to you right away." She had already changed out of her costume and removed her stage makeup. Without the usual dark layers of eye shadow and mascara she looked like a reasonably civilized teenager. I led her back into the nearly-empty auditorium where we found a pair of secluded seats.

"Will this do?" I asked.

Lorna looked around. "I guess so," she said uncertainly.

"So what's so urgent?" I asked.

"Francis told you about the stranger in the woods," she said. I nodded. "Well, we've been arguing about this. I saw the stranger was a woman."

"And Francis?"

"He thought it was too dark to see anything."

"But you feel pretty sure?"

"Yes. Women notice things," she said with a note of challenge in her voice. I thought of Agnes directing crowd scenes, seemingly able to watch everyone at the same time, or Priscilla, apparently giving her full attention to Marie in the Piano Lesson scene but still noticing that Winthrop—horsing around during the dress rehearsal with some of the towns children while waiting for his entrance—was about to tumble into the orchestra pit. I was willing to grant the point, though I felt amused at this seventeen-year-old's confidence in spouting off about gender differences.

"So what did you notice?" I asked.

"Men and women don't crouch the same way," Lorna said.

"They don't?" I asked. This was news to me.

"No," she said. "The whole dispersal of weight is different. A woman will reach out for a branch for support, favouring her non-dominant leg, where a man will tend to balance his weight evenly." I tried to imagine myself crouching in the woods and couldn't find anything in the image to contradict her picture. "And so's the contour. I'm not talking about a woman's figure but the way her back will curve and the way she'll hold her shoulders."

I had to concede that Lorna noticed details that I would never even have considered; clearly she'd been giving this question a good deal of though. "You make a pretty strong case," I said.

"Darn right," she said, with an air of satisfaction that an adult was actually taking her seriously. "I don't know why Francis won't believe it."

"I appreciate your telling me this," I said. "It might really make a difference."

"Do you think so?" she asked. All the put-on sophistication had vanished; I welcomed her genuine response.

"A real difference," I added, watching Lorna depart to rejoin her friends. If Lorna's eyes were to be trusted, despite the darkness of the woods outside the church, this would remove Dean Tapley from the suspect list, I observed with relief. Much as I disliked working for the man, I felt reluctant to cast him in the role of murderer.

I returned to the lobby where the last of the audience members were making their way to the parking lot. I found Agnes heading toward the dressing rooms to pick up her coat.

"You must be relieved to put this behind you," I told Agnes, who was still holding a cellophane-wrapped bouquet from the cast of the show.

"You can say that again. You know how it is: you select a show in June and envision an extraordinary success. Then you start working with volunteer actors in September and wonder how you're ever going to pull it off. Then they all learn their lines, you work on blocking, and everything seems to be going all right. But when they try to talk and move at the same time you recall Lyndon John's unprintable description about Gerald Ford."

"Who couldn't walk and chew gum at the same time?"

"But in the remark it wasn't 'walk.' Finally it all pulls together. Then you put them in the theatre and it's as if they've never seen a set before and keep bumping into it. Yes, I'm relieved it's over."

"I've spoken with Herbert. I guess you're also relieved that the Historical Society will get to keep its home."

Agnes smiled, then turned her head and gave me a quizzical look. "Oh, no. You're thinking that this gives me a motive for killing Mark."

I lifted an open palm. I'd collaborated with this woman for eight months even though we didn't actually work together—I'd be in one room rehearsing one group's singing while she'd be in another room directing another group's acting. Following this line of inquiry felt like an act of betrayal. Agnes didn't seem any more comfortable than I. We remained silent for several moments before she spoke.

"All right, Axel. I guess I don't have any choice but to betray a confidence, but I truly hope you can keep this to yourself."

"I'll do my best."

"You must have observed the differences in personality between Mark and Herbert."

"That's not too hard."

"They'd talked about investing in a new ski development, pending an investigation of the ski company's financial position. When the initial report came back favourable, Mark was heavily involved in the production so Herbert went ahead with the investment, knowing how much Mark loved skiing and intending to tell his partner as soon as he could. But Mark was sometimes away from the office for days at a time."

I thought about the number of hours Mark had spent with me, and nodded.

"Then the final report came in, reversing the initial estimation. Herbert was embarrassed to confess his mistake and looked for another way to recoup the investment which, after all, hadn't gone bad yet, although it looked as if it might. Herbert started losing sleep—keep in mind that he's been in poor health ever since his heart attack, and the stress of our show only made things worse. Miriam urged him to admit his mistake but Herbert was afraid that Mark would accuse him of disloyalty and the partnership might founder."

Now I understood why Herbert had been so discountenanced when I'd asked him about the company's investments. He'd thought that somehow I knew about his potential fiasco.

"I think there's still something you're not telling me, Agnes."

She reddened, frowned, and said, "In for a dime, in for a dollar. What I told you about Thursday night wasn't completely accurate. I did speak with Lorna and Francis just the way I said, but I didn't drive Miriam home. Her car was still in the parking lot when I left."

I gave Agnes a hug and thanked her for putting up with all the frustrations. We'd put on a grand show, the two of us, and made a great many people happy with our efforts.

Agnes dropped me off at my apartment and as we rode in contented silence I recalled the day she had put the dean in his place. "This is my cathedral," she had said. Then I thought about the church where I worked. "This is my cathedral," Dean Tapley could have said, though I never heard him utter any such words. "You are the master of all you survey," Agnes had said. Well, wasn't that appropriate? The dean had ultimate responsibility for what went on at the cathedral: he wrote the sermons, composed the liturgy, chose the hymns (and corrected the organist's tempo if he went astray). I had taken his actions personally when they had been entirely impersonal—the dean had no interest in trying to control me; he was just doing his job. "Business is business," Mark might have said.

In fact, as well as in principle, I was master of my own little domain. I chose my preludes, postludes and offertory selections. I selected music for the choir on the rare occasions when we had enough singers to deliver even a unison anthem. Dean Tapley wasn't my enemy; he was just the dean.

I had the impression that I'd forgotten something important when the words of my college physics professor came to mind: "You can neither prove nor disprove a theory with a thought experiment." For all my play-acting with Francis or imagined stances with Lorna I had never visited the scene of the crime, having assumed that the police, with their sophisticated forensic techniques, would have learned everything there was to learn from a close examination of the site. Then it occurred to me that from their point of view no crime had been committed. Moreover, with rain having kept the ground moist since Thursday, the woods at St. Matthias might still be very much as they had been on Thursday night. I quickly changed my clothes and pedalled out to the church.

Leaving my bike in the deserted parking lot I walked up the stairs of the pathway that been so much in my mind and conversation during the last three days. The sound of traffic on the highway, though reduced on this holiday afternoon, still seemed disturbingly close. I soon found the broken bushes through which Mark Stanstead's body had tumbled.

My college physics course came to mind once again: momentum in physics is the product of a body's mass and its linear velocity. If would have taken a fair amount of momentum to knock Mark off the path, through the bushes, and onto the highway, although not as much as I would initially have thought—I still had minor bruises from Francis' demonstration in the cathedral. If Lorna's powers of observation were to be trusted, a woman assailant would probably have attempted to compensate for lower body mass with higher velocity. She would likely have made a running start before hurling her body against Mark's.

I walked slowly into the woods, trying to maintain a straight line from the break in the bushes. Nothing insured that the murderer didn't come at Mark from an angle, either from the front or the back, but it made most sense to attack directly form the side, so as to minimize the distance Mark's body had to travel before reaching the deadly flow of truck traffic in the lane closest to the bushes.

The earth varied in moisture, with drier areas on higher ground near the trees; this was probably where Francis and Lorna had concealed themselves. A direct line to the path carried me through ground which, though not exactly muddy, seemed wet enough to preserve the impression of a shoe. I kept walking. If I were going to make the attack, with my fairly slight build, this was more or less where I would have stood. No sign on the ground nearby betrayed the presence of a human intruder.

Suppose the woman had been heavier than I, and perhaps less confident of her running ability. She probably would have waited closer to the path. I retraced my steps as carefully as I could. Then I saw it, concealed by the late afternoon shadows: the impression of a sports shoe, with a curious pattern of lines broken by tiny diamonds. I looked around for other marks but though someone had evidently been standing here I could find no other distinctive trace. I knew where I had to go next.

Chapter 20

By the time I changed my clothes and rode my bicycle to the Whately residence it was late afternoon, the cinematographer's "magic hour" when the particular angle of the sun bathes the world in a golden glow that shows off every detail to best advantage.

"Herbert is sleeping," Miriam said when I knocked at the door. "I'm just about to go off for a ride; would you like to join me?" She fetched her bicycle from the garage and we set off down the street. "The city looks lovely at this time of day. Let's ride up to the park. It's been several days since I've had any exercise."

Named Sunset Park before the onslaught of revisionist nomenclature, the grassy knoll atop a promontory served as a favourite destination for athletic cyclists and hikers by day and a notorious lover's lane for newly automobilized adolescents by night.

Miriam Whately was more than equal to the challenge of the climb but eventually the gradient proved too much for both of us and we walked our bikes the last hundred yards to the summit.

"I once saw a television story about a man with a heart condition," I told Miriam as we walked. "He came to a psychiatrist complaining about a recurring dream of a roller coaster whose track ended in open space. Each night his dream brought him a bit closer to the gap in the tracks, to the point that he was afraid to sleep, certain that if the car in his nightmare went off the track, he would die of fright. Trouble was, the lack of sleep was wearing him down to the point that he feared for his heart. Whether he slept or didn't sleep, he was bound to die."

"What did he do?"

"In the story he ended up jumping out the psychiatrist's window."

"Wasn't there any other way?"

"I imagine that's what you asked yourself when you watched your husband impaling himself on the horns of a dilemma. If he told his partner what he had done, he faced disgrace and ruin. Yet the strain of not telling threatened to kill him. You did what you did to save Herbert's life."

"It's an interesting theory, Axel, and I don't deny that I might have killed Mark given the opportunity, but it never presented itself. I left the choir rehearsal with Agnes and by the time we got home—we stopped for a drink along the way, as I'm sure she'll tell you—the police had already informed Herbert of his partner's death. I don't deny that the accident, or suicide, or whatever it was, makes life a lot easier for Herbert but I can't take any credit for it. Ah, isn't this gorgeous!"

We had reached the highest point of the climb and stopped to lean our bicycles against the chest-high iron railing separating the bluff from the steep scree-covered slope leading to a drop-off to the river. The city of Rochambeau extended beneath us like a toy town. I could make out the tower of the Anglican cathedral, the school where we had put on the musical, and further away, alongside the ribbon-like Boulevard des Laurentides, the small parish church of St. Matthias.

At the far edge of the panorama stretched the city's two principal bridges. I had spent many a Saturday afternoon cycling the riverside paths that these bridges—one a truss, the other an arch—turned into a circuit, but this was the first time I had ever come to this lofty lookout. All my attention was absorbed by the majestic view. Then I happened to glance at a patch of mud that we had crossed just before arriving at the lookout. Beside our tire marks and the waffle pattern of my running shoes I noticed a different pattern: a series of lines interrupted by tiny diamonds.

Suddenly I found myself slipping under the rail, a swift sideways blow having sent my front wheel off the pavement. Unable to grasp the railing I seized the only object within reach, the front wheel of Miriam's bicycle, which slid under the railing, bearing its rider with it. I let go of her bike as I bumped down the incline, still entangled in my bicycle, scarcely noticing as small loose rocks scraped against my bare skin. The pitch became steeper and I began to gain speed despite the friction of my body against the rock. To one side I saw a shrub growing improbably out of the inhospitable surface and I grabbed it, more out of instinct than intention.

My brother-in-law once described three kinds of holds for assisting one's ascent or descent in the mountains. Mineral holds you could trust—places where fingers or toes could securely grasp the rock. Animal holds you could trust—the support of a hiking companion's clasp. Vegetable holds were not to be trusted—branches snap or become uprooted, leaving one off balance and vulnerable.

For once a vegetable hold sustained me—the branch somehow held, my slide ended and my bicycle, tangled in my sneakers, came to a halt. Little by little I pulled the bike up toward me, then relying on the friction of rubber tires against rock, and the more reliable mineral holds that gradually disclosed themselves to my searching fingers, I made my way back up the slope and under the railing to the roadway.

Miriam was less fortunate. The angle of her fall had taken her beyond reach and neither rock nor branch had interrupted her descent as she slid down the slope, just above her bicycle, and then over the edge and down into the river, so far below that I could not be sure that I heard a splash.

Chapter 21

"WHAT SHOULD I DO?" I wondered as I descended the hill toward the city. Should I call 911 or leave an anonymous tip for the police? I felt totally confused and almost instinctively made my way to Cathy Stanstead's house. Surely she would know what to do.

Judging from the look on Cathy's face, I must still have been in a state of shock when I knocked at the door, unable to say by what route I had come. She led me inside, told me to wash off my arms and legs, and applied disinfectant and bandages to the worst of my abrasions.

We sat in the living room and I described my misadventure with Miriam. "Like a mother bear protecting her cub," was all she said when I had finished.

"Was Herbert in such jeopardy as he imagined?" I asked her.

"I don't actually know," Cathy said. "Mark and Herbert had been partners for their entire careers, like their fathers before them. On the other hand," and I recited with her, "'business is business.'"

"But what should I do?" I asked her.

"Axel," Cathy said, looking me straight in the eye, "I think you've done enough."

"But ..."

"Really."

We sat in silence for a few moments.

"Her body will be discovered."

Cathy nodded.

"And Herbert?"

"Let it be an accident. It *was* an accident."

"But shouldn't I ..."

"Axel, do you really think it would improve Herbert's state of mind to know that his wife murdered his partner for his sake?"

"I suppose not. But after all my questions, won't there be rumours?"

"There are always rumours, Axel, but if you're willing to let people conclude that you were a bit of a twit, Mark's death will go back to being a suicide. I can live with that; can you?"

I nodded.

"All the same, to avoid embarrassing questions you might do well to keep your arms and legs covered for the next several days."

I nodded again.

"And Axel ... thank you." Cathy kissed me on the forehead and then watched from the doorstep as I pedalled home in the gathering twilight.

FIRE AND ICE

Some say the world will end in fire,
Some say in ice.
From what I've tasted of desire
I hold with those who favor fire.
But if it had to perish twice,
I think I know enough of hate
To say that for destruction ice
Is also great
And would suffice.

—Robert Frost

Chapter 1

I WAS TRYING TO TEACH trigonometric identities to a class of 11h-grade hooligans when the fire alarm ended the lesson, to my frustration and their unconcealed delight. Filing down the hallway we repeated a drill we had already executed the month before and that returning students knew by heart through repetitions every month of the school year. Each of the 95 boys, grades 4 through 12, at the Galton School lined up in the parking area near the entrance to the school, in alphabetical order by grade. Each of the nine prefects checked off the boys in the grade assigned to him and reported the results to the assistant headmaster, Carl Kitchener, who would normally turn to the headmaster, Harold Bromley, and announce in a loud, military tone, "All present and accounted for, sir!" (The adults—twelve full-time teachers, the office staff, kitchen crew and maintenance workers—were expected to look out for themselves.)

This October morning differed from last month's drill in two important respects. First, it appeared that there really was a fire, judging from the excited murmurings as those boys who had actually seen the flames ignored the assistant headmaster's demand for complete silence and described them to those who had not. And second, Carl Kitchener's usually confident voice faltered when he announced, "One missing, sir."

"Who's that?" Bromley demanded.

"Ratley, sir."

That would have been Eric Ratley, universally known as Eric the Rat, the worst misfit in a school primarily populated by misfits. Unable to tolerate the bullying and petty thievery of the boys in his dormitory, Eric lived in a kind of nest he had built for himself under the stage in the school chapel. The headmaster hadn't made life any easier for Ratley. More than once I had heard Bromley publicly belittle the boy in school assemblies for his complete unwillingness to embrace the Galton spirit, as expressed in its official brochure.

Galton is a residential school for boys occupying 600 acres of wooded hills and open fields nestled in the bosom of the Laurentians. How do you spell adventure? Begin with a capital "G": Galton offers white-water rafting, alpine and cross-country skiing, winter camping, and White Mountain backpacking as part of its outstanding outdoor education program. Galton promotes the development of strong legs, sound lungs and gritty determination. The words "academic excellence" nowhere appeared in the remarkable document.

Yet for all his disdain of the unathletic Ratley, the headmaster unhesitatingly turned, bounded up the steps to the main entrance, and disappeared into the building. The original Galton School had been destroyed by fire eight years earlier. Its replacement, at least in its central area, resembled a ski lodge more than a preparatory school, with its high ceiling, irregular angles, tall windows and wooden beams. A row of stone steps led to the entrance doors. One passed administrative offices on either side of a small hallway which opened onto the main lounge whose sudden immensity must have been designed to impress prospective parents. Rows of wooden trestle tables on the right marked the communal dining area, followed by the library, a classroom wing and the dormitories, with offices and the school chapel located on a wing to the left. Above the entrance to the lounge hung flags representing each of the countries that had contributed to the student body. The sheer number of these ensigns suggested that the school continued to display the flags long after the students had departed.

As we waited for the headmaster to return I gazed at the tall trees surrounding the school. A goodly proportion of evergreens asserted their place among the red, orange and yellow foliage of deciduous trees, producing an unusually rich autumnal palette. As one of my colleagues had said when I remarked on the scene, "There's no prettier place on earth—at least when the boys aren't here." Behind the boys stood the teachers' parked cars, each with a key in its ignition. No one had more than a half mile to walk from residence to school, and in good weather some came in on foot, but the over-packed schedule made every minute count and it was often easier to drive. One of my colleagues had clued me in about the keys. It didn't matter now but during the several months of snow cover it made it easier for the maintenance crew to move the cars themselves instead of searching for their owners when it came time to plow the parking lot.

A murmur went over the assembled student body at the sight of the headmaster emerging with the inert body of a young teenager. As the village fire truck could be heard mounting the hill, siren screaming, Bromley lay Ratley's inert form on a blanket of jackets donated by several of the boys and begin to administer artificial respiration, pressing hard on the boy's back.

The first time I saw the headmaster stand before the student body I thought he could as easily have been a male model—not a young, buff athlete but the silver-haired, clear-eyed purveyor of shirts or automobiles or whiskey for "men of distinction." Hair immaculately brushed, monogrammed handkerchief poking discreetly out of blazer pocket, he beautifully filled the part of front man for the school.

This morning he was all business, a grim look taking the place of his normal commanding demeanour. I remembered practicing these moves back in scouting days; there was something fearful about seeing them applied in earnest. The headmaster finally surrendered his position when a fireman took over. Only Ian Townsend, the worst of a bad lot in the junior school, dared make a joke of the fireman's efforts to revive Eric with mouth to mouth resuscitation.

Ordinary measures of time seemed incapable of calculating the interval during which the fireman laboured. Surely we all must have continued breathing but I had no recollection of it. Few of the boys, if asked, would have confessed to praying, yet all of us at one level or another hoped, even prayed, for the man to succeed. It would not be so. When the fireman finally abandoned his efforts and Eric Ratley's lifeless form disappeared into one of the school vans, it seemed almost impossible to abandon the fiction that all this had just been part of the drill.

Chapter 2

By DAY'S END THE PICTURE had become a bit clearer. The fire, for all the excitement it produced, had been largely confined to a single classroom, that of history teacher Geoffrey Hanshaw. Ratley, according to the headmaster, had died of smoke inhalation rather than actual burns. The discovery of a gasoline can in the burnt-out shell of the classroom led the headmaster, without awaiting the report of the fire marshal, to order a full locker inspection. While the boys waited in the chapel, some more apprehensive than others, a crew of six teachers went through every locker.

The locker area presumably did not appear on the itinerary of the school tour. Occupying a dark, concrete-walled area in the lower level of the school just past the gymnasium, the lockers had been installed as an afterthought when the spartan dorm rooms proved to offer insufficient space for students' belongings. In an open area beside the lockers sat a barber's chair, the previous headmaster having determined that it made more sense to bring a barber to school than to transport the boys to the nearest town offering such services.

I drew Corinne Hanshaw, the English teacher, as my partner, and as we went through the section assigned to us, she answered my question as to why none of the lockers had locks.

"You want the public reason, Axel, or the real reason?"

"I guess I'll have time for both," I said as I looked down the rows of lockers.

"According to the headmaster, locks would betray the ideal of a community based on mutual trust."

"So has the ideal been working?"

"Humph! You've been here only a few weeks, Axel, but would you trust any of these boys?"

"So what's the real reason?"

"They tried using combination locks during the Old Man's last year as headmaster."

"Before Harold came."

"That's right."

"What about the ideal of mutual trust?"

"Even the Old Man had begun to recognize that our current crew of sociopaths wasn't the community of young gentlemen that he envisioned when he built the school in the 30s."

"Did the locks help?"

"They only made things worse. Boys would tell each other their combinations in order to lend books or notes, and then complain when something went missing. But that wasn't the worst of it. To save time, a lot of boys would just hook the locks in the holes without actually locking them. Then some joker would switch the locks and activate them so that we'd have to come down here to compare locker serial numbers with the master list to sort things out. It was a complete mess."

Corinne's voice contained a note of bitterness that I assumed went beyond frustration with the boys' locker antics. As I looked at her light brown hair, slightly greying, and trim figure, I could imagine that Corinne had once been an attractive woman. Was teaching at Galton enough to kill one's spirit?

Our search turned up nothing more incriminating than contraband food. Corinne told me about the flourishing black market in junk food, with a doughnut going for two to three dollars. One enterprising chap cleared enough by selling food at a 500% mark-up to buy two skateboards.

Teachers at the other end of the locker area discovered small quantities of marijuana and some pornographic magazines, which they simply confiscated. There was no point in trying to prosecute: the boys' lawyers (and you could be sure that their parents would engage lawyers) would simply say that someone else had placed the material in the locker, and you'd have no way of proving otherwise.

Peter Perkins's locker was a different matter. Perkins, I learned from Corinne, subscribed to *Soldier of Fortune* magazine and kept his classmates spellbound with methods for creating home-made bombs, producing weaponry and killing adversaries. Given the nature of our student body, it seemed miraculous that nobody had followed up on

Peter's provocative suggestions. I had visions of students—or worse, teachers—hanging upside down in a Malayan mantrap, but Corinne assured me that so far, it had all been just talk.

Perkins openly expressed his desire to burn the school down and boasted about his pyromaniacal exploits at previous schools. In his locker had been discovered a crude cartoon of a boy with an enormous cock urinating on a burning school, along with a receipt from a local gas station for a ten-gallon can of gasoline. Before day's end, Peter Perkins had been expelled and his parents summoned to remove him from the school. Evidently the headmaster was not bound by strict rules of evidence when it came to expulsion. Each boy's parents having paid for compulsory tuition insurance, the school suffered no financial consequences of a disciplinary dismissal.

Chapter 3

PERHAPS BECAUSE OF GALTON'S GEOGRAPHICAL isolation and the intensity of its regimen, the staff banded together with an unusual degree of loyalty, cooperation and compassion, in contrast to university life of individual professors on individual islands. On Labour Day weekend, before the start of classes, the entire staff gathered to renovate the cabin by the lake. The kitchen staff catered lunch and the "work day" took on a festive flavour in part, I suspected, because we could see real results from our labours. Some took eagerly to the task of re-shingling the roof and scampered up the ladders. Not for me! At one point a tool needed to be taken to the roof. I carried it up the ladder and handed it to one of the roof crew, but the very thought of actually climbing around on the inclined surface made me dizzy.

I opted instead for painting the interior, a task that I shared with Julie Woodrow, the school librarian, nurse and tennis coach. I don't care much for painting, but at least I could stand on solid ground, and the prevailing atmosphere of conviviality would have made just about any chore tolerable.

Julie and I finished our task before the others, and when I asked Corinne if she'd like assistance, she suggested instead that I take Julie for a canoe ride around the lake. I didn't wait for other tasks to materialize but located the canoe, and with Julie's assistance, launched it.

As I paddled lazily in the afternoon sun I enjoyed looking at Julie's chestnut-coloured, pony-tailed hair—tucked through the opening of a white baseball cap—and her lithe, athletic body, dressed in khaki shorts, deck shoes and a Galton T-shirt. I liked listening to her infectious laugh as I described my misadventures in previous jobs. I took pleasure in her ironic sense of humour and irreverent attitude toward regulations and the self-important people who promulgated them. And I confess that I appreciated her decision to sit facing me on a pillow on the bottom of the canoe so that we could converse easily, when we both knew that she could easily have matched me as a canoeist had we been aiming for speed.

"I've never had an experience like this," I told Julie, "with all my colleagues gathering together and enjoying each other's company."

"Don't university music departments ever get together for cocktails?" Julie asked, with the faintest hint of mockery.

I thought about the antagonistic souls at Monongahela University and shuddered. "It's hard to organize a social event when half the group isn't on speaking terms with the other half," I said.

"Faculty meetings must have been quite an experience."

"You have no idea." I recounted a few stories then returned to my first idea. "Why doesn't this kind of thing happen more often? These people clearly have fun together."

"Wait until the boys arrive," Julie said ominously. "Each period lasts only forty minutes, so a free period barely gives you enough time to photocopy a test or telephone about a missing book order or go down to the storeroom for more chalk."

"I understand the days are too full, but suppose we took one Friday evening a month and got everyone together?"

"Only way you could do that would be to put it on everybody's schedule. Why don't you suggest it to the headmaster?"

We passed the rest of the afternoon in pleasant conversation under a sun that provided warmth rather than oppressive heat. Poetic words like "halcyon" ran through my head, and I wondered what my life would be like once the actual teaching began.

Harold Bromley liked the idea of staff outings—said he wished he'd thought of it himself—and offered me a budget of $50 a month to cover incidental expenses. So at the end of September, as Galton was enjoying a bit of Indian summer weather, the entire staff gathered for a softball game on the village diamond. The teachers barely numbered enough players for a single team but when we invited the maintenance and secretarial staffs and their spouses to augment our ranks we had more than enough players to cover all the positions (with an extra "shortstop" to play short right field).

The elaborate athletic facilities seemed all out of proportion for the village, and I suspected some kind of provincial boondoggle at work. The village had neither an elementary nor a high school, nor did it support any professional or even semi-professional teams. Yet the field came equipped with full lighting, bleachers and refreshment stands in addition to the usual backstop and fence. I learned that the field received constant use during the summer with kids playing during the day and informal leagues of adults in the evening: a fine illustration of the principle, "if you build it, they will come." Happily, by September the field received only sporadic use and I was able to reserve it for our band of irregulars.

Dolly Canfield, the school bursar, produced the game's winning run. With men and women equally divided between the teams, it's often the quality of the women's hitting and fielding that decides the issue. Our team managed to turn two double plays, thanks in part to the slowness of the opposing runners, but we were still down by a run in the last inning when Dolly came to bat. A large woman of indeterminate age—she had been engaged by the Old Man in his later years—Dolly had no pretensions about her athletic ability, but neither would she accept the label of an "easy out."

Carl Kitchener, the assistant headmaster, pitching for the other team, both looked and acted the part. As head of outdoor education he spent more hours under the sun than anyone except the maintenance crew, and his normally blond hair had been further bleached by exposure to the summer sun. One couldn't have called him over-competitive in a derogatory sense, but he took everything he did very seriously, which accounted for our team being on the short end of the score.

Carl would not have deliberately given Dolly an easy pitch, either because she was a woman or because, as bursar, she cut his monthly pay check. More likely he was tiring toward the end of the game in a less familiar sport—hockey was his forte. One way or another, when the ball came right across the middle of the plate Dolly belted it over the left fielder's head driving in two runs, to our delight and the grudging admiration of our opponents. She was the belle of the barbecue following the game.

Chapter 4

IN MANY WAYS THE START of a new school year in September is the same everywhere. Teachers hope, despite previous painful experience, that this year they will actually get through the syllabus. Students hope, against all logic, that they can pursue the same study strategies as in years past and yet achieve higher grades. This year Galton students took particular interest in testing their new teacher, Axel Crochet, engaged to teach math and start a choral music program. At my interview, Harold Bromley had told me that he was looking for someone who could also lead rock-climbing. When I explained my fear of heights, he shrugged his shoulders, said "Two out of three isn't bad," and signed me up for the standard one-year contract allowing me to serve the school "at the pleasure of the headmaster."

The boys had no idea just how new their teacher was, for in fact I had never taught school before, having spent my previous career in the groves of academe. But denied tenure at Fleur de Lis University, and unable to locate a position as a musicologist anywhere else, I had used an undergraduate double major in mathematics and music and a masters degree in information science in support of my new career. Lacking a teaching certificate I could never teach in a public school, but my credentials proved adequate for a private school such as Galton, and having a doctorate in musicology, though of no practical use, looked good in the school's faculty roster.

For a scholar accustomed to teaching six hours a week, life at Galton came as something of a shock, since one might easily do that amount of teaching in a single day, especially if you counted in the school sports commitments. A typical morning saw me up at 6:45, to the dining hall for breakfast at 7:30, playing the piano for and helping to keep order in chapel at 8:05, teaching 10th-, 11th- and 12th-grade math classes in the first three periods, overseeing the Student Bank during break (while other staff members enjoyed coffee), spending a free period or two, then attending tutorial period, a daily meeting with half a dozen tutees and anyone else with questions about math.

Dinner came in the middle of the day, a full meal frequently including a roast that the teacher sitting at each table was expected to carve. Teachers were also expected to maintain a minimal level of table manners. There seemed to be no level beneath which two or three boys at my table could not sink, so at nearly every meal I had at least one boy standing by the wall, Galton's standard punishment for mealtime infractions.

The afternoon brought two more periods, alternating between 9th- or 10th-grade computers and 5th-7th-grade music. At 2:55 I would change for sports, train with the cross-country team, shower towards 5, eat supper at 6, and spend an hour practicing the piano, except for Monday, when I met with the Math Club, or Thursday, when I directed the newly-formed all-school chorus. I prepared classes until ten, with a half-hour break to drive down to the village to pick up the New York Times. Barely enough sleep, then the same routine again.

Saturday classes occupied me in the morning, followed by dinner and various activities, leaving me perhaps a couple of free hours in the afternoon. Saturday nights, when I wasn't on duty, I would drive a van-load of 10th graders to the movies as a reward for those who had done well on tests (or shown improvement on retests), leaving at 5:30, returning around 10:30. (This represented positive reinforcement; negative reinforcement for uncompleted assignments took the form of academic detention between 5 and 6. This sounded good on paper but didn't always work in practice, and I had heard one staff member muse on the desirability of reinstating corporal punishment.)

Sundays, despite the absence of a set routine, remained no less charged. Mid-September brought the 10 kilometre Terry Fox Run in the rain (Galton maintained a non-recognition policy with respect to weather); late September saw me co-leading a day trip to the Montréal Art Museum, followed by responsibilities as Master-on-Duty.

The MOD regime, falling every sixth day or so, put one in charge of the school, leading the chapel service, saying grace at meals, responding to crises large and small, making sure that the younger boys took showers after sports, etc., a duty extending until 9:30 except on Tuesdays (the Senior Housemaster's night off), when it ran till 11:00, and on weekends, when it seemed to drag on interminably.

Perhaps the most disorientating part of life at Galton for me lay in the inadequacy of hitherto reliable coping skills. In the past I depended on sheer energy to carry me through difficult challenges, like Horse in *Animal Farm*, whose response to trying situations was to pull harder. In the end, of course, he simply couldn't pull any harder, and died. I tried not to dwell on that aspect of the analogy. Galton swallowed all your energy and asked for more. In the past I counted on careful organization to relieve deadline pressures. At Galton it took maximum efficiency just to put me a little behind.

Teaching math requires a fair amount of writing on the blackboard, which the 11th graders recognized as a splendid opportunity to disrupt the class by throwing pennies at each other across the room. University students never behaved that way and I found the behaviour thoroughly disconcerting. I experimented unsuccessfully with keeping an eye on the students while writing behind my back or over my shoulder. And of course the boys were not above time-honoured tricks like placing thumbtacks on my chair while I wasn't looking.

Then there were the boys—not part of the class—who thought it amusing to stand outside the classroom and kick the metal door with all their might, scuttling around the corner before I could come out to identify them. I put up with this kind of nonsense without complaint, but I began to regard math teaching as a term of penance for past misdeeds or advance payment for rewards in the hereafter, and wondered if there weren't some easier profession to which I could flee.

When Carl Kitchener, the assistant headmaster, got wind of what was going on he chided me for not approaching him. "We're all in this together, Axel. This is the boys' idea of hazing, and every new teacher gets subjected to it, but that doesn't mean you have to take it lying down." The next day Carl concealed himself in the hallway, nabbed the perpetrators red-handed, and made them spend an afternoon hour kicking soccer balls about the perimeter of the field. The boys in class still threw pennies but at least the kicking stopped.

My fiercest antagonism came from Sylvain Desrochers, an 11th grader who seemed to have taken me on as a special project to give purpose to his life by adding misery to mine. A short but wiry lad, Sylvain had a long thin nose and sharp chin that made me think of a fox, not the charming foxes of French literature but the fox who kills your chickens and then laughs at your efforts to stymie him. Sylvain seemed to regard the back corner of the room as his private domain and performed whatever misdeed was necessary to be consigned there, from which vantage point he would continue to heckle me and the rest of the students in the class.

I responded to the boys' disruptions by trying to make the class more interesting. Once a week we would take a break from the usual routine of finding yet one more method for factoring polynomials to take up math problems not in the curriculum. I tried to show students how mathematical thinking can help with real-life problems by showing them what they could do when they got stuck: try a special case; alter the problem to one they could solve; simplify; draw a diagram; look for a pattern—but a discouraging number of students had already given up on themselves and refused to engage their minds. Their attitude toward problems of all kinds—not just math problems—appeared to be to let someone else do it (their parents seemed to have dealt with all their problems so far), or else to hope the problem would simply go away.

One boy turned up every day during extra-help period. "I can't learn anything in class," he said, and who could blame him? I kept devising different ways of looking at a question until I found one that worked. To present inverse proportions, for example, the textbook invoked the pressure/volume relationships in a gas. This may have worked for students who liked chemistry but for the rest of us (I always hated chemistry), it seemed easier to think of the elevation of a hot air balloon in terms of the number of sandbags it carried, or the value of a car in terms of its age, though I had to abandon that example when one student told about vintage cars and their *appreciating* value. But I despaired of getting students to remember the quadratic formula.

My sole satisfaction came with the two students in my 12th-grade calculus class, one the Head Boy of the school, the other a bright chap from Japan who did fine so long as we stuck to mathematical symbols. He had no trouble differentiating the formula for the volume of a sphere in terms of its radius, but I found his next question a trifle unnerving: "What's a sphere?"

Chapter 5

As MASTER ON DUTY ON the Saturday before Halloween I finally had an opportunity to take stock of my first six weeks at the Galton School, an existence that had now become as familiar to me as the endlessly turning wheel of a hamster cage to its furry occupant. On weekends the deserted school office served as centre of operations for the MOD and, sitting in the school secretary's accustomed spot, I surveyed the school from her perspective. A large window onto the hallway gave her a view of anyone entering or leaving the building, with advance warning coming from another window looking out onto the parking lot and beyond that a view down the hill to the playing fields. A locked door behind the desk led to the headmaster's office.

Just after lunch most of the boys signed out food and lantern oil for overnight stays in the huts scattered through the woods around the school. In the old days, when the Old Man taught most of the classes and his wife served as the entire kitchen staff, the hut system provided the couple with one evening a week to themselves. The present headmaster had seen no reason to alter the tradition.

Of course, this being Galton, no interval of time could be entirely uninterrupted. In mid-afternoon a boy came to me complaining that his Frisbee had landed on the school roof and demanding to know what I intended to do about it. I fetched a ladder and held it while he retrieved the errant disk, climbed down and went back to play. On reflection, I thought that perhaps this had not been the most prudent course of action, so when two more boys came to the office a little later, both claiming to have lost Frisbees on the roof—and presumably envious of their companion's exploit—I told them they would have to wait for the maintenance crew on Monday and they went away crestfallen.

Meanwhile boys serving detention were doing schoolwork, or at least appearing to do so, at tables in the dining area of the main building. With Parents Weekend but seven days past I had no occasion to locate some boy for familial visitors. In a school occupying six hundred acres, such searches could often consume a fair bit of time, especially if the boy in question was not eager to see mom and dad.

I recalled my meeting with Eric Ratley's parents a week or so before his death. One evening Mr. Ratley and his estranged wife took me out to dinner in the village to discuss their son's problems, which included getting regularly beaten up by all and sundry. The dinner lasted more than four hours, ample time to hear more than I ever wanted to about Mr. Ratley's occupation—selling bubble gum, soft drinks and refrigerators to Inuits. ("You may laugh," Corinne had told me beforehand, "but he has become extraordinarily well off as a result of this peculiar enterprise.")

Over dinner I listened more times than I thought possible to Mr. Ratley's favourite adjective ("mind-boggling") and forced more smiles than I could have imagined as the former Mrs. Ratley described her son, over and over again, as "just a happy-go-lucky guy," a phrase that betrayed a colossal gift for denial. I recommended that Eric undertake some kind of assertiveness training in order to break out of his scapegoat role.

Returning to school at around nine, we met with Eric himself, who complained that everything in his dorm and book locker was constantly being ripped off, to the point that he had to keep a single pen and pencil on his person at all times since the other boys wouldn't let him keep even a pencil case. The parents seemed a bit shocked. "Welcome to Galton," I felt like saying, the school where returning students routinely asked new boys, "What school did you get thrown out of before you came here?" This is where I worked.

I used the afternoon hours to correct old math quizzes and create new ones. Dinner proved to be an unusually quiet repast with so many of the boys "roughing it" in the huts. I actually had time for a bit of reading during the evening. My thoughts turned to Julie, visiting her sister in Ottawa. Since our canoe ride Julie and I had become close companions. I found in her a sympathetic ear as I tried to find my footing in an unfamiliar situation. She found in me a kindred spirit in appreciating the ridiculous aspects of our role as teachers cum zookeepers. I had turned to her to regain my balance after the strange encounter with the Ratley's.

Julie had smiled when she greeted me at the door of her apartment.

"More tales of woe?" she asked with a mischievous smile. She invited me in and we sat on the sofa as I described my evening.

"What is it with these parents?" I asked.

"At least they seem to care about their son," she said. "For a lot of parents Galton serves as a dumping ground for kids they don't know how to handle."

"Parents Day didn't produce much of a crowd."

"No. Some of the boys won't see their parents until Christmas, when a lot of parents will be counting the days until we take over again."

I asked Julie whether she knew anything about Sylvain Desrochers, my 11th-grade nemesis.

"He's an interesting case," she said. "He regards Galton as refuge more than exile, like many of the boys."

"Problems at home?"

"His father is an alcoholic who seems to take pleasure in abusing his son. The mother couldn't stop the abuse but she knew one of the trustees and managed to get Sylvain here on a scholarship."

"Galton has scholarships?"

"Not many, but Sylvain is actually a very bright kid."

I recalled our lesson on the Triangular Inequality, which says that in any triangle the sum of the lengths of two sides must be greater than the length of the third. A bit of play with toothpicks or straws will show that to be the case: if the sum of two sides doesn't exceed the third the whole thing just collapses. But students tend to find the principle too abstract so I introduced the concept by asking them to draw a triangle with sides of 5, 8 and 14 units. A few scoffed at my effort to engage them and just sat at their desks. Some others just drew any old triangle and then labelled the sides 5, 8 and 14. "No," I insisted. "The triangle has to be drawn to scale." A few actually worked at it, using rulers and measuring lines until they convinced themselves that it couldn't be done. Sylvain remained, as usual, apart from the fray in the rear corner of the classroom. But when the forty-minute period ended and a new class of math students came in, Sylvain rushed to the front of the room and told them in the tones of a experienced huckster, "I'll give $5 to the first person who can draw a 5, 8, 14 triangle to scale," a wager that incited a flurry of activity among normally unengaged boys.

"Given the nature of the students here, don't you find it incredible that there's no psychologist on staff?" I asked.

"I've often wondered the same thing," Julie said. "I think the answer lies with the trustees."

"How's that?"

"They're the ones who control the budget and they're all Old Boys who still think of Galton as a university-preparatory school the way it was in their day."

"So you don't think they know what we're dealing with?"

"Axel, they don't want to know. Let me tell you about the so-called meeting we had with the trustees last year when they came for a tour of the new facilities."

"What was new?"

"The computer room, new baskets for the gym, new rope tow for the ski slope—not really a lot to show but it gave Harold a chance to meet with the trustees here for the first time since becoming headmaster."

"So what happened?"

"Each of the teachers was instructed to put up displays of student work. We used the library conference room to show off the model castles that some of the boys had built for a unit on the Middle Ages."

"And the trustees were impressed?"

"They loved it—they kept talking about how much they would have enjoyed having such a nice lounge and dining hall when they'd been students here, not to mention the computers."

"So when did you meet to discuss the problems of our current clientele?"

"Are you kidding? It never came up. The headmaster needs the trustees to continue raising money to keep Galton in business. How enthusiastic do you think they would be if they knew what the place was really like?"

"Didn't anyone speak up?"

"I heard Corinne talking to one of the trustees, who seemed a bit confused. 'We'd known that Galton had one or two problem kids,' he said, 'but you're telling us that nearly all the students have psychological, social, or learning problems?' 'Yes,' Corinne answered, 'and often all three.'"

"Did he believe her?"

"He wouldn't even look at her statistics on reading levels. He just mumbled something about the students being 'basically good kids' and went on to talk with someone else."

Our conversation had begun in Julie's living room, a rather plain affair whose institutional furnishings suggested that she hadn't made many changes in the more or less public area of her dwelling. The school nurse part of her position required her to occupy an apartment off the kitchen and she was evidently accustomed to administering first aid of one sort or another at odd hours. I recognized a large flat bowl, hung ornamentally on the wall, as being in the same style as the pottery I had seen at the headmaster's welcoming party, which he described as the work of local artist. On the adjacent wall a copy of an etching depicted a field with a picket fence. "Good fences make good neighbours?" I had asked her at our first visit. "Or a reminder to keep one's boundaries in good repair," she had replied. I thought of the contrast between the matter-of-fact, even somewhat impersonal, manner Julie preserved during school hours and the uninhibited, even impish, attitude she displayed when we were together.

As our conversation moved from the problems of the school to the pleasures of our relationship the venue had shifted to Julie's bedroom, which seemed sybaritic by contrast. What appeared to be silken fabric hung from the centre of the ceiling to the walls, effectively erasing the room's stark right angles. Other richly-coloured fabrics hung over a portable screen in one corner and a nearly full-length mirror tilted on an elaborate wooden base beside the closet. The bed cover featured intricate patterns in red, black and gold. A large Moroccan electric lamp over the bed set the theme for smaller candle-powered lamps of vaguely Mediterranean design on the bureau top and bed tables.

Julie caught my look of amazement. "I actually made it to Morocco one summer after grad school," she said. "Some of the silks come from there. The lamps I had to search for in Montréal." She lit the candles in the small lamps then turned out the overhead lamp; an unearthly blue light suffused the air.

"Is that a belly-dancer's belt I see hanging on the screen?"

Julie giggled. "I took a few lessons when I got back from Morocco but I haven't worn that belt for a long time."

I had taken off my shirt and lay on the bed, taking in this vision of voluptuary delight, and was so engrossed with our exchanged words that I scarcely realized that I was half-dressed while Julie lay naked on top of me. Time to let the conversation drop.

Chapter 6

When I entered Dolly Canfield's office early in November to pick
up dinner money for the grade 5-7 choir trip, I could see why so many
of the boys considered her as a substitute mother or grandmother. The
chocolate chip cookies on a plate near the door had clearly come from
her oven, not from a box, and Dolly's manner indicated a genuine
interest in whatever you had to say, as if she regarded visitors to her
office to be guests rather than intruders.

The filing cabinets I'd expected to see dominating the room instead
seemed deliberately to have been stowed in an out-of-the-way corner.
At stage centre sat Dolly's desk, positioned so as to offer a view of
whoever passed her door. Bowls of candy occupied the corners of the
desk nearest the visitor, who sat in a comfortable chair rather than a
utilitarian piece of institutional furniture. Framed pictures of skiers
and mountaineers seemed aimed at an adolescent male—rather than
adult female—audience, as did the collection of baseball caps hanging
from the branches of a coat-rack. The only concession to femininity I
could discover was the yellow sweater hung over the back of Dolly's
high-backed swivel chair.

"So your choir's already touring, eh?" Dolly asked with only a gentle
hint of disbelief. It took me a moment to figure out the complicated
pattern of widths in the black and white stripes of her blouse. Dolly
wore her hair up in one of those elaborate coiffures whose secret I have
never understood.

"Command performance," I said. "The headmaster evidently wants
to justify my salary to the trustees. We're singing a few numbers for a
gathering in Montréal."

"You must be a wonder-worker to turn some of these little rascals
into choristers!"

"I had a lot of help," I said. "Harold suggested I'd have better luck getting the kids to sing than trying to teach them music theory or appreciation."

"Sound advice, I'd say."

"But after a week I was ready to throw in the towel, there being no way I could conduct a choir, accompany them at the piano, and maintain order at the same time."

"So what did you do?"

"I went to Harold and told him I couldn't cope. 'No need to apologize,' he said. 'I wouldn't want to face that group singlehanded myself.' So he called in backup in the form of Gloria Kitchener."

"Good move," Dolly said. "The boys call her the Blond Witch."

"Well, she's made all the difference in our rehearsals. She sits at the back of the class with her metre stick and when anyone starts to get out of line she doesn't even need to wave it in the air: she just casts a glance at the miscreant, raps her ruler once on the floor, and the disturbance stops before it even gets started."

"That's what a reputation will do for you, Axel," Dolly said. "You can be sure that Gloria's metre stick has rapped a few knuckles in her science classes. Some lessons the boys learn fast."

Dolly pushed the plate in my direction and I happily accepted. I'm a pushover for chocolate chip cookies.

"Of course I don't reckon they come to her for advice the way they do to you," I said.

Dolly smiled. "You have to remember, Axel, that I don't have to teach the boys. And in here it's just one to one—there's no question of keeping order."

"But still—I don't think at most schools the bursar's office would be a source of solace."

"I daresay you're right," Dolly laughed.

"You know, I've been thinking about Eric Ratley—I met with his parents shortly before his death, and his mother struck me as completely clueless. Did you ever serve as substitute mom for him?

"Oh, poor Eric! I can't tell you the number of hours he spent in here. I sometimes put him to work filing for me—he was so eager for someone to talk to."

"I guess being a loner helped contribute to his death," I said.

"How do you mean?"

"Well, when there's a fire drill people look around to be sure everyone leaves the building, but nobody looked out for Eric. Where was he found, anyway?"

"Harold said he discovered him in a corner of the library," Dolly said. "I guess Julie must have been wearing her nurse's cap that day."

The passing bell sounded in the corridor, followed by the commotion of boys changing classes, but I had another question I wanted to ask Dolly before returning to the fray.

"What about Peter Perkins?"

"He's definitely one disturbed lad," Dolly said, "but I have trouble seeing him as a simple arsonist."

"Why do you say that?"

"The term is too prosaic for Peter. He would have liked 'pyromaniac' better."

"Did he ever do any large-scale damage?"

"I keep forgetting you don't know all the boys' records. Yes, 'large-scale damage' would definitely describe the situation at his former school. But that's just what bothers me."

"What's that?"

"Peter made no secret of his intention to burn Galton down, but considering his experience and cunning, it just doesn't seem likely that he would have been content to destroy a single classroom. He had much more grandiose ambitions."

"But the evidence …"

"Yes, there's that. Well, I hope he's happier where he is now than he was here. Galton is a hard enough place for the stable-minded and even harder for boys like Peter."

I gathered the envelopes into which Dolly had placed the meal money for each of the choir members and made my exit.

Chapter 7

LATE IN NOVEMBER, WHEN THE school dispersed for Adventure Week, I found myself as trail-sweeper in a White Mountain backpack trip led by Carl Kitchener. A former professional hockey player, Carl also had some kind of military background; the boys maintained that he had been in the CIA and Carl evidently found it advantageous not to deny the rumours. His motto "Always forward," which may have served him well in sports and spookdom, seemed less well suited to leading a band of perfect tenderfeet on a trek that included what the guidebook described as "the most difficult mile of the Appalachian Trial."

Up at 5:30 a.m. on Sunday, we actually left as scheduled at 6, Carl having insisted that the boys load their packs into the van the night before. Breakfast at McDonald's outside Montréal and a midday meal in Colebrook provided refuge from a driving rain, unpromising weather in which to begin a backpacking expedition. We drove slowly toward the trailhead, hoping that the rain might let up, but to no avail. So thirteen boys and two leaders hoisted packs onto shoulders and strode off into the woods.

Almost immediately we encountered an unexpected obstacle: the rain-swollen river had covered all the usual fording rocks, leaving no recourse but to take off our socks, replace our boots, roll pant legs to the knees, form a human chain, and wade through the icy water. Emerging from the river after twenty minutes as anchor man Carl, wearing famed Peter Limmer boots, emptied the water and had dry feet for the remainder of the trip. For the rest of us, it was three days of wet feet.

Trial by cold followed hard upon trial by water. The rain turned to snow and soon the golden carpet of the forest floor was completely covered in white. The footing turned treacherous and some became frustrated to tears by their unaccustomed burdens. Bringing up the rear I had to pick up items that escaped from badly-fastened packs: frying pans, shoes, tent pegs, flashlights.

At last we stumbled with relief into Carlow Col Shelter. Abandoning the plan to pitch three tents, we squeezed all fifteen into the twelve-man shelter. Carl insisted on doing all the cooking for the two of us and I had no complaints about our steaks, but many of the boys crawled, dinnerless and dejected, into their sleeping bags to escape from a waking nightmare. Even Sylvain, normally full of remarks putting down whatever activity he was engaged in, seemed unusually subdued.

Morning brought the eerie sight of ice-clad tree branches and a snow-bedecked landscape. Boys who had carelessly left their boots outside the shelter had to force their feet into shoes rigid with ice. Huddled inside, reluctant to emerge from the modest protection of the shelter, they watched a Canada jay nibble at an abandoned steak and finally fly off with the whole thing. Amid sounds of disgruntlement we broke camp and headed up the mountain under a shower of snow melting from tree branches. As the day wore on, and the distance between vanguard and rearguard increased, I alternately cajoled, encouraged or tongue-lashed tearful teenagers convinced that they could not take another step.

Afternoon brought views of incredible loveliness—autumnal oranges, red and yellows viewed unconventionally from above, with range after range of mountains extending into the distance and snow-clad Mount Washington rising majestically over all. Some who during the morning had been ready to abandon trip, comrades and life itself found new energy after lunch and exclaimed over the unfamiliar sights. Others, who had already pushed themselves to their imagined limits, now seemed defeated by the new ordeal of treading over treacherous icy rocks and fields of deep mud. By the time we at the rear had crossed the summit of Goose Eye Peak and descended to Full Goose Shelter, there was just enough time to cook supper before nightfall and an early bedtime.

In contrast to the exhausted boys, soon silenced by sleep, Carl, apparently invigorated by the exercise, seemed happy to sit up talking by the campfire. Unconstrained by Galton's usual tight time limits, Carl gladly answered my questions about the origin of the school. Light from the fire made his boyishly blond hair look almost orange. The scar at one side of his mouth, far from detracting from his rugged good looks, seemed rather to enhance them.

Galton was founded by the Old Man, who built the school with his own hands in 1939 and served as its original headmaster. Until this year, he dwelled in a house in the very centre of campus, a situation reminiscent of the James Thurber cartoon depicting a nude woman (stuffed? lurking?) atop a bookcase beside which one man says to another, "And that's the *first* Mrs. Perkins." His eventual departure to a retirement home occasioned a general house shuffle, which gave Carl the central house and opened up the small house in which I lived.

The Old Man, in his 80s, had a girlfriend in Montréal, as stubbornly loyal to city life as he to the country, so once a week one of the school's maintenance workers, a monolingual Francophone, would don chauffeur's garb and drive the Old Man, a monolingual Anglophone, to the city to visit his paramour.

"But how did the school end up with its current clientele?" I asked.

"You mean sociopaths, psychopaths and general nogoodniks?"

"Well, yes."

"What's the primary responsibility of a private school headmaster?" Carl demanded.

"I don't know—present a model of academic excellence and intellectual inquiry?" I said.

"Not even close." Carl looked at me with a touch of disdain. "Fill the beds."

"Oh."

"We had some trouble maintaining our quota of boys in the 70s. Then one chap who had flunked out of every other private school in the province got turned around at Galton—I think it was our outdoor education program that did it—and that spelled disaster."

"But wouldn't that be a good thing?"

"Only on the surface. Western Psych saw our success and rejoiced to discover a place where they could send their hard cases. The Old Man couldn't afford to turn them away and the rest is history." One log slid off another sending a shower of orange sparks into the sky.

"What happened when the Old Man retired?"

Carl snorted. "Harold Bromley came in with his idea of 'no bad children.'"

"And this didn't work?"

"Are you kidding?" The assistant headmaster spoke more openly than he might have done on school property. "His liberal philosophy took a beating at the hands of malicious, street-smart criminals who, suddenly freed from the constant threat of corporal punishment, ran amok." I recalled Corinne's words one day after chapel when we discovered the hymnals scattered all over the room. "Some of them really are no-good little bastards."

"So what happened?" I asked.

"We managed to dismiss fifteen of the worst offenders—at least one is currently in jail—but we still had to contend with the likes of Peter Perkins."

"Do you think he really set the fire?"

"Who cares? At least he's gone. He did plenty of other things without managing to get caught. One excuse is as good as another."

"Was Eric Ratley the first boy to die at school?"

"So far as I know, but we had a close call last winter."

"How so?"

"You can imagine that a lot of boys try to run away from this place." I thought of Eric's attempt to create a safe haven and could easily imagine that others might prefer outright flight. "Most of the fugitives hike down to the village and then try to hitch to Ottawa. But one lad—a student from Korea—made the mistake of heading in the other direction."

"Not a smart move?"

"Going that way you head into a thousand square miles of federal forest land. As soon as we learned of his absence I headed out on snowmobiles with two of the older boys. Fortunately our chap had let one of the faculty dogs go with him so we had an extra set of tracks to follow. But we had to find him—if he'd been out overnight he would have perished." The logs had now burned to embers and rather than add new wood we decided to call it a day.

The original schedule called for us to hike over one mountain, through the Mahoosic Notch, up a steep ridge to Old Speck Mountain, then down to Speck Pond Shelter. Overcoming all his principles, Carl opted for a change in plan. On Tuesday we enjoyed a leisurely brunch and then I headed off with two members of the cross-country team, marvelling at how much more fun it was to share these mountains with the appreciative instead of constantly listening to the imprecations and complaints of the stragglers. We emerged at a logging road, changed to running shoes, and ran the several miles to the point where we'd spotted the lead van. Soon the rest of the group appeared, in high spirits over their accomplishments and relieved at the curtailment.

At the end of the excursion one 9th-grader confided that he was looking forward to going home where he would be hugged and kissed for an hour and a half. I found this touching, perhaps because of the realization that not all the boys could say the same. One chap's parents were still in Europe and many came from unhappy homes, or from parents who had sent them to Galton just to get rid of them.

Chapter 8

EARLY IN DECEMBER MY ALGEBRA class arrived at a section on word problems. A more experienced colleague had warned me that faced with word problems students would take the first two numbers they could find and perform the simplest possible operation upon them, a procedure I came to think of as "Galton math."

"We don't do word problems," my charges announced.

"I'm too old to learn word problems," one fifteen-year-old earnestly assured me.

"Nonsense," I said. "It's like this. If a farmer can plow a field in 2 hours and his son can plow the same field in 3 hours, how long will it take them to plow the field working together?" Common sense alone would tell you that two people working together would finish a job in less time than either person working separately. But no. "5 hours!" came the inevitable triumphant response, even after we'd spent a day and a half on just this kind of problem. When I gave them a test the entire class failed.

"All right," I said. "We'll concentrate on one type of problem each day for a week. We'll do three examples in class and then you'll have three to hand in as homework." At the end of the week I gave another test. Only three students passed, but all the students' scores were twenty points higher than before.

Two days later Corinne circulated a sheet indicating that my best students were reading at a comprehension rate of 50% for their grade level. Small wonder. I felt like a person putting the shot for the first time. He gives a mighty heave and the thing travels two feet. "Weight training," a friend advises. "That'll do it." So he trains with weights for an entire week, returns to the pit, and manages to put the shot two feet and two inches.

Earlier in the fall I had decorated my classroom by hanging, on the wall above the blackboards, a banner six inches high and about twenty feet long containing the first seventy-two digits of pi, the number that begins 3.14159265358. I taught my students the sentence *"How I wish I could calculate pi,"* in which the number of letters in each word stands for one digit in the succession. One morning, when I entered the room, someone had repeatedly written the words "Axel sucks" in magic marker all down the length of the banner. What was that about? Then I remembered. The previous day Joel, a 7th grader and a true math prodigy—don't ask me how he ended up at Galton—came into the room at the beginning of my 11th grade math class to announce that he had memorized all seventy-two digits shown on the banner. He turned away from the board and proceeded to recite them. Some of the 11th graders followed the numbers on the banner to check his accuracy; others couldn't understand what all the fuss was about. When he finished several boys applauded. Then Sylvain uttered an obscenity for which I made him stand in the corner.

Looking at the defaced banner I saw no choice but to pull it down. When the 11th-graders came in for class only a couple of students noticed its absence but I saw Sylvain smirking at the back of the classroom. I supposed it was nice to know that I was an on first-name basis with one of my students.

Still, Galton occasionally had its lighter moments. When Rennelle, the school seamstress, who had something of a reputation as a practical joker, approached Dolly to ask whether the buttons she'd ordered had arrived, Dolly handed her the box and told her she had to count them to be sure that we had received the proper number. "Come on!" Rennelle protested.

"Yes," Dolly said. "And from now on you're supposed to keep track of how many buttons you sew for each boy and how much thread you use so we can bill the parents accordingly."

"No way!" Rennelle exclaimed, and stomped out of the room. When Harold heard the story, he drafted an official memorandum corroborating the new "cost-effectiveness procedures," and sent it to Rennelle. Later he reported that when Rennelle stormed into his office to inquire whether he had taken leave of his senses, he had trouble keeping a straight face. The two housemasters decided to play along by requesting that Rennelle maintain separate accounting sheets by house and to indicate the actual day on which any given button was sewn.

The first major snowstorm in December brought the opening of the Galton ski hill, a novel experience for some boys. One afternoon I came out of class and found Geoffrey Hanshaw and Carl Kitchener laughing in the hallway. I asked what had happened.

"Yesterday I started the rope tow going and young Clarence, the 6th-grader from Africa, found himself on skis for the first time," Carl said.

"So his classmates taught him how to snow-plow?" I asked.

"You wish," Carl said. "Ian Townsend took him to the top of the hill, convinced him that turning was for wimps, and schussed straight down the hill with Clarence right behind him."

"But Ian's an expert skier," I said. "Clarence is lucky he didn't get killed."

"Apparently he had the time of his life. I had a hard time trying to sell him on the wisdom of skiing under control."

"At dinner I heard some of the boys call him kamikaze," Geoffrey said.

"Was he offended?" I asked.

"No way," Geoffrey said. "The kids meant it as a compliment."

One evening earlier that same week, returning home from the movies, I noticed a skunk in my backyard. I reported the incident to Julie the following evening when we had taken refuge in her bedroom from the pervasive craziness of the school. "And like any other male dodo-head you decided to take decisive action," she said with a good-natured smile that took the sting out of her words.

"No, I thought he probably had a better claim to the place than I did."

"Wise move. Last year one of the maintenance people's dogs got into a fight with a skunk just outside the front door, provoking a blast that rendered not only the dog but the entire contents of the first floor intolerable. All the food had to be thrown out, while the dog suffered the indignity of repeated immersions in tomato juice. We called it the week of the pink poodle."

"Doesn't sound as if anyone was to blame."

"Perhaps not, but two nights later a skunk managed to get into the Old Man's house. The Old Man took after it with an air rifle and the animal matched him discharge for discharge, finally giving up the ghost after the sixth volley. Needless to say the skunk, though vanquished, clearly emerged as victor. The stench pervaded the area for more than a week."

I thought of the story Corinne had told me at the softball game. Before the arrival of Harold Bromley and his two golden retrievers, raccoons learned to open the screen windows from the outside and used to roam inside the school at night, once getting into the headmaster's office, scattering papers all over the room and depositing a ceremonial offering on his desk. One time, on the eve of the headmaster's daughter's wedding reception, a raccoon got into the kitchen, found a jar of strawberries (we're talking 64-ounce containers of industrial strength strawberries here), dragged it into the dining room, already set up for the occasion, unscrewed the top, and spread the sticky fruit all over the official white carpet.

"So you haven't had any set-tos with Galton varmints?" I asked.

"Not the kind you're thinking of. My battle came with creepy-crawly things that get into people's hair. I had to treat every boy with anti-lice shampoo. In fact, that's what I was doing the morning of the fire."

"So that's the reason you didn't discover Eric in the library."

"What are you talking about?"

"That's where Harold said he found Eric."

"How is Eric supposed to have died?'

"Smoke inhalation is what they told us."

"And what does that require?"

"Smoke, I guess."

"Right. But the fire never reached the library, thank goodness. I barely have enough of a budget for new acquisitions. We could never afford to replace the books. The damage seems to have been confined to Geoffrey's classroom."

"Wouldn't there have been smoke in the corridor?"

"That's possible, but the library doors close automatically—they can't be left ajar—so we didn't get any smoke in the library.

"Do the boys use the library a lot?"

"Not as much as I'd like. When compelled to do research in the library they'll consult the encyclopedia, but most of the other books receive little use. But I have a book I'd like your help with."

"From the library?"

"Not a chance." Julie laughed as she produced a slim volume explaining how common yoga postures could be turned into uncommon sexual positions. Naturally I was happy to assist her research.

Chapter 9

THE CHRISTMAS CONCERT TOOK PLACE in the school's main lounge, a somewhat astonishing achievement under the circumstances. When Harold told me that he wanted me to start a chorus I explained the inverse relationship between the size of a choir and the quality of voices necessary to make it successful. "In that case," he declared, "we'll need the entire school." Anticipating the obvious problem of maintaining discipline he invoked his authority as headmaster to make the choir mandatory for teachers as well as students.

"But where would we put on a concert?" I asked. "The stage in the chapel wouldn't hold a dozen people, much less a hundred."

"How about here in the lounge?" Harold proposed.

"You'd have to build risers," I said.

"Show me."

I sketched a design on a piece of paper, indicating how permanent risers could fit into an oblique angle of the room, and Harold summoned the chief of maintenance and told him to drop everything else and set his crew to building risers."

"But what about the leak in the dormitory roof?" the man protested.

"Forget that," Harold said. "We need risers if we're going to have a choir."

To my surprise the risers, covered with the same carpeting as the lounge, appeared in less than a week, in ample time to hold our initial rehearsal the first week of classes. No sooner had we gotten the entire student body assembled on the risers than the boy on the end of the top riser tumbled off the edge, victim of a "domino effect" launched by one of the boys in the centre. I looked up and saw Sylvain Desrochers' mocking face, defying me to do anything about it.

Yet I discovered that music really does have charms to soothe the savage breast—and they didn't come much more savage than those of the Galton student body. Most of the boys at our Thursday night gatherings had never sung before, considered singing sissy, and wouldn't be there at all unless compelled. For the first fifteen minutes of a rehearsal they'd make as much trouble as they dared, but after awhile music began to work its spell and they found themselves participating willy-nilly, even those who preferred to grumble along an octave lower than the actual notes. By the time of the concert a fair number of them seemed to be taking well-concealed satisfaction in getting the music right and showing off their skills for their parents.

The simple program came off admirably, including a unison piece that I had composed for the group, a musical setting of a carol from Kenneth Grahame's *The Wind in the Willows*. After the concert I saw Harold Bromley happily accepting congratulations from one of the parents, though when he spotted me he hastily threw in a phrase about his sagacity in hiring "this talented young man."

The previous night I had seen Dolly sitting at the back of the lounge during our dress rehearsal. She must have spoken to the headmaster because after the concert he invited everyone to the dining area for a reception for which Dolly had evidently done all the baking: Christmas treats as well as her trademark chocolate chip cookies. Dolly looked resplendent in a long red skirt decorated with green wreaths, a matching green blouse and a red vest bordered with white snowmen. When I went over to thank her for her labours she gave me a big hug and afterwards I saw tears in her eyes. I didn't know what that was all about but was glad to have an appreciative auditor.

At the staff meeting the following morning I noticed relief on every face as the absence of the boys and the anticipation of Christmas Break meant a temporary reprieve from the constant state of stress. I recalled the fall Tutee Draft, modelled after the National Football League player draft. Each staff member had half a dozen tutees, to be met on a daily basis, whose parents had to be regularly informed concerning their sons' progress or lack thereof. Teachers were given the opportunity to protect former tutees from the draft and then the remaining students were selected, one at a time.

During the early rounds people chose the best-behaved students. Then came those with problem parents ("Your phone's going to melt down") or problem kids with generous parents ("I'll keep Ian—I can use the bottle of gin at Christmas," Geoffrey Hanshaw had said.) When we finally came to the most difficult kids some chose cannily—if your kid got expelled, that would be one less tutee.

Of course we couldn't leave for vacation before writing comments on every student in our classes. Where October remarks could be optimistic ("With a bit more effort your son could improve his performance in class"), now we had to prepare parents for spring grades ("Unless your son makes a decisive change…"). The lucky few got to write remarks like "Jürgen has consistently been one of the best students in the class. I shall sorely miss his enthusiastic participation," written of a German exchange student returning home.

But the staff bubbled over with wit and good humour. During my previous career as a musicologist I had never encountered such a supportive, friendly group. The same spirit of camaraderie prevailed during the staff party that evening, in which Harold confessed to Rennelle that the button caper had been a gag. I learned that I had been the subject of a pool betting on whether I would survive even as long as Christmas (and this among people unaware that I'd never taught school before). If only we had each other to teach instead of the boys!

Chapter 10

WE RETURNED FROM HOLIDAYS TO the sombre news of Dolly Canfield's death. Evidently the bursar had slipped on the icy front steps and broken her neck in the fall.

"A freak accident?" I asked Corinne before the memorial service.

"Not that strange," she said. "A few years back the headmaster instructed two boys from Indonesia to clean the snow off the front steps. Keep in mind that before coming here they'd never experienced snow. They thought they could make the job easier by just hosing the steps down."

"Did it work?"

"Like a charm, but you can imagine the results."

"Probably turned the whole entrance into a solid sheet of ice."

"You got it. The maintenance crew had to spend two days sanding, salting, and chipping away to remove the ice without dislodging the stones."

With the chapel filled to capacity I'd be hard pressed to accompany hymns on the small upright piano so I opened the top in order to increase the volume level, only to find that some joker had dropped a hymnal inside the instrument. I pulled it out and prepared for the service.

We called it a chapel but the room had at one time served as the venue for an operetta and there was nothing in the décor to prefer one function over the other. As a chapel, it boasted neither pews nor a cross, neither organ nor display Bible, neither communion rail nor wall hangings of ecclesiastical nature. As a theatre, it offered neither footlights nor orchestra pit, neither klieg lights nor a projection booth. Tall windows on both sides of the room offered views of the woods. The upright piano of uncertain pedigree had to take the place of either churchly or theatrical instruments. Three steps on either side led up to the stage, where a lectern had been placed for the use of those conducting the memorial service.

Dolly had been beloved by more than one generation of Galton students and the congregation numbered many Old Boys in addition to the trustees, the staff, and people from the village. The widowed Dolly had no relatives to deliver a eulogy but Corinne, representing the staff, offered a heart-felt appreciation of what Dolly had meant to the school, both as our colleague and as a friend to the boys. "Perhaps because she no longer had children of her own Dolly took on the responsibility of friend in need to the boys of the school. She kept a special eye out for the victim and the outcast, to whom she unfailingly offered a sympathetic ear." I learned from Corinne's remarks that some years earlier Dolly's only son had died from a drug overdose at the age of our older students. Apparently he had been a singer and guitarist, which may have accounted for Dolly's emotional response at the Christmas concert. No wonder she showed such empathy to boys like Eric Ratley. It would be dismissive to use a phrase like "maternal instinct" to explain the depth of feeling that Dolly shared with and inspired in others.

I found it surprising that the headmaster summoned such muted language when his turn came to speak of Dolly's place in the Galton community, describing her as "competent, kind and concerned." When he announced that "Galton has suffered a great loss," I got the impression that he was thinking about the position he would have to fill rather than any personal sense of bereavement.

After the service I complimented Corinne on her eulogy, and then asked what she thought of Bromley's remarks. "I think there's been some kind of ill feeling between them of late," Corinne said, "and Harold simply doesn't have the ability to completely conceal his emotions." Then one of the trustees approached, depriving me of an opportunity to pursue the question.

As I was gathering up my music before leaving the chapel I happened to glance at the stowaway hymnal and thought I saw something white protruding from it. I turned back the cover to reveal a business envelope bearing the name Mr. Gilbert Ratley, followed by what was presumably his address.

After supper I took the unopened envelope to Julie's apartment and told her how I had discovered it.

"So what's in the envelope?"

"Gentlemen don't read gentlemen's mail," I said a bit stiffly.

"I'm not a gentleman," she said, "and besides, the envelope isn't even sealed." She opened the flap and withdrew several sheets of paper covered with columns of figures. "What do you make of this?" she asked, passing the sheets to me.

"Afraid I'm not much good at accounting," I said. "It's got the kinds of words you'd expect: 'disbursals,' 'income,' 'subtotals,' and so on—but I don't know what it means."

"Don't give up so easily," Julie said. "Here's a column labelled tuition payments. It wouldn't be too far-fetched to think that it was generated inside this school."

"And we can probably assume that Eric put the envelope in the hymnal and concealed it in the piano."

"It certainly couldn't have gotten there accidentally. But why didn't he mail the envelope instead of hiding it?"

"Maybe it was something he wanted to be able to show his father should the need arise."

"Or something he was supposed to send his father but preferred not to. In any case, we're not going to get much further without understanding these numbers."

"I could ask Kyla Bromley. Evidently she's serving as interim bursar for the rest of the year."

"I don't know. That might not be such a good idea. How about Corinne—she teaches an accounting course along with her English classes."

I took the mysterious envelope with me and told Julie I'd let her know when I learned more.

Chapter 11

THE CANADIAN SKI MARATHON, LISTED in the Guinness Book of World Records as the longest cross-country ski tour in the world, ran approximately one hundred miles from Lachute to Gatineau, near Ottawa. The two-day tour covered ten sections, separated by checkpoints where officials punched the appropriate squares on skiers' bibs, inspected their faces for frostbite, then sent them to revivify themselves with hot water and honey, peanuts, raisins and cookies before striking out on the next section. Prizes were awarded not for times but for the number of sections covered. Those hardy souls intending to ski all five sections each day started two hours before the main pack of around 1500 skiers. A gold medal went to skiers who covered all ten sections.

The entire Galton School participated in the event with greater or lesser degrees of enthusiasm. A handful of intrepid gold-medal seekers had breakfast at 4:30 a.m. and then departed for a 6:00 a.m. start in Lachute. The rest of us ate at 6:00 in order to begin at 8:00.

The start of the race surprised me with the intensity of the cold, and a substantial contingent of the younger boys, perhaps prudently, turned around and returned to the bus. ("No way I'm staying out there, sir!") Under the old regime they would have been summarily shot. Harold, more sympathetic than his predecessor, let them warm up in the bus and then drove them to the next checkpoint. Leniency or not, each boy still had to cover two sections of the course each day.

The rest of us, endeavouring to ignore the assault of polar air on our lungs, pressed on across meadows and pastures, straight through a couple of barnyards, across frozen lakes, through woodland glades, undulating wilderness and open ridges, along an abandoned railroad right-of-way, though an occasional tiny village, and up hills of daunting gradient.

Eventually the sun broke through the clouds, warming the air to a relatively cheery zero degrees Fahrenheit. The crowds of skiers thinned out dramatically after the first checkpoint and I found that I could swing along easily at around eight kilometres an hour. The great difference between a ski marathon and a running marathon lay in the glide you could get by pushing off with your arms. I covered thirty miles the first day—a bit longer than a running marathon—and another thirty the second.

Section three ended with an extended "bobsled run." I enjoy skiing fast but I like to ski under control, a subtlety not permitted by the narrow, twisting trail. On alpine skis I might have had the opportunity to do a few check turns, and if I had mastered some of the older ski techniques, like the Arlberg turn, that one could execute on cross-country skis, I might have still have avoided disaster. Instead I found myself travelling faster and faster with nasty challenges coming at me more rapidly than I could address them. Soon I was relying entirely on instinct in trying to deal with plank-width bridges, ill-placed saplings, sudden declivities and reverse-banked turns.

I finally met with calamity on a precipitous icy spiral that Nordic skis, lacking metal edges, had no hope of negotiating. For one breathtaking moment I found myself airborne, magically delivered from the hill's abundant perils. Everything seemed unnaturally quiet, as if time had frozen like the surface from which I had taken leave. Then the spell ended and I fell heavily on an obdurate rock, producing more pain, and subsequent larger bruise, than I'd hitherto experienced in my adult life. Julie, when I recounted the misadventure, sounded surprisingly unsympathetic. "Why didn't you just sit down in a deliberate fall when you got going too fast?" she asked. "Men!"

By the time I reached the end of section eight on the second day, Geoffrey Hanshaw, waiting at the checkpoint with a school van, told me that I was his only passenger. "A few of your cross-country runners sailed by here an hour ago; the rest of the boys fulfilled their quota for the day and have already gone back to school."

As the van headed out into the wintry landscape I glanced at my chauffeur. Geoffrey Hanshaw—nobody called him Geoff—had a round face and the florid complexion of a heavy drinker. One of Galton's most popular teachers, he made history come alive, with an emphasis on battles and deeds of physical daring that appealed to his adolescent male audience. To his wife Corinne's protests that he made too free with the facts, Geoffrey responded that the important thing was to hook the students—details would take care of themselves later on.

Geoffrey walked with a cane on account of a vague unspecified military wound that inspired hair-raising speculation on the part of the boys and that excused him from obligatory physical activity such as the ski marathon. Evidently he'd been quite a jock at university, where he began his drinking career. Now overweight, and occasionally short of breath, he lived on his reputation rather than on current performance.

"I'm amazed at the organization of this event," I said. "It's not just the officials at each checkpoint. Somebody had to set one hundred miles of trail."

"That task involves many hands," Geoffrey said. "Carl Kitchener has been out with the snowmobile for the past several weeks setting and grooming the portion of the trail that crosses the Galton property, and there are many other volunteers all along the route."

"I'm impressed with those who have the stamina to complete all ten sections. It took all my strength to complete six and I'm a marathon runner."

"There's an even higher level."

"Really?"

"They call it *coureurs de bois*: skiers who complete all ten sections while carrying camping equipment on their backs to spend the intermediate night outdoors."

"You're making this up!"

"Swear to God," Geoffrey said.

"I can understand why the entrance fees are so high. I'm grateful to Harold for taking care of it for us."

"It doesn't come out of his own pocket, Axel."

"But still…"

"I know you're impressed with the way the headmaster got your risers built so fast, but I don't think you'd be wise to trust him completely."

"What do you know that you're not telling me?"

"It's all just rumour—you know how these things are—and I'd prefer you didn't quote me, but rumour has it that Bromley, let's say, awards himself a bonus in addition to his salary."

"How could you do that and not get caught?"

"Oh, you eventually get caught—that's the way the game works."

"I don't get it."

"Say a headmaster rewards himself a bit too generously."

"Embezzles."

"That's a harsh word, Axel."

"So what happens?"

"The board of trustees tells him he's been caught, awards him a glowing letter of recommendation, and sends him off to become headmaster somewhere else."

"Without warning the next school."

"Nary a whisper."

"It all sounds a bit unreal."

"Welcome to life in a private school, Axel." The light faded as we drove past snowy fields empty of crops or cattle. "Let me offer you a word of advice."

"What's that?"

"If the headmaster ever asks you if you'd be willing to get your license to drive the school bus, don't do it."

"Why?"

"You'll spend the rest of your career at Galton doing it. Only a few of us have that license. I sort of had to," Geoffrey gestured at his leg, "but you don't want to do that if you value your free time."

"What free time?" I said.

"Exactly." We went on in silence for awhile then Geoffrey said, "My craziest experience with that bus came on the way back from a school trip a few years ago. I was driving down an incline when the front wheel came off the bus and rolled ahead of us down the hill. Funniest thing I ever saw."

"Was anybody hurt?"

"Nope, but I heard a lot of jokes about gimpy bus, gimpy driver."

Chapter 12

SOMETIMES THE IMPUDENCE OF THE younger boys during our music class tested even Gloria's ability to maintain order. I'd been teaching the students "McNamara's Band" for St. Patrick's Day, and had managed to get the whole class to whistle enthusiastically after the chorus. But at one rehearsal early in February Ian Townsend had arranged with a number of his cronies to clap their hands or stamp their feet when I tried to give instructions. Naturally the rest of the class was happy to follow their lead. Or they would shout out, rather than sing, certain words in the song: "Oh the drums go BANG and the symbols CLANG the horns they blaze AWAY." On such occasions one took solace in short periods. It occurred to me later that such coordination probably had entailed a fair amount of rehearsal on the boys' part and supposed that I should take a bit of ironic pleasure that they were actually practicing for choir.

After the rehearsal I thanked Gloria for her continuing support. "It's hard to avoid words like 'monster' for some of these kids," I said.

"You're thinking of Ian."

"Yes."

"You don't know the half of it." They say that after forty, people are responsible for their own faces, since half a lifetime of using certain muscles and not others creates a distinctive, indelible pattern on one's physiognomy. I speculated that what kept the boys in order when Gloria was around was not her long blond hair, braided in the back, or even her willingness to use the metre stick, but the hard expression conveyed in her mouth and eyes. I didn't know this woman's story but I imagined that it had included a good deal of unpleasantness.

"Really?" I said.

"After Christmas Break Ian came back to school with several hundred Ritalin pills that his grandmother had found in the medicine cabinet."

"Aren't the boys supposed to turn over all medicine to Julie for distribution at mealtimes?"

"Not Ian. He sold them to his friends as downers."

"But isn't Ritalin a stimulant?"

"That's the paradoxical part. I don't really know why a stimulant calms down hyperactive kids, but it seems to work."

"What happened?"

"Eventually the affair came to light, the rest of the pills were confiscated, and the participants set to running miles at 6 a.m. One eighth-grader, when we asked him why he had taken the pill, said he thought it would help him to sleep."

"Did it?"

"I don't know. His teachers have observed that he never has any trouble sleeping in class."

"I can't imagine what it will be like to have Ian as a student by the time he hits 11ᵗʰ grade."

"It's not a pleasant prospect. He's already made a shambles of the 8ᵗʰ-grade sex education class."

"Oh no."

"When the teacher asks for questions Ian demands to know details of sodomy, bestiality and D & B."

"D & B?"

"Discipline and bondage. What's the matter, Axel. Don't you and Julie ever spend any time watching blue movies?"

I thought Gloria was going to be the one to blush, but it turned out to be me. I tried to turn the conversation back to Ian. "How does he get into this stuff?"

"His parents went on a cruise over Christmas Break, leaving Ian with well-intentioned but ineffective grandparents. I understand he spent the entire vacation watching porno films on the restricted channels."

"Why don't we get rid of him?"

"His father's a trustee."

"Oh." We began walking toward the classrooms for the start of the next period. "Seems ironic that we're stuck with a boy like Ian when it's an inoffensive misfit like Eric Ratley who dies in a fire."

"Eric the Rat," Gloria said. "I don't know why the Old Man ever admitted him."

"You mean he was here before Harold came?"

"Lord yes! Hadn't you noticed the way Harold hated him?"

"Eric didn't exactly fit the model of the Galton boy."

"Eric didn't fit any model. He hated sports, he hated classes and he hated his teachers." Gloria's intensity suggested that she had had Eric as a student in one of her classes.

"I guess Dolly was his only friend at school," I said.

"You might say that."

"You don't seem to approve."

"I shouldn't speak badly of the dead, but I'm not sure Dolly was a healthy influence on Eric."

"But nobody else would talk to him."

"Maybe she talked too much."

"How do you mean?"

"One afternoon in the fall I saw Eric coming out of Dolly's office looking as if he'd just swallowed a canary."

"Did anything come of it?"

"Not that I know of, but I recall that for the next several days Eric walked around as if he were concealing a guilty secret."

"Probably Dolly just told him he was a good kid, and the unfamiliarity of the expression left him dazzled."

As we entered our respective classrooms I wondered whether Dolly had provided Eric with the documents I had discovered in the hymnal. It didn't seem like her—for all her big-heartedness, Dolly had a pretty strong sense of appropriate behaviour. Still, it bore thinking on.

Chapter 13

I EXPECTED CORINNE HANSHAW'S CLASSROOM to be decorated with framed pictures of famous authors, with perhaps a bust of Shakespeare or Milton. Instead I saw walls covered with posters of movies made from great works of literature. A boyish smile from a still-youthful Albert Finney advertised "Tom Jones," with James Dean representing "East of Eden." Other walls contained posters from more recent films: "Oliver," "Out of Africa," "A Passage to India," and "A Room with a View." Presumably as a concession to masculine tastes Corinne had included posters for "The Godfather," "Platoon," and "The Untouchables." A VCR machine in one corner suggested that Corinne employed actual films to sustain the interest of her print-phobic students.

Corinne and I met in her room in late February to clear up the last of the fallout from what I thought of as the Great Galton Bank Fiasco. At the headmaster's request, Corinne and I had opened the Galton School Bank in the fall to give the boys a safe place to keep their money and, incidentally, to give students experience in using and running a bank. One of the 12th graders served as manager and half a dozen boys rotated as tellers. As a safeguard we set up a double-entry bookkeeping system: one book contained all the individual accounts, another recorded each day's transactions. In principle, an enlightened idea; in practice, a disaster.

The system came crashing down at Christmas, or so I discovered in January. Just before vacations, the boys would regularly take out a lot of money, more than we usually kept on hand in the school, so we had them fill out withdrawal slips a day in advance. The bank manager would tell me how much he needed and I would drive down to the village to withdraw the necessary funds from our account there. Just before Christmas vacation I gave the manager nearly $2000 in cash, which he distributed into labelled envelopes to be given to the boys on the buses to Montréal or Ottawa or Toronto, to forestall the possibility of pilferage in the school. We thought we'd covered all contingencies.

No, the manager didn't lose the money; all the envelopes went to their proper recipients. But instead of making the tellers enter the withdrawals into the two books, the manager put the slips under his pillow, whence they disappeared. From here on, the scenario turned into a Bob & Ray routine, those gifted comedians who spent four decades perfecting their parodies of every aspect of radio broadcasting.

Now the trouble with Bob & Ray routines is that they ruin your ears for regular radio. One skit had the Chemical Corn Exchange Bank of New York announcing that it had misplaced its records during a recent move. "So we're asking each of you who had accounts in the old office to come in and tell us how much money you had in the bank. We'll take your word for it. If we all play fair, we can get through this situation."

After Christmas the manager asked everybody who had taken money out before Christmas to let him know how much he had withdrawn. In this fashion he was able to account for $375. I assumed he had resolved the problem until the next time I went to the village to take out money for the boys and found out that we didn't have any.

When I questioned each boy in the school individually, I was able to account for nearly $1000, but that still left a gap of more than $800, so I went back to the books and discovered, with Corinne's assistance, that the Galton School Bank had been an exceedingly generous institution. Tellers had credited deposits instead of withdrawals, had added in the boy's *account number* instead of the amount of deposit (and since the average deposit was around $5 and there were 95 boys in the school, with accounts numbered from 1 to 95, the chances were very good that the bank lost money on virtually every such transaction), and added another $20, $30 or $40 by faulty addition or subtraction, or had made a figure that the next day's teller had misinterpreted when calculating the new balance. In some cases, a withdrawal had simply been omitted. All this came to light as I cross-checked every transaction that had taken place since September (including some of the younger boys who turned up at the bank every day to deposit or withdraw the same $3). Of course after Christmas the boys, discovering that their Christmas withdrawals had never been entered, happily withdrew the same money a second time.

After we had gone as far as we could and there was still $600 unaccounted for, Corinne and I went to the headmaster and after discussion we decided simply to bill everybody in the school $8, in addition to whatever else they owed. Students to whom I tried to explain the situation saw no reason why they should have to give back the money they had withdrawn for a second time. "It wasn't my mistake," they insisted. So we went over their heads to their parents, most of whom eventually made good their sons' debts, but some of whom, though paying $13,000 a year in tuition, made a fuss over the $8.

Once we'd rebalanced the books, we reorganized the entire system, canned the bank manager, gave the job for the entire junior house to the junior housemaster, changed banking hours, and gave the bank a room where it could keep people from crowding around and screaming in the ears of the tellers. I hoped it would work.

After Corinne and I had settled accounts in the bank to the best of our ability I was about to depart when she said, "Oh, by the way, Axel, I've been meaning to return that envelope to you."

"You mean the Ratley envelope?"

"Yes."

"Were you able to make any sense of its contents?"

Corinne gave me a funny look. "This is a bit awkward, Axel."

"Really?"

"I know you don't like to think ill of anyone—your naïveté is one of your charms—but I have to be sure of your loyalty on this before I say anything further."

"Goodness! You make it sound like a cloak-and-dagger story."

"You may not be far wrong. To be completely blunt, if it came to a choice between me and Bromley, which way would you lean?"

"I'm grateful to the headmaster for giving me a job after a year of being unemployed, and I guess I'll always maintain that gratitude, but you're my friend and that bond goes deeper in my book."

Corinne seemed to have been holding a deep breath, for she exhaled now in what I took to be relief. "I thought that was true, Axel, but I just had to be sure."

"So what's this all about?"

"The records you gave me make it clear the Bromley's been keeping two sets of books and pilfering thousands of dollars from the school."

"How did he manage that?"

"It's a little complicated, but part of it lay in not listing the activities fees that that parents pay on top of tuition. Bromley used tuition fees to cover the activities and pocketed the difference."

"And now his wife is keeping the books."

"I don't know whether Kyla is in on these shenanigans, or whether she even knows about it, but it's hard to imagine her being completely in the dark."

"I'd heard rumours about the headmaster, but you're saying this is conclusive proof."

"Oh yes. If this were to reach the board of trustees, he'd lose his job immediately."

"But the envelope was addressed to Eric's father."

"If that went to a parent—at least one who knew anything about business—Bromley wouldn't just lose his job; he'd go to jail."

"So he wouldn't just get a nice letter of recommendation and move on to another school?"

"No way! From the trustees' point of view, the headmaster looks after the boys. From the parents' point of view, the headmaster looks after their money."

"That sounds awfully cynical."

"How long have you been teaching in private schools, Axel?"

"About six months."

"You have a lot to learn."

As I left Corinne's classroom I knew who I needed to talk to next.

Chapter 14

THE AUBERVILLE THEATRE HAD MANAGED to resist the trend toward multiplexes through a combination of geography and demographics. As the only theatre in a thirty-minute radius it would never want for paying customers. On the other hand, the total population it served would never justify its expansion. An art deco sign reading "Odeon" hung above a glass-enclosed ticket booth, a convex protrusion in front of tall doors whose perimeters were outlined by parallel silver lines.

In the last year before movies went from ninety minutes in length to two hours, Auberville Theatre's twin screens each showed a double feature. You had to choose which combination you wanted to watch when you bought your ticket—the theatre frowned on efforts to see just the main film from each bill—but on occasion I had managed to do just that, switching from one side to the other under the guise of buying candy or using the restroom.

I had telephoned to make an appointment with Peter Perkins, currently employed as the theatre's projectionist, and he invited me to join him in his booth, warning me that our conversation would be interrupted every ten minutes or so by the need to change reels for one auditorium or the other. With two projectors for each of the auditoriums and several reels for each film there wasn't a lot of extra space in the booth, but Peter opened a folding chair for me against the metal cabinets that lined one wall of the cubicle. Open metal shelving on the facing wall held empty reels; a clock occupied the only available space on the wall.

Peter was wearing blue jeans and a "Poison" T-shirt and when he caught me looking at it strangely he said, "We don't have a very strict dress code in the projectionist's booth."

"Have you been working here long?" I asked.

"Every since October, sir," Peter said.

"You don't have to call me sir any more, Peter," I said. "Axel is okay."

"It feels strange, but all right."

"I've probably been here couple of dozen times since you left school," I said, "without knowing I was the beneficiary of your skills."

"With all due respect, Axel," Peter said, "I didn't exactly 'leave school.'"

"My fault," I said.

"I've seen guys from Galton here all the time but I always keep out of sight so they won't make fun of me."

"I imagine that some of them consider you something of a hero."

"Axel, I didn't start that fire."

"Given your record you make an awfully good suspect."

"Did you come down here to listen to my story or are you just going to make more accusations?"

"Sorry," I said. "Let me shut up for awhile and hear what you have to say."

"Just a sec," Peter said as he deftly made the change from one projector to the other, and then replaced the spent reel with its successor. "All right," he said. "I grant you that I've set my share of fires, and that I'd made no secret about intending to burn down Galton, but given my record, how would you rate me as an arsonist?"

"That's a funny question," I said, "but I'd have to say you are pretty good at it." I thought of the unsettling stories I had discovered when, after talking with Dolly, I read Peter's file.

"And if I announced plans to burn down the school and then torched a single classroom?"

"A pitiful effort, from your perspective."

"Exactly."

"So how come the fire didn't spread further?"

"Surely you know the school's history! When the original buildings burned down eight years ago, they were determined that such an accident would never happen again, so they used special flame-retardant materials for the panelling and cinder block walls between each room."

"And more sprinklers than I've ever seen before."

"Right. So a ten-gallon can of gasoline isn't going to go very far, even if you managed to disable the sprinkler system."

"But you thought you could overcome those obstacles?"

"Oh yeah!" Peter's face shone with an intensity that I found disconcerting. I'd observed the boy's quiet competence in managing the technical demands of the equipment he ran, but realized that he could be no less skilled in manipulating instruments of mayhem. What went on in the dark recesses of this boy's mind?

"But what about the evidence?" I asked.

"Puhleeze. It would have taken a lot more than ten gallons of gasoline for that place. I didn't plan on using gasoline in any event. But knowing what you do about me, do you really think for even a minute that I'd save all my receipts and store them in my locker?"

"When you put it that way ... And the cartoon?"

"Not a bad idea, but not my doing." My mind balked at trusting an arsonist's account of not setting a fire, but Peter's story sounded entirely plausible.

"Do you feel badly about Eric's death?" I asked.

"That's another thing. I didn't like a lot of those guys, but no way would I let anyone die. My plan was to wait for a vacation, say March Break, when the school would be unoccupied."

"I guess that way it would take longer for the fire to be discovered."

"See how easy it is to start thinking like a pyromaniac? Whoops. I have to change reels." Peter moved to the second set of projectors, serving the second of the theatre's screens, and performed his duties. I didn't think I had much more to learn, so I thanked Peter for his help and went to catch the remainder of the "B" feature.

Chapter 15

THE VILLAGE, LOCATED FIVE KILOMETRES down the hill from the school, though too small to support its own movie theatre did boast the world's largest log cabin, an enormous resort hotel on the banks of the Laurentide River. In summer months wealthy yachtsmen would tie up at the hotel, enjoy dinner and drinks while their laundry was being done, restock with food at the local grocery store and gasoline at the hotel's dockside pumps, and then resume their journeys.

You didn't have to be wealthy, I discovered, to visit the main lounge of the hotel on a weeknight and nurse a ginger ale while listening to the harpist playing from the balcony. With a good novel to complete the picture, and a well-developed sense of compartmentalization, one could manage to escape the Galton horror, at least until conscience pricked with a reminder of unmarked math quizzes.

I never saw many of the village folk at the hotel, nor did the village betray any of the usual signs of a posh hostelry in its midst: no T-shirt stores, no photo shops, no tiny shacks offering ice cream and homemade fudge. The village offered only the usual liquor store, grocery, a few small restaurants and gas station found in any small town in Québec.

Just after March Break I headed to the village's single gas station. Where Standard Oil Company stations in the States had gone to the assertive angularity of "Exxon," with its rectangular signs, Canada preserved the curved signs and rounded consonants of "Esso." The station consisted of a single pump and a tiny *dépanneur*, or convenience store. Gone were the days when you could get an oil change, or even replace an old tire or worn windshield wipers, at your local gas station.

I filled the tank of my car and then did my best to strike up a conversation with the proprietor, dressed in a mechanic's overalls, his gray hair partially covered by a long-billed engineer's cap. I had heard that the railroad used to pass through the village but that was many years ago and the tracks had long since been removed. It was nice to see some last vestige of the railroad. Business seemed slow and with nothing better to do he apparently didn't mind putting up with my imperfect French, never correcting me but cocking his head quizzically if what I said didn't make sense to him.

"As I recall, the nearest gas station going east is ten miles to Thurso and the nearest going west is about twenty miles to Hawkesbury."

"Sounds about right," he said and spat a wad of tobacco into a garbage container three feet away.

"Do you get many people running out of gas in between?"

"You mean people walking down the highway looking to lug a can of gas back to their car?"

"Right."

"Nope. Folks around here are too smart to let themselves run out of gas."

A trailer truck breezed by on the road behind me. Although the highway doubled as the village's main street, and the posted speed limit called for a maximum of 50 kilometres an hour, truckers rarely observed it except during school hours, factoring in the occasional speeding ticket as part of their operational expenses.

"How about tourists?"

"I think tourists are afraid of us. You teach up at the school, don't you?" I acknowledged the fact. "Thought I'd seen you before. I recognized your jacket. No, tourists seem to think that if they ever broke down this far away from the city they'd never be heard from again. I've never known of a tourist running out of gas, at least not at my station." He offered to check the oil in my car but I'd had an oil change only two weeks earlier and figured it was probably all right.

"But you do sell gas in cans?" I asked.

"Oh, sure. Mostly people buy gas that way for lawnmowers. Sometimes for a Ski-Doo, but in wintertime they just ride them up to the pump."

"I'm thinking about last October. You ever sell a can of gasoline to a teenager?"

"Can't recall I ever did. Not much call for gas in cans in October. But let me ask my nephew. He sometimes works the pumps when I'm not here." He shouted toward the interior of the small building. "Hey, Robert," placing the accent on the second syllable of the name.

After a few moments a younger man emerged from the building wearing jeans and a woollen plaid shirt. He moved with the slow steps of someone who preferred sports on television—preferably accompanied by an ample supply of beer—to activity on the field. "What's up?" he asked.

"This fellow wants to know whether you sold a can of gasoline to one of the kids from the school last fall."

"We don't see you folks here too often," Robert said. "I thought you had your own gasoline pump at the school."

"That's only for the maintenance vehicle. Teachers still pay for their own gas."

Robert drew closer and looked at my bright red Galton jacket. "I've never seen any of the kids stop here, but a man dressed like you came to buy gas—sometime before Halloween, as I recall. Course his jacket didn't read 'Galton Coaching Staff' like yours."

"No?"

"Nope. His said 'Galton School Headmaster.'"

I thanked him, paid for my gas, and headed up the hill.

Chapter 16

THE HOTEL, IN ADDITION TO a harpist, offered the only curling rink in the area. For our March staff outing I arranged a fondue dinner at a local restaurant followed by an evening of curling. The rink, tucked away in the lower level of the hotel, boasted two curling sheets, their white surfaces brilliantly illuminated by overhead lamps. Bulls-eyes with concentric circles of blue, red and yellow could be seen clearly through the ice.

As it turned out, I was not the only neophyte in the group, nor was I alone in finding curling to be an exquisitely frustrating game. One endeavours to launch a massive, smooth granite stone down a strip of ice in such a way that it comes to rest within a designated bulls-eye area. Each team propels eight stones and scores one point for each stone within the bulls-eye area which lies closer to the centre than the opponents' closest stone.

The frustration lies in correctly judging the launching force. The smooth surface of the ice and the massiveness of the stone combine to carry even a moderately launched stone down the length of the ice, through the bulls-eye area and on out of bounds. In contrast to bowling, our February staff outing, where you want to release the ball with enough force to knock down ten pins, curling requires a delicate touch in light of the stone's considerable weight and the near-frictionless surface. Advanced technique calls for knocking enemy stones out of position and prolonging the flight of launched stones by feverishly sweeping—and thereby melting—the ice along the stone's path. We swept like mad but I think anybody could tell we were mere tyros. Beyond the brightness of the curling area the rest of the room remained in shadow so that our every gesture, successful or more often not, took place as a kind of theatrical display.

Poor Kyla Bromley proved unable to keep a single stone in bounds all evening. I commiserated with her as we sat beside each other on the bus back to school.

"You don't know your own power," I said.

"Tell me about it!" Kyla said. Kyla was a tall woman—taller than I, as any rate—and kept her hair cut short in the style of an active athlete. Her skin was ruddy from many hours out of doors and it seemed to be her vitality that made her beautiful. 'Pretty' seemed too dainty an adjective for such a powerful woman.

"There are so many sports where your strength would be an asset: baseball, basketball, golf, bowling, tennis."

"I like all of those sports and I'm pretty good at them, if I do say so myself."

"It must be frustrating to be penalized for strength."

"'More finesse,' my teammates kept telling me. I know they were just trying to be helpful, but it only made things worse."

"It's like American tourists abroad," I said. "'They don't understand English,' one will tell the other. 'Talk louder!'"

Kyla laughed, probably for the first time all evening. "Finesse," she muttered.

"I had an experience something like that. I worked one summer as a clerk-typist in a military arsenal. I considered myself to be a pretty fair typist but this was the first time I had ever encountered an electric typewriter."

"Didn't that make it easier?"

"Not for me. This was the era before photocopiers. We had to type on a manifold consisting of an original and twelve copies: the original and a complimentary copy went to the addressee. Other copies went to every department down the line with a mandatory copy of every document going to the commanding general. The catch was that there could be no errors. If you made a mistake you had to throw away the whole manifold and start over."

"Sounds challenging."

"It was awful. I'd get to the bottom of the page, make an error and have to begin again. But this time I'd be more nervous and got only halfway down the page before making an error. Eventually it got to the point that I couldn't get through the first line: the machine seemed so sensitive that it would type by itself when I merely looked in its direction."

"What did you do?"

"The second day I discovered that the machine had a touch control that the previous typist had turned to its most sensitive setting. I turned it to the opposite extreme and got along fine for the rest of the summer."

"Maybe I could roughen up the bottom of the stones or stick some sandpaper to the surface."

"Sounds illegal but it might do the job."

"I want to thank you, Axel, for organizing these monthly get-togethers. We've been having so much fun with softball and basketball and bowling and the rest that it's hard to believe we never had anything like this before you came here."

"It's fun for me, too. And I want to thank you for the nice job you did on 'O Holy Night' at the Christmas concert. You've been so busy that this is the first time I've seen you since Christmas. We miss your voice."

"I had no idea the bursar's job would be so demanding when Harold asked me at Thanksgiving about taking it on. No, I guess it must have been after Christmas."

"Do you make chocolate chip cookies for the boys?"

"Oh, Axel, I don't have time for that. And besides, it doesn't really seem very businesslike, does it?"

The next morning I accepted an invitation to play hockey against the eleventh grade, figuring that you don't often have the opportunity make a fool of yourself in two different sports on successive days. Never having held a hockey stick before I figured I'd best travel light, so borrowed only helmet, gloves and a stick from one of the boys. We played by Québec provincial school rules, which forbid checking, so there was no great physical danger (despite Sylvain's greeting as I entered school in the morning: "I hear you're going to play this afternoon, sir. That's great! I'm going to break all your ribs.")

Happily Carl Kitchener had played professional hockey and the headmaster had played semi-pro so they could take up a lot of slack from an inexperienced math teacher on figure skates who still managed, with an assist from a junior master, to score a goal (ribs intact).

Chapter 17

OUR "WHEEL OF FORTUNE" STAFF meeting in April took place in an all-purpose function room at the rear of the library that had served as Geoffrey Hanshaw's classroom while the fire damage to his room was being repaired. Geoffrey's history lessons would have had to be exceptionally compelling to keep his students from being distracted by the panoramic view down the hill to the playing fields. The same folding tables that I had placed against one wall for a Math Fair just before March Break were now gathered at the centre of the room. We sat in chairs placed around them like Knights of the Round Table, except our table was square.

I thought of the Round Square Conference, an international association of private schools to which Bromley had somehow managed to affiliate Galton. The headmaster had given us a written description of the program and asked us for nominations. *"Round Square schools are founded on a philosophy which embraces a series of six pillars or precepts which can be summed up in the word IDEALS. They are Internationalism, Democracy, Environment, Adventure, Leadership and Service. Students at Round Square schools make a commitment to addressing each of these pillars through exchanges, work projects, community service and adventure. The overriding goal is to ensure the full and individual development of every student as a whole person through the simultaneous realization of academic, physical, cultural and spiritual aspirations."*

I had difficulty picturing cultural and spiritual, much less academic, aspirations on the part of most of our boys, but membership in the association seemed to have increased our international enrolment, for good or ill. Boys from other countries, attracted by the idea of Canada and the emphasis on outdoor activities, found themselves surrounded by juvenile delinquents. Some, like my 12th-grade calculus student, maintained an internal dignity that kept them above the fray. Others went native, so to speak, and became some of our worst offenders.

Still others wrote frantic letters home to parents certain they must be exaggerating—how could a school with such an attractive brochure, and an international clientele, really be the den of vipers their sons described? Many remained but a single year.

When the headmaster announced the meeting to give advance notice of which students would be invited not to return, I thought of several troublemakers I'd be happy to see go. But Corinne reminded me that our prospective salary increases were predicated on enrolling one or two boys above the break-even number of eighty-five, as well as a general increase in tuition.

"It's like 'Wheel of Fortune,'" observed Geoffrey. "For three thousand dollars, is Peter Perkins going to stay or go? The wheel spins … uh oh, BANKRUPT!"

"If they can't do the work," I persisted, "we should just let them repeat the grade."

"But many parents will tell you that if their boy doesn't advance to the next grade," Gloria countered, "they'll take him out."

In the event, we decided to give two boys the boot and let the fate of a dozen others ride on their final exam results. "Pass or history," as Geoffrey put it.

There'd been an accident during the afternoon but Carl, the Master on Duty, reassured us. "Ian Townsend fell, but he landed on his head so there wasn't any damage." Townsend polluted the younger boys, filled the air with foul language, and generally constituted a strong negative influence in the school. Had his father not been a trustee we would have gotten rid of him long ago. Dad understood that his kid was something of a monster but we needed to get the goods on the lad and so far he'd been clever enough to avoid getting caught. The boy looked like a cherub and sang well in the choir, but appeared to be utterly without moral values. Scary. Unfortunately neither Ian nor Sylvain made it to the dismissal list.

That evening, when I visited Julie, she had news for me. "I have a friend who teaches at Bayfield."

"Bromley's previous school."

"Right. She thinks he embezzled from them."

"Does she have any proof?"

"Come on, Axel. You know the way things are. By the time the facts filter down to the staff all that's left are hearsay and innuendo."

"But at least it suggests a pattern." I told Julie about my conversation with the gas station owner in the village.

"That doesn't really prove anything, Axel. Bromley could have been buying gasoline for his lawnmower."

"He's the headmaster, Julie. He doesn't mow lawns or shovel sidewalks. The maintenance crew takes care of all that stuff."

"How about the Ski-Doo?"

I shook my head. "That school has its own gas pump to supply all the maintenance vehicles."

"So you think he bought gas in the village just to get a receipt and a can to frame the Perkins boy?"

"That's the way it looks to me."

"But what's the point? If the headmaster wanted to get rid of Perkins, he just had to say so. Everybody would have supported him— the boy was a menace. I mean, how could a school recently destroyed by fire even think of admitting a known arsonist?"

"Guess they must have been really desperate to fill the beds."

With the school day ended, Julie had let her hair hang long to her shoulders. As she led me into the bedroom she doffed the prim housecoat in which she had answered the door. Now she wore only a diaphanous green nightgown that left little to the imagination.

"Your long hair reminds me of the Tower Scene in *Pelléas et Mélisande*. The scene is virtually impossible to portray credibly on an opera stage—in some productions it seems downright ridiculous—but as a mental image I find it incredibly erotic."

"What happens?" Julie pressed her body more closely against mine.

"Pelléas is standing on the ground outside Mélisande's balcony. She's combing her hair and lets it fall so that it envelops him."

"I can see where that might be hard to stage."

"But he sings, 'I never saw tresses as lovely as yours, Mélisande. How soft they are, as though they had fallen from the sky. They feel alive like little birds in my hands, and they love me.'"

"What does she say?"

"Mélisande is afraid someone might see them, but Pelléas ties her hair around a branch to make her his prisoner."

"Sounds kind of kinky to me."

"Then he sings, 'My kisses creep along your hair.'"

"What does she think of that?"

"She complains that it's hurting her."

"Downright abusive if you ask me. What happens next?"

"Golaud comes along."

"Golaud?"

"Her husband."

"You mean the girl is married!"

"It's a romance."

"I don't know, Axel. Sometimes I think you have some pretty strange ideas of turn-ons."

"Maybe you need to hear the music as well."

"But I can think of some other things we can do with my hair," Julie said with a suggestive smile. And she showed me.

Chapter 18

BEING MOD ON SUNDAY MEANT a relaxed start—breakfast at 8:30 instead of 7:30; no classes—but by day's end one was as exhausted as after a full day of teaching and sports. By late April I'd learned to treat life at Galton like a marathon and paced myself accordingly.

The first few hours after breakfast saw the Galton disciplinary system working for once. Minor infractions carried blocks—walking outside around the school buildings during morning break. Major infractions or major accumulations of minor infractions led to the imposition of hours that boys had to approach staff members to work off. The previous day, for example, the junior housemaster had set a bunch of little kids to polishing all of his shoes. On Sunday I put six boys to work pasting inserts into the chapel hymnals, my aim being to provide texts for a number of fine hymns that didn't appear in our book.

I organized them into two teams of three each, had them bring the hymnals up from the chapel, and then sat them at dining room tables for the chore. They dug into their labours with great fervour, some working for punishment, some voluntarily, just looking for some way to fill empty hours on Sunday, but after about twenty minutes one of them complained that he was bored and didn't want to do it any more. I suspected that the boy had never had to work at anything menial in his entire nine-year-old life. The downside came later when I had to go back and spend half an hour redoing about twenty of the hymnals myself, but that was to be expected.

Another lad worked off half an hour by going through all the junior-choir folders removing staples that an over-zealous copy-service employee had mistakenly inserted, then going through the same folders to correct the disorder created by some of his dyslexic classmates who had put all the music in reverse order several weeks ago during a similar exercise. Of course, in correcting the first series of mistakes he introduced new mistakes that I subsequently had to fix.

In the afternoon a telephone caller identifying himself as the King of Greece asked whether the headmaster could be reached. I was tempted to say, "Yeah, and I'm Babe Ruth," and give him the telephone number of the local pizza parlour. Happily, I resisted the impulse, for it turned out that he really was King Constantine of Greece, calling with regard to the International Round Square Conference with which Galton had recently become associated.

An hour later a self-appointed vigilante duo came into the office to announce that they had detected two boys coming out of the woods, reeking with deodorant which nonetheless failed to mask the telltale odour of cigarette smoke. One of the culprits, moreover, was seen carrying a pack of cigarettes. What was I going to do in the face of this damning evidence? Pass the buck, of course, and I scribbled off a note to the head of the discipline committee.

Late in the afternoon I posted a note on the office door saying that I would be back in ten minutes, and then walked to the school chapel. It took me awhile to discover how to get under the stage, the location of Eric Ratley's secret lair. I kept looking for stairs at the back of the stage but no stairs were to be found. I returned to the main level and examined the front of the stage looking for an opening—still no luck.

I climbed back on stage and examined the floor more carefully. Sure enough, a trap door had been cut into the surface of the stage floor, probably for some drama production. I recalled how rapidly the chorus risers had appeared and figured that the director of a play had asked the headmaster to install a trap and he had turned to the head of maintenance the way a ship captain might turn to his first mate and order, "Make it so!"

It didn't take too much longer to discover the mechanism for activating the trap. I turned on all the stage lights, having neglected to bring a flashlight, and lowered myself into the opening. I examined the trap door from the underside and discovered that someone—probably Eric—had nailed two small pieces of wood at the edge in such a way that by swivelling them into place the trap door could not be opened from above. Eric must have wanted to forestall the possibility of being attacked while he slept.

I discovered the sleeping bag and pillow that Eric had preferred to a dormitory bed and the several cartons in which he had stowed his few possessions. But everything was in disarray, the contents of the cartons scattered about the area. I could only conclude that someone had been conducting a hasty search without troubling to conceal the fact. I examined each item carefully without finding anything of interest. What did Eric possess that anyone else might want? Then I thought of the hymnal hidden in the chapel piano.

Chapter 19

MAY BROUGHT THE 9ᵀᴴ-GRADE COMPUTER exam. Some boys learned
computer programming as naturally as children learn spoken languages.
A few of the 9ᵗʰ graders, with a first-rate textbook on structured BASIC,
delighted in jazzing up their assignments in ways that would have cost
me considerable effort to duplicate. Others lacked the patience to try
something new and a number of the boys, frustrated to discover that
if you don't give the computer exact instructions, it won't work at all,
preferred typing obscenities on the screen or attempting to down the
system by random banging.

During the previous two weeks, to review the year's material, I
had assigned the students to write a number of programs from which
I would choose two for the final exam. Now the moment of truth had
arrived, in a windowless bunker whose cinder-block walls remained
unadorned by panelling or even pictures. The school's Commodore
PETS were rather outdated by 1987 but Galton's mandate hardly
included keeping on the cutting edge of computer technology.

A number of boys diddled around for awhile then left the exam
without even waiting to have their work evaluated. A few got a halfway working program going, and a few actually coded the couple of
dozen lines in the order necessary to make the machine perform its
function. By contrast with earlier tests, where students would nickel-
and-dime me to death with requests for help—by fixing enough "just
this one line, sir"s, you find that you've done the whole program for
them—I tried to hold firm to judging only the finished results, so the
room remained relatively quiet except for the tapping of keys and the
occasional expletive. The beauty of a computer exam from the point
of view of the instructor, and its terror from the point of view of the
student, is that you can't possibly fake it. Either the program works, or
you get error messages ("Syntax error, 60," "Type mismatch in 120,"
"FOR without NEXT in 50," "Out of data in 80").

In the afternoon came the Point-to-Point race, a half-hour dash across four mountaintops. One section of the course had become completely familiar since the entire school ran it every Monday afternoon, a roughly three-kilometre dash up a mountain, through the woods, down a ski slope and across several soccer fields, an experience I found reminiscent of the blurry forest chases in "The Return of the Jedi." Even by the time the first snows had put an end to the weekly ordeal I found the experience bewildering—racing full tilt through the woods, tearing past other competitors on a narrow trail, hoping not to turn an ankle or break a leg. Students had to complete the course within 150% of the average time of the first five finishers or be compelled to repeat it. I recalled seeing Eric Ratley calmly walking the course, knowing that he would have to do the whole thing again but refusing to give the school, or its headmaster, the satisfaction of seeing him push himself in an obligatory athletic event.

That course turned out to be the easiest stretch of the Point-to-Point, which began with a hand-over-hand scramble up a mountain to Point One. I'd enjoyed a lifetime of experience hiking in the White Mountains and remembered the special pleasure that came in rocky summits that required both arms and legs to negotiate particularly steep sections, and I thought of myself as a reasonably agile climber. But I'd never actually raced to the summit in a state of panting exertion.

If the trail up to Point One had seemed indistinct, the way down the other side of the mountain had no trail at all, just a bushwhack past branches seemingly bent on putting your eye out and over roots intent on capturing your sneakers and sending you sprawling. Leaves left over from the fall covered rocks, many of them unstable, and low-lying scrub seemed designed to lacerate bare legs. The pathless ascent to Point Two seemed even more arduous than the rocky approach to Point One, but the tree-dodging descent to the school road proved a good deal more frightening, like a slalom course with leaf-hidden burrows and jagged rocks hungering for toes or ankles.

One had but a few moments to enjoy the regularity of the road before having to run up a ski slope. No roots or bushes here but only an unyielding gradient that tortured already-exhausted legs and worn-out lungs. From there the trail led into the woods again to Point Three, the course of the weekly run, then along a ridge (where one hoped to avoid potholes, fallen logs and mud pits) en route to Point Four, then finally another jumping, tumbling, slip-sliding descent to the road again.

Some students took this competition very seriously, scouting out what they considered the most advantageous route through the bushwhacking section of the run, and marking their path with secret signs. Running the steady four-and-a-half hours of a twenty-six mile marathon left one wary of stairs for the next several days. Running panting and out of breath for half an hour took its own peculiar toll. Why push so hard? The obnoxious Sylvain Desrochers had announced in class that he intended to kick my ass all over the course (both obnoxious and disrespectful, one might say), and I was willing to endure a good deal of physical discomfort to avoid giving him the satisfaction. Happily I finished two seconds ahead of him at 28:03, seventh overall behind members of my cross-country team.

The following day we spent white-water rafting on the Rouge River. Arriving at base camp we writhed our way into wet suits, bootees and helmets until we looked for all the world like the sperms in Woody Allen's "Everything You Ever Wanted to Know about Sex."

A school bus drove us to the launching point where we scrambled aboard the eight-man rubber rafts. A professional pilot coached us on basic maneuvers ("When I say 'Paddle!' you keep paddling until I say 'Stop!' or you'll find yourself in the water") and then we were off. You've doubtless seen "The African Queen" or "Deliverance," so you know what white water looks like, but until you've actually been in it, you can't appreciate the sensation of seeing a gigantic hole in the water, then plunging into it. The raft gets tossed about a lot and you take a good deal of water aboard that has to be bailed out during the next calm stretch. We went through four sets of rapids, paused for lunch, and then bussed back upstream to do it again. The second time around the boatman took us straight into major maelstroms that we had skirted the first time through. I moved from second-to-rear to second-to-front (when possible, I take my adventures in carefully measured increments) in order to experience the shiver of delight of each approaching peril without actually getting thrown from my perch.

Then back to camp to peel off wetsuits, empty booties, and sit down to a steak dinner that served as the incentive for boys who didn't care that much for rafting. As Carl observed, not only did we get to do all this for free, but we got paid for it as well.

After dinner came the obligatory viewing of the videotape (after all, nothing really happens until you've seen it on TV). Watching each of the dozen rafts hit the canyon waves and flip in the air, usually spilling half a dozen passengers, raised my esteem for our pilot's skill in getting us through unscathed. I could have sworn that the video caught Sylvain shoving another boy into the drink, but no harm seemed to have been done. What would the term have been? Not defenestration; perhaps *deraftisation*. I reflected that Galton was not a bad life if you could survive the downside.

Chapter 20

THE FOLLOWING NIGHT I DREW Senior Study, the most dreaded of MOD responsibilities. Galton maintained a system whereby students capable of studying quietly in their rooms were permitted to do so. The forty or so students incapable of such self-discipline were herded into a single large room—formed by opening the dividing wall between two adjoining classrooms—presided over by the Master on Duty. It occurred to me that throughout the year my duty schedules had fallen on weekends, when there was no formal study, or Thursdays, where choir rehearsals relieved me of this chore.

But I had seen how the headmaster or Carl or Geoffrey had kept the boys in line with a whip-crack voice and was confident that I could do the same. The main thing was to let them know who was boss. Study began quietly enough. Boys opened their textbooks and notebooks with at least a pretence of working. Some used small metal rulers to underline important phrases in their notebooks. I saw one boy insert earplugs into his ears, and imagined that others would have put on headsets to listen to music had this been permitted. Others made little show of working, stretching out their legs under the tables and staring blankly at textbooks, occasionally looking up at the clock to calculate the time remaining in their enforced incarceration. One boy asked permission to use the restroom and I granted it. Two boys moved together to confer on an assignment but they kept their voices low so I saw no reason to object.

Then two of the 11th graders, sitting on opposite sides of the room, began an argument that others soon joined. I had noticed no provocation and could see no reason for a dispute but the raised voices broke the stillness irreparably. I employed my whip-crack voice with approximately the effect of waving a red cape in front of a charging bull. Wads of paper, chalk and erasers began flying around the room, and I had about as much chance of stopping the commotion as Mickey Mouse of turning back the flood in "The Sorcerer's Apprentice."

At this point the assistant headmaster entered the room and, with a whip-crack voice, set everything to right. The boys resumed their seats as suddenly as they had left them; eyes went to textbooks with an intensity that insisted they could never have been anywhere else. Carl gazed about the now-quiet study hall then turned to me and said quietly, "You can go home now, Axel." When I protested he said, "Really, Axel. Take the rest of the night off." Somewhat bewildered I gathered my things and walked the dark road home.

The next day the headmaster summoned me into his office. "Axel," he said sympathetically. "You wouldn't say that this has been the happiest year of your life." I muttered a few words of demurral. "Perhaps Galton isn't really the best place for you to spend the rest of your career." He clearly did not want to prolong the conversation. I left shaken.

During the next several days I reflected on the lessons I had learned from watching my advisor Leon Nelson during the year I spent as a visiting scholar at Magnolia University. I had no hope of imitating his Socratic style as he subjected students to a daily catechism—indeed, when I had tried to model myself directly after him at Fleur de Lis University the results had been disastrous. I grew to understand that the secret was to know who you are as a person and be that as a teacher. Could the same lesson apply to being a disciplinarian?

I had a chance to find out the following night when I ended up being assigned to Senior Study again. Once again, the boys gathered for the nightly ritual in which some would concentrate to the best of their limited ability while others would simply serve their term. This time, however, when one of the boys attempted to break the silence by making a show of sharpening one pencil after another, I walked over to him, dropped to a crouch, and murmured so that only he could hear, "You're disturbing my study."

To my astonishment he said, "Sorry, sir," and went back to work. I made only two other such visits the entire evening. When Carl Kitchener walked past the room, as he did several times during the two-hour session, he saw a model of tranquillity. I couldn't swear that every boy was actually studying during the entire interval, but no one was interfering with the process.

The next morning Harold called me into his office again. "I don't know how you did it, Axel. I've never seen such a quick turnaround. But if you can keep on managing the boys the way you did last night, you can stay at Galton as long as you like."

As I walked to my next class I thought about the Point-to-Point Race and at the end of the period asked Sylvain to remain a moment after the others had gone.

"What now?" he asked with a sullen expression.

"I wanted to tell you I thought you had a pretty good run the other day."

"Didn't beat you."

"Did you train for the event?"

"Put out a couple of markers to get through the bushwhack section."

"I mean, have you done any regular roadwork or intervals?"

"Just running with the soccer team."

"That's pretty impressive: the only guys ahead of you were on cross-country, and they'd been training for weeks for this event."

"And you."

"I'm a marathon runner, Sylvain. I do twenty-mile runs every Sunday. If you trained the way the runners do, you'd be outpacing me too."

I only got a grunt from Sylvain as he left the room, but I noticed that he managed to stay out of the corner for the entire next week.

Chapter 21

ON SUNDAY AFTERNOON JULIE CAME over to my house, the last building on the road past the school. Galton's demanding schedule made it feel as if I scarcely spent any time there. I took all my meals at the school, except for an occasional pizza on the way to the movies, so the kitchen remained clean and orderly, although clearly unrenovated. If I'd spent any time using the kitchen I would have felt right at home: it looked just like my parents' kitchen when I was growing up, right down to the linoleum floor. For the remainder of the house the school had covered the floors with what appeared to be a mishmash of carpet remnants. How else explain the jarring juxtaposition of blue, orange, green and red shag rugs?

My bookcases filled the living room and study, my collection diminished by the recent donation of all my books on music history to a university outside Ottawa. "What happened?" someone had asked the music librarian when the bequest became known. "Did Crochet die?" No. I simply couldn't face the prospect of daily reminders of a bygone career.

Today Julie appeared in off-duty garb: a short brown skirt and a sleeveless blouse in a flattering shade of peach. ("Mango," she corrected me.) Julie looked around at the framed photos on the wall beside the sofa, the Lake of Zurich, a snow scene from the French Alps, a hotel doorway in Paris, and a shot of the impossibly narrow houses in Amsterdam, all dating from a six-month sojourn in Europe during graduate school days. "I've been trying to make sense of the strange goings-on at this school," she said, "and so far the pattern eludes me."

"Let's try a change of perspective," I suggested. "If we just look at events we have a fire, two supposedly accidental deaths and an expulsion, combined with some peculiar evidence: financial documents hidden in a hymnal, a receipt for a container of gas (even though we've never actually seen the receipt), a hidden lair hastily searched, and a headmaster who seems to have no qualms about misappropriating funds."

"And if we can rely on Corinne's analysis, evidence that would spell jail time, not just an easy move to another source of cash," Julie said.

"An unscrupulous person in that situation might resort to extreme measures."

"So what if we looked at the deaths as murders instead of accidents?"

"You mean Dolly, too?"

"Why not?" Julie said.

"In that case the fire could be just a diversion," I said.

"But then how did Eric die?"

"I've been thinking about that a lot. Eric is supposed to have died of smoke inhalation in the library."

"And we know that the fire never reached the library."

"Here's another possibility. Let's say Bromley visits Eric in his lair the night before the fire, smothers him to death with a pillow, and leaves his body there. When he re-enters the school, he doesn't go in the direction of the fire but goes in the opposite direction to the chapel. He brings the body outside then tries to 'revive' him."

"Why does he need to kill Eric?"

"Eric had information that could put Bromley in jail, at least so Corinne says."

"Do you think Dolly gave it to him?"

"That's been bothering me. I don't think so, at least not the way you mean."

"How then?"

"Eric was miserable at Galton and the headmaster only made it worse with his personal remarks. Let's imagine that one of Bromley's little jokes at Eric's expense leaves the boy speechless with rage. The ever-sympathetic Dolly indiscreetly mentions that the headmaster himself is not without faults and injudiciously alludes to a file she's been keeping which, if made public, would more than disgrace the headmaster."

"Isn't that putting Dolly in a pretty poor light?"

"I don't think it was intentional. Let's look at her side of it for a moment. She's discovered what Bromley was up to. What's she going to do?"

"Dolly was a straight shooter. She would have gone to the headmaster and laid it on the line," Julie said.

"That's the way I see it, too," I said. "And what do you imagine he would have said?"

"He probably gave her a choice between maintaining her silence and keeping her job and breaking one and losing the other."

"I imagine the same. And what's Dolly going to do?"

"Not much she can do, with no other means of support."

"But the situation eats at her. I think her remarks to Eric would have just been a guilty secret forcing its way to the surface."

"And with her rosy view of the students at Galton she might not have been aware that a boy like Eric could get past any lock in the school. But how would Eric know what file to take and wouldn't Dolly have noticed its absence?" Julie asked.

"This doesn't have to be a quick effort. My guess is that Eric came to Dolly's office night after night until he came across something that she had set aside. Remember the arrows and exclamation marks. Eric could have photocopied the file and put it back."

"So how does Bromley get wise to this?"

"My guess is that Eric, unsophisticated in the ways of the world, goes to the headmaster and says something like, 'Get off my back or I'll tell my father what you've been doing.' Eric didn't really have any idea how he would expose Bromley if it came to that and Bromley didn't really know how much Eric knew."

"But Bromley knew what would happen if Eric's father ever learned what was going on. Bromley didn't even have to know about Dolly's file, but Eric had to die before he could cause any damage," Julie said.

"It didn't take all that much planning. Bromley just had to buy some gas to get the receipt, draw a crude cartoon, and then plant them in Peter Perkins' locker after the fire. He would have known that Geoffrey didn't have a first-period class, so he could have spread the gasoline while the rest of us were in chapel, then start the fire once everyone had settled into classes."

"But for Bromley, Dolly represented a dangerous loose end."

"Kyla let it slip that Harold had asked her about serving as bursar at Thanksgiving—well before Dolly's death."

"Wouldn't the police have found Dolly's death suspicious?" Julie asked.

"The local police chief probably would have accepted Bromley's story, especially when he told that charming anecdote about the Indonesian boys and the hose. An overweight woman breaks her neck falling on ice—I don't think the police would even have opened an investigation."

"I'm still bothered by Eric's death," Julie said. "How did Bromley pass off a cadaver twelve hours old as a body recently overcome by smoke inhalation?"

"You're thinking of rigor mortis."

"Not just that. A lot of chemical changes take place when a person dies, and they keep on occurring for the next several days."

"Well, you noticed that the headmaster didn't give mouth-to-mouth respiration but pounded Eric on his chest and back."

"Still, his face should have given away the difference."

"You're thinking like a person with an advanced medical education. We're talking about a volunteer fireman with a bit of first aid training. But you're overlooking the most important point."

"What's that?"

"A successful headmaster commands compliance. He's the alpha dog in any situation. If he tells someone Eric has died of smoke inhalation, it would take a very strong-minded individual to stand up to him. People tend to see what they want to see, and I think the village fireman accepted Bromley's version over the evidence of his senses without giving it a second thought."

"So what do we do?"

It had grown dark as the afternoon neared its end and I turned on a couple of lamps in the living room. "All we have to show the authorities are suppositions and an incriminating financial statement," I said.

"I guess it would be unrealistic to go to Bromley and appeal to him to do the right thing."

"Look what happened to Eric when he approached Bromley and presumably appealed to his better nature."

"The same thing would happen if we tried to make a public announcement at the next staff meeting."

"Right. Bromley would just ask for my resignation in return for a recommendation or fire me on the spot. It's hard to find allies in a situation where everyone serves 'at the pleasure of the headmaster.'"

"So what's left?"

"I think I need to meet Bromley in a public place, lay out the story and ask him to confess to the police. If not, I'll present the story to the chairman of the board of trustees that very night. They might be willing to overlook embezzlement but I don't think they'd condone murder, or even the suggestion of murder."

"Are you sure you'll be safe?"

"I don't think the headmaster's going to shoot me in the main lobby of the hotel."

"So when do you plan to approach Bromley?"

"No time like the present," I said.

Chapter 22

SWEET SOUNDS OF THE HARP drifted down from the balcony as I sat in the lobby waiting for the headmaster to appear. Fifteen minutes past our meeting time and still no Bromley. A hotel employee entered to add a log to the fire in the oversized fireplace. Even in May the evenings could be chilly but the fire was probably mostly for show. I finished one ginger ale and ordered another. Finally the headmaster turned up, dressed in a double-breasted navy blazer, school tie and grey slacks. "Sorry, Axel," Bromley said. "I had a dinner meeting that ran late."

We found a secluded table. I drew a deep breath and began. "I have an unpleasant story to tell you." I laid out the scenario that Julie and I had worked out. It occurred to me as I spoke that while we had no hard evidence against Bromley, he had no way of knowing if I made up a few details to support the accusations. So in addition to my actual conversation with the gas station owner I told him that Dolly had explained the meaning of the financial statement. I told him that someone had seen him carry the gasoline can into the classroom and that someone else had seen him spray the steps to the school to make Dolly's "accident" seem more plausible. My years as a university professor had given me an air of authority, or so my friends told me when I uttered some preposterous falsehood with a straight face and it took them a moment to realize that I wasn't in earnest.

Bromley didn't try to deny anything I said, nor did he mention the absence of real evidence for his murders. A professional criminal would have known whether or not anyone had observed his actions. An amateur like Bromley had no reason to doubt the existence of the fictitious witnesses I'd cited.

"All right, Axel," he said. "I accept your terms. But I hope you'll be gentleman enough to let me consult my lawyer to arrange the circumstances of my surrender."

I hadn't planned on delay. I was all ready to telephone the chairman of the board of trustees if Bromley didn't turn himself in this evening. I wasn't sure how to handle this turn of events. "I'll give you twenty-four hours," I said.

"Done," Bromley said, and without offering to shake my hand on the deal he rose and strode out of the lounge. I finished my ginger ale, walked to the parking lot, got into my car and prepared to drive up the hill. I turned the key in the ignition and nothing happened. Gas level? Adequate. Battery? No indication of problems. I had no intention of opening the hood and staring into the engine as if I had the slightest clue of how to proceed.

Bromley drove by in one of the school vans, saw me, and stopped. "Problems?" he asked.

"Car won't start. I'll call the CAA."

"Could take hours on a Sunday night and no garage here in town. Let me drive you up the hill."

This definitely wasn't the scenario I had planned. Should I trust this man, a more or less confessed murderer? I decided to risk it, but remained on high alert on the drive back to the school. Bromley seemed only abashed and penitent.

When we got to the maintenance garage Bromley opened the large door with an automatic device and we drove in. He pressed the button again and the garage doors lowered noisily. I'd only seen the corrugated metal structure from the outside and marvelled that so many vehicles could be crammed into such a small space. I walked to the pedestrian door and was just about to open it when I caught a glimpse of something moving near the side of my head. Then I felt a strong blow and fell unconscious to the floor.

Chapter 23

"Welcome back." I identified Julie's voice before I recognized my surroundings—a bed in the school infirmary. The divider curtains had been pushed back—I was the room's only occupant. A combination scale and height measure stood by the door. White drawers and locked glass cabinets lined one wall. The room had no formal decoration but a large window admitted sunlight and offered a view onto the woods; I thought I could catch a glimpse of one of the huts. My vision had cleared but this definitely did not feel like waking up in the morning. Then I felt a tender spot on the side of my head.

"Okay, I won't ask 'where am I?' I've figured that part out, but you'll need to fill me in on the rest."

"What's the last thing you remember?" Julie was wearing a green sweater over a tan skirt in place of her usual nurse's smock, and her face conveyed her concern for my condition.

"Being in the garage with Bromley. What did he hit me with, a sledgehammer?"

"Tire iron, but it did the job. He must have had it at the ready beside him in the van. What possessed you to ride with him?"

"My car wouldn't start."

"Interesting coincidence, don't you think?"

"Not likely." The car had never let me down before, and had given no signs of trouble on the drive down to the hotel. "So what happened next?"

"I was watching for your return. When Bromley drove past in the school van I thought I spotted you in the passenger seat so I kept watching as the van pulled into the garage. When Bromley came out and you didn't, I called the police, but I warned them not to use a siren. I didn't know what plans he might have for you."

"Then what?"

"I flagged the policeman down and we walked to the maintenance garage. There seemed to be an awful racket coming from inside. We found Bromley nearby—he appeared to be watching and waiting. While the policeman spoke with him I ran into the garage but I couldn't see anything for the exhaust fumes. Bromley had turned on every van, truck, snowmobile and even the school bus. Fortunately he'd left you next to the door where you'd fallen and I was able to drag you out. Don't worry. I had some assistance transporting you here."

"What about Bromley?"

"I didn't see that part. The policeman said that Bromley had put his hands out in front of him ready for handcuffs."

"A bit melodramatic, don't you think?"

"That's the part the policeman was reluctant to tell me. Apparently it was just one more trick. The policeman went off his guard when Bromley acted so accommodating so he was taken by surprise when Bromley grabbed his gun and shot himself in the head."

"Fatally?"

"Yes." It flashed through my mind that what we had attributed to decisiveness in the headmaster might really have been impulsiveness.

"So what do we do now?"

"Your job is to rest—that was a nasty blow you took. Happily Bromley didn't know too much about anatomy. Another few inches toward the neck and you could be in the same state as he is."

"You saved my life—thank you."

"A life worth saving, as they say. Besides, I've got plans for you when you recover."

About the Author

Arthur Wenk loves music, mathematics, movies, mountains, mysteries, magic and marathon running. He has published books and articles on Debussy, music and the arts, music history and bibliography, programming graphing calculators, and the bookstores of Toronto. As a speaker he has recently offered presentations on psychotherapy, film, and a history of western culture. In the summer, he enjoys hiking in the White Mountains of New Hampshire. Wenk's teaching career has taken him to southern California, Boston, Pittsburgh, Québec City and Southern Ontario, where he has founded a succession of *a cappella* choirs and served as a church musician in addition to academic duties. Axel Crochet, introduced in *The Quarter Note Tales* (Wingate Press, 2006) represents a nod to Claude Debussy's alter ego, Monsieur Croche, the dilettante-hater. You can learn more about the author at his website, www.arthurwenk.com